The Little Victim

Also by R. T. Raichev

The Hunt for Sonya Dufrette
The Death of Corinne
Assassins at Ospreys

THE LITTLE VICTIM

R. T. Raichev

Constable • London

Constable & Robinson Ltd
3 The Lanchesters
162 Fulham Palace Road
London W6 9ER
www.constablerobinson.com

First published in the UK by Constable,
an imprint of Constable & Robinson, 2009

First US edition published by SohoConstable,
an imprint of Soho Press, 2009

Soho Press, Inc.
853 Broadway
New York, NY 10003
www.sohopress.com

A copy of the British Library Cataloguing in Publication
Data is available from the British Library

UK ISBN: 978-1-84529-536-3

US ISBN: 978-1-56947-575-1
US Library of Congress number: 2008048830

Printed and bound in the EU

1 3 5 7 9 10 8 6 4 2

Mixed Sources
Product group from well-managed
forests and other controlled sources
www.fsc.org Cert no. SA-COC-1565
© 1996 Forest Stewardship Council
FSC

To Michael
in gratitude for the Gulf

Author's Note

This is a work of fiction. All the characters are imaginary and bear no relation to any living person.

R. T. R.

Contents

Alas, regardless of their doom,
The little victims play!
No sense have they of ills to come,
Nor care beyond today . . .

Thomas Gray

1

Lady Macbeth of Noon's Folly

'He kisses her bedroom door each time he passes it. He thinks about her *all* the time.' Lucasta Leighton made a despairing gesture. 'He keeps talking about her. I do tell him to forget her. She's gone. She's made her choice, appalling as it is. She is no longer a *child*. She's never going to return, she said so. He can't do anything about it. She's thousands of miles away. Well, he says he can't give her up, not just like that, not his only daughter. He still believes she might be persuaded to come back, you see. When I tell him she won't, he gets angry. He snaps at me.'

Lucasta's voice was steady but her eyes were red, as though she had been crying. 'Do have some more coffee, Iris,' she urged her sister-in-law as she picked up the silver pot.

'Thank you . . . Where's Toby now?' Iris Mason-Stubbs turned her mild bespectacled face apprehensively towards the door that led into her brother's study. Toby had always made her nervous.

'He went for a walk. He said he'd be back soon. He left forty-five minutes ago. He should have come back by now, really. I hope he's all right.'

Noon's Folly Cottage overlooked the woods. It was half past eleven in the morning but the sky outside was so overcast, it felt like late afternoon or early evening. The streetlights were on. Not the best day for a walk, Iris thought. She sat facing the french window. The chill mist had caught the back of her throat and made her cough the moment she had got out of the car and started walking towards the house. Swirls of mist – floating and clearing and rolling sluggishly back – like the tentacles of some fantastical creature from the very depths of the ocean – exploring – looking for prey? Something mesmeric about it. *Below the thunders of the upper deep, Far, far beneath in the abysmal sea – His ancient, dreamless, uninvaded sleep – The Kraken sleepeth.* Did people still read Tennyson? The trees and giant ferns were obscured into shadowy silhouettes – everything outside appeared submerged – the streetlights were turning into blurs of watery, acid-green phosphorescence. So quiet too.

Toby would never come back. Toby had been snapped up by the monstrous Kraken. Iris felt at once disturbed and oddly comforted by the fanciful idea.

'This is better, isn't it?' Lucasta had turned on the two table lamps. 'Shall I put another log on the fire? Are you warm enough?'

'I'm fine. Thank you.'

'Are you sure? You look pinched.'

It was an attractive room done in silver-blue and maroon – Laura Ashley and Liberty's – everything in its appointed place – the glass-top coffee table gleamed – not a speck of dust anywhere – *quite* unlike the cosy chaos that reigned in Iris's drawing room. Iris didn't really see any point in keeping her drawing room tidy. No matter how often they had it tidied up, it was a mess again in no time. Lucasta blamed the dogs and she kept telling her to get rid of them. Once Iris admitted she actually found muddy paws endearing and Lucasta stared at her as though she thought her completely off her head. They were *so* different. Henry said he could well imagine old Lucasta blowing off Fido's head with a shotgun and not batting an eyelid.

Iris glanced at the books that lay on the coffee table. *An Englishman's Garden* and *An Englishwoman's Home.*

Shouldn't it have been the other way round? A novel by someone called Antonia Darcy – a detective story, judging by the cover – a gloomy Victorian Gothic mansion and *such* a sinister-looking tree. Iris thought she might enjoy it. Were the man with the pipe and the woman in the mink coat the detectives? Heaven knew what kind of danger awaited them inside, what fearful mystery, what tangles in need of tackling.

'I am sure exercise is good for Toby,' Iris said brightly and she raised her cup to her lips.

'Maybe, but *not* in this damp weather.' Lucasta's face assumed a severe magisterial expression. 'Yesterday he complained of chest pains. He sat slumped in his chair for what seemed like ages, his hand pressed against his heart. I was terribly worried. I wanted to ring for an ambulance but he wouldn't hear of it. He refuses to go to the doctor, you see. He tells me not to fuss. Oh – that girl! That girl! It's all her fault!'

'I did think Toby looked ill the other day.'

'He *is* ill. Hardly eats anything. Broods. Sleeps badly. Talks in his sleep. Keeps calling out her name. He gets up in the middle of the night and walks about the house . . . I pretend I'm asleep,' Lucasta went on, 'but I get up too and follow him. He has no idea I have been watching him. Please, Iris – not a word!'

'My lips are sealed.'

'He sits at his desk and writes letters to her. He always tears up the first draft and starts again. I've read all his letters. I piece them together, you see – in the morning. He holds conversations with her – imagines she is in the room with him – begs her to come back – promises her things – tells her how much he loves her – addresses her as his "dearest girl". Then his mood changes and he gets angry and starts calling her names – oh, such dreadful names. Last night he started reminding her about the fire, when he saved her life and was nearly killed in the process.'

'Ah, the fire.' Iris nodded.

The fire had taken place sixteen years before. There had been an explosion – the mightiest of bangs followed by a ball of flame that had been seen for miles. Swaylands – her brother's holiday cottage – had burnt to the ground. Imogen – Toby's first wife – had suffered her first nervous breakdown as a result. Poor Toby had lost part of his little finger. There had been the suspicion that it was her niece who started the fire, after being refused something she'd set her heart on, ballet shoes or a pony, Iris couldn't remember which. Spoilt, terribly spoilt.

'D'you know what he said? He said he wouldn't mind having *all* of his fingers chopped off, if that was the price he had to pay to have her back! I am afraid he's losing his mind. He's had the absurd idea of going and bringing her back.' Lucasta shook her head. 'Flying thousands and thousands of miles to the subcontinent, can you imagine? As though she'd listen to him! He's going mad. Well, I do believe that's her intention. *She wants to drive him mad.* That's her revenge. She is a wicked, wicked girl!'

There was a waft of Hermes perfume as Lucasta rose from her armchair and crossed to the window. A tall, stately woman with a Roman nose and neatly arranged ghost-grey hair, she was wearing a high-collared purple dress and a brooch in the shape of what looked like a triton. She held her torso erect and, though clearly agitated, clasped her hands firmly before her. There was a hint of the monarch about Lucasta, a demeanour that was *plus royaliste que la reine*. She had kept her figure through gardening and good genes – she was a Furness – and of course she had never had any children.

Lucasta stood beside the french window, gazing intently into the gathering darkness. Like some faithful old dog, Iris thought. Iris knew everything about dogs – she had five. Such comedians! She could sit and watch their antics for *hours*. Iris had eaten a dog biscuit once and declared it actually tasted quite nice. She was also a voracious reader of books about dogs. Her favourite story came from the annals of 1930s Hollywood and concerned a male dog named Pat, a sort of canine drag artist. Pat had played Lassie in one of those marvellous old films and had become famous around the film studios as 'the only star who could play a bitch better than Bette Davis'.

Would a story about a transvestite mutt lighten Lucasta's mood? Of course it wouldn't. Now, wasn't it peculiar that Lucasta should detest dogs and yet dote on Toby, the most difficult of men? Her brother was impossibly opinionated, unutterably insensitive to anybody's feelings but his own, given to the highest dudgeons imaginable, overbearing, short-tempered – the list was endless.

Lucasta and Toby had got married a year before, only two months after Imogen's death. Lucasta had known Toby for more than thirty years. As it happened, she and Imogen had been childhood friends. Lucasta had nursed Imogen during the latter's short illness and she had been there when the end had come. It was Lucasta who had made all the arrangements for the funeral, hired caterers for the baked meats, paid the nurse's wages and provided her with references, had the house cleaned from top to bottom and despatched Imogen's clothes to various charities, all neatly labelled. Lucasta had taken care of – well, of everything. She was that sort of woman. Fearsomely efficient. She makes me nervous, Iris thought.

Lucasta was fifty-seven or -eight and she had never been married before. Everybody had been surprised at the match, but in all fairness it had to be said that Lucasta and Toby actually had a lot in common – a fondness for country walks, the diaries of James Lees-Milne, gardens, the local Conservative club, the theatre. They also did the *Times* crossword and Sudoku together. Toby let Lucasta 'manage' him – he actually *listened* to her the way he did to no other woman. Well, they would have been leading a happy life together – a comfortable, quiet, mildly eccentric, pleasantly autumnal sort of life – but for this dreadful business of Toby's daughter.

(How curious – not once so far had they referred to her niece by name! So far it had been 'she', 'her', 'Toby's daughter' or 'that girl'. Beyond the pale – that was where, by unspoken consent, they seemed to have relegated her niece.)

'I don't understand her. I really don't,' Lucasta was saying. 'Personally I've never had any problems with her, mind. She's always been perfectly civil to me. She never cast me in the role of the wicked stepmother or anything like that. She used to ask me questions about the garden.'

'I don't suppose Toby lets you read her letters?'

'No. He's extremely sensitive about them. With good reason!'

'Oh? You don't mean . . .?'

'*Yes*. I've read all of the letters. Toby has no idea. I know where he keeps them – inside Volume 5 of *Famous Trials*. You won't breathe a word, will you, Iris? Toby would be furious if he knew.'

'Haven't you tried to intercept them – stop them from getting through to him?'

'As a matter of fact I did try a couple of times, but he always manages to get them before me. He seems to have developed a sixth sense, so he is always up particularly early on the day they arrive. I even considered bribing the postman but we keep getting different ones.' Lucasta sighed. 'Toby stands in the hall in his dressing gown, perfectly still, staring at the door, waiting for the letter to hit the mat.'

'How dreadful.'

'He then takes the letter to his study, reads it several times, makes notes, and starts writing his reply.'

'So she's given him her address?'

'She has. You seem surprised. That's part of her game, don't you see? It's clear she *expects* him to write back, so that she can laugh at him and gloat over his misery and frustration. Each time a letter arrives Toby hopes – believes – she'll tell him she's coming back!'

'What – what does she write about?' Iris hoped her sister-in-law wouldn't think her too ghoulish.

Two very bright red spots appeared on Lucasta's cheekbones, but she spoke in a composed enough voice. 'Well, she tells him in some detail about the kind of things she does.'

2

The Most Dangerous Game

The kind of things she does.

Iris Mason-Stubbs had only a vague notion what they might be, these things. Nobody so far had actually put any of it into words. For some reason she thought of it in terms of an invasion. The invasion of the Home Counties by . . . by . . .

She frowned, her cup of coffee poised in mid-air. No, she couldn't think by what. She had to admit she was a bit out of her depth. She had had no experience of such matters. One *heard* stories about girls like that, but of course it wasn't the sort of thing that happened to people one knew. Certainly not to members of one's family. *To her own brother.* It was awful – the stuff of nightmares – the kind of hideously lurid story that sold tabloid papers to hoi polloi. Well, not only to hoi polloi, sadly. Henry relished the rags – he said he found scandal 'irresistible' – he couldn't help it, he said. Henry claimed to be the reincarnation of a roofer from Romford. So droll! (On no account must she tell Henry.)

APPEAL COURT JUDGE'S DAUGHTER TURNS –

No. She couldn't say the word – not even in her mind. Well, the rags *would* make the most of any opportunity for sensationalism. But that's what it was all about, wasn't it? *Yes.* She wasn't such a dim bulb after all. That's what it was all about. No point in clinging to the hope it might turn out to be something completely different, because it wasn't something completely different. Rather inconsequentially Iris remembered how her poor mother had once maintained that a gentlewoman's name should appear in newspapers only twice: on her marriage and on her death.

Hitherto Toby and Lucasta had contrived to keep the situation under wraps, which was perfectly understandable – no one in their right mind went about broadcasting their dark personal secrets! It was the kind of embarrassing private drama that at any moment might explode into an even more embarrassing public one. Toby wouldn't be left alone if the tabloids were ever to get a whiff of any of it.

Her brother had already been in the news. He had made certain public statements – 'pronouncements', the liberal press had called them – concerning some of his bugbears: single mothers, immigrants, the Archbishop of Canterbury and his beard, queers in the army, state schools. Not surprisingly, the liberal press had taken against him. The liberal press would have a field day – oh, how they would gloat – if only they were to learn of Toby's predicament!

It occurred to Iris that she wouldn't be immune either. If she were to be identified as Toby's sister – as the 'aunt' – they would think her worthy of their attention. News reporters and suchlike would besiege their house and they'd keep ringing the bell. They'd bang on her front door and shout impertinent questions through the flap and demand interviews. They'd flash their cameras. It would drive the dogs potty! (Columba and Tailwagger became frantic each time someone rang the front door bell.) Henry might actually get it into his head to go out and talk to them. Henry would probably think the whole thing a hoot. *How are the mighty fallen.* Henry was bound to say something like that. He and Toby didn't get on. Toby liked to refer to his brother-in-law as 'that buffoon'.

She asked where exactly her niece was at the moment.

'Well, she was in Dubai to start with, that's in the United

Emirates, then in Bahrain, but since last month she's been in Goa.'

'Go-ah? Where exactly is Go-ah?'

'South India. On the Arabian Sea coast. She is at a place called Kilhar.'

'*Killer?*'

'Kil-*har*. Ghastly place, by the sound of it. Toby looked it up on the map. He's got *two* maps on the wall in his study – one of the world, which he's covered with stars and dates for the places she's been to – the other of Goa, Doesn't allow me to go anywhere near them. He's like a general conducting some military campaign!' Lucasta gave a mirthless laugh. 'He's marked Goa with a red flag.'

Red for danger. 'Killer'.'Kill her'. Either association was extremely unpleasant. Iris thought: *Toby is obsessed with his daughter and Lucasta is obsessed with Toby. Nothing good can come of it.*

'He's got someone spying on her.'

Iris sat forward alertly in her chair. 'Not a – policeman?'

'A policeman, yes. A retired one. A man called Bishop – no, Knight – some such name. He's English. He's lived in Goa for years, apparently. Knight tails her, writes everything down, then reports his findings to Toby. Toby spends *hours* on the phone, talking to him. You should see our phone bill. Oh, Iris, that's not how I imagined our lives would be! This is complete madness. Toby doesn't deserve any of it!'

'Of course he doesn't. Oh, my dear, I can't tell you how sorry I am. Such a pretty girl too. Who'd have thought it? Well, Toby didn't like her doing modelling. Isn't that when the whole trouble started?'

'Toby disapproved of the *company* she started keeping while she was modelling.'

In search of high-octane thrills. Henry had used that expression once – apropos of something completely different. Oh, how Henry would enjoy this!

'She met some man, didn't she? Some – foreigner?' Iris

peered into her cup. 'She said he was one of her "sponsors", I remember, but of course it turned out he was something completely different – or have I got the wrong end of the stick?'

'The man was an Arab. He was an escort agency owner. Terribly rich.' Lucasta spoke in measured tones. 'He was the head of an international escort agency. Branches in London, Paris, Shanghai, Bahrain and so on. He made her an offer, apparently, which she accepted. All that came out later on, mind. Sorry, Iris. I am a bad hostess. Would you like some more coffee?'

'Yes, please.'

Lucasta picked up the pot with a steady hand. 'Toby learnt the exact nature of what was going on entirely by chance. The exact nature of – of what she did. It came to him as a bolt out of the blue. He happened to open her diary, you see. *Quite* by chance. Oh well, you might as well know the whole story. He saw names – dates – a record of the payments she'd been receiving – instructions – addresses.'

'Instructions?' At once Iris wished she had held her tongue.

The redness on Lucasta's cheeks intensified and her lips pressed tighter. 'Instructions from clients. Concerning their ... particular ... *tastes*. Lists of outfits and – objects – paraphernalia – even lines of dialogue. He confronted her at once, asked for an explanation. She accused him of snooping. She was terribly rude to him. At first she prevaricated, told him it was none of his business, but then she came out with it. She looked Toby in the eye and told him what she did. In some detail.'

Only once before had Iris felt the discomfiting fascination of the appalling – on lifting a fallen branch in her garden one day and finding a dead squirrel crawling with maggots. (Dulcie had barked her head off. Max, the coward, had run off.) That, Iris reflected, was how those watching the corpse of Pope Pius XII, embalmed by an amateur taxidermist, turn green and then explode, must have felt. Objects? Paraphernalia? *Clients?* The dreaded headline swum before her eyes once more and this time it wrote itself out in full.

APPEAL COURT JUDGE'S DAUGHTER TURNS HOOKER.

'She probably exaggerated, but it all sounded horribly convincing. Toby turned white as a sheet. He went up to her and slapped her face. She slammed out of the room – left the house. Toby broke down and cried. I'd never seen him in such a state. He was distraught. He wouldn't let me go anywhere near him. Kept pushing me away.' Lucasta's voice quavered. 'He didn't sleep a wink that night.'

'Poor Toby,' Iris said. 'Poor you.'

Toby's portrait hung above the fireplace. It was by Andrew James, an awfully fashionable painter, much in demand, Iris had been told, and it had cost the earth, apparently. Toby had ordered it to mark his retirement from the bench the year before. The portrait showed Toby wearing his judge's wig and rather majestic scarlet robes. It was a theatrical kind of picture. Toby had been depicted holding a pair of scales in his right hand and a parchment with a blood-red seal on it in his left. His lips were a bit too full and nearly the same shade of red as the seal, giving him a somewhat dissolute air. There were bluish shadows about the eyes. (Henry insisted that Toby had been *en maquillage.*)

The portrait made Toby look like an actor *playing* a judge. It put Iris in mind of Alec Guinness. She'd always found Alec Guinness a little creepy, especially when he smiled. Well, Toby had a strong histrionic streak in him, but then that could be said about most judges. As a boy Toby had excelled at charades and he had been unrecognizable as Charley's aunt in the school production of that play. So droll! Papa had laughed so much, he'd had hiccups followed by a giddy spell. 'A highly sinister talent,' Toby's headmaster had declared with a little shudder, Iris remembered. (Did people still find jokes about aunts and nuts coming from Brazil amusing?)

She went on gazing at the portrait. Something cruel and sinister about the mouth and the eyes. The painter had clearly taken liberties, though Toby had liked the portrait immensely. So, for that matter, had Lucasta. They were *such* an odd couple. Henry had dubbed Lucasta the 'Lady Macbeth of Noon's Folly' – a woman of dark and impenetrable passions, about whom an opera should be written.

Iris suppressed the sudden urge to giggle. Terrified that Lucasta would notice, she pretended to cough.

'A frog in my throat,' she croaked, jabbing her forefinger at her collarbone. She had nearly exploded earlier on, when Lucasta had said 'tastes' and 'paraphernalia'. She had had to dig her nails into her arm. She must ask Henry what paraphernalia that could be. Whips? Outsize syringes? Silk stockings? She had actually read somewhere – Stop it, she told herself. Handcuffs? She was as bad as Henry! If she went on thinking about it, she would become hysterical and that would never do.

I must be serious, Iris reminded herself. This is no laughing matter. She tried to be as positive as she could about her brother and his achievements. Toby had devoted his life to justice. Toby had high moral standards. Toby was passionate about the truth. He had become notorious for his sadistic sentences. He had been hated and feared. Fifty years ago he would most certainly have been known as a 'hanging judge' –

No – that wasn't particularly positive! Iris sighed. She wished she liked her brother more.

Lucasta was speaking. 'She came back the next day. She talked to me as though nothing had happened, but pretended Toby wasn't there. He tried to speak to her but she ignored him. She went up to her room and started packing. Toby went after her. He looked terrible – like death warmed up. Then they had another row and she managed to reduce him to a state of near-collapse. After that she left. Her parting words were that she was never coming back. Good riddance, I thought, I felt relieved, but then . . . then . . .'

'Her letters started coming?'

'It's all calculated to drive him mad, or to kill him. She insists on recounting her exploits. I did consider writing to her and telling her to stop. All right, do whatever you like, it's your life, but, for heaven's sake, *stop bothering your father* – something on those lines. I don't dare. I am afraid she'd tell Toby. She might, just to cause trouble between us – she's that kind of girl. Toby would never forgive me. He's already accused me of interfering – of being a "meddler". Well, perhaps, if I had been her mother, things might have been different.'

'She was a real handful as a child. I am afraid Imogen couldn't cope. She was very much Daddy's little girl. Toby spoilt her, rather.' Iris lowered her voice. 'They kept changing nannies.'

'I try to put a brave face on it, but the truth is I am at my wits' end. My marriage is being wrecked. I watch Toby being destroyed – slowly, methodically, relentlessly – and I can't do a thing. *Not a thing.*'

Once more Lucasta crossed over to the window and stood there, staring out into the garden, her hands clasped before her. 'Our poor maple tree,' she murmured.

The last few leaves on the maple tree in the front lawn had been shrivelled by early frost but still clung to the nearly bare branches. Dead leaves, as far as Iris could see, lay everywhere, dark and wet, a blackened coating on the ground. And the mist went on swirling round – swirling round – something mesmerizing about it.

The Kraken . . .

'It's been an hour. He said he'd be back in twenty minutes. It's very cold outside. He's weak as a kitten. Am I a fool to worry so much?' Lucasta had a somewhat manic look about her. 'What do you think?'

Iris blinked through her glasses. 'You – you don't mean we should go and *search* for him?'

'Would you mind awfully?'

The idea of a ramble through the misty forest was far from inviting. 'Of course I wouldn't mind. Not a bit,' Iris assured her.

She in fact felt the reluctance of a dog about to be led to its bath water.

3

Flowers for the Judge

My dear girl, Lord Justice Leighton whispered as he leant against the ancient oak tree and shut his eyes. *My dear sweet girl.* Just now I had the very strong feeling that you were here with me. This oak – do you remember? *Our* oak. Of course you remember. It looks and feels exactly as it did twenty years ago. Gnarled and misshapen and bunioned and covered with patches of moss.

The same. Unchanged. How is it that *you* changed so much?

We used to walk in the woods, you and I. You were five or six at the time. The loveliest, cleverest little girl. You had such a winning way with you. If I forgot to take your hand you pushed it into mine. We always ended up beside the oak. It had become *our* oak. You kept asking for stories. You loved nothing better than a good story. Andersen, the Brothers Grimm. Andersen, in particular. Little Ida, Gerda, the Snow Queen! All a little too spooky, I thought, but then you were fond of Winnie-the-Pooh as well ... Funny fellow, Milne. Wrote all those books for the parents, rather than the children, or so it's been claimed. Christopher Robin hated him, apparently. Read about it somewhere. Christopher Robin said he felt 'exploited'. Wrote a memoir on the subject. Talk about unsatisfactory fathers!

You adored that bouncing Tigger. You said you were going to marry Tigger when you grew up, remember?

When we tired of playing at Pooh-sticks, pretending to be Heffalumps, and having 'expotitions', I started making up stories for you. One particular story became your favourite – about a little squirrel who lived inside the oak. The squirrel had a squint, got squiffy on squash that had been laced with liqueur, squandered her acorns and quarrelled with her squaddies! It was all unbearably silly nonsense but that was the way you liked it. I made things up as I went along. How you laughed! I would give anything to hear your laugh again.

The squirrel's name was Ria. You liked that name so much, you started calling yourself 'Ria'. You still do. Ria. That's how you sign your letters. It gives me a jolt, every time. Ria. The name suited you, I thought.

It's as though none of it ever happened.

I am still in a frightful state about you. About you becoming that – that other person. I don't understand it. It defies logic. Sometimes I think it is all a bad dream. Why choose the gutter when you could have had the sky? You had beauty, brains, every social advantage. You'd never wanted for money either. I sent you to the best schools. Queen's Gate, Kensington, then Mont Fertile in Switzerland, to be 'finished'. Such a marvellous place, Switzerland. All those mountain peaks glittering like wedding cakes.

You had a string of the most eligible suitors. Young men from good, distinguished families. I keep thinking of Prince Norbert of Wchinitz and Tetau. You met him in Geneva. At a *thé dansant* – they still hold old-fashioned social events like that there. I found him a charming young man – such excellent manners and so taken with you! You would have made the perfect princess. I rather wished – I rather hoped – in fact, for a while I *did* believe that he and you . . . but it wasn't to be. You were not interested.

I know I mustn't upset myself – must take care of my heart – that's what Lucasta keeps saying, damn her. I didn't bring any pills with me.

Was it all my fault? I keep racking my brains, but I haven't been able to get a satisfactory answer. It couldn't have been Lucasta's fault. It would be so easy to blame Lucasta for our estrangement, the wicked stepmother and all that, but the problems started *before* Lucasta appeared on the scene.

You didn't like the discipline I tried to impose on you. You began to rebel, to act in a wilfully disobedient manner. You started defying me. You seemed to *enjoy* defying me. You took particular pleasure in saying outrageous things. You seemed to find some of my reactions amusing. Well, I do tend to over-emphasize, pontificate and use Latin phrases – to enunciate orders as though they were papal encyclicals! There was that scornful look in your lovely eyes. That upset me. You don't know how much that upset me. *Stop treating me as though I were one of your criminals*. That was what you said.

Did I treat you like a criminal? It's my unfortunate manner, I know. *Mea culpa*. I am sorry. Perhaps after so many years on the bench, some kind of professional deformation does take place? I was never aware of it – not until you mentioned it.

I am sorry I hit you that day. I should never have done it. I am haunted by the memory. That last day, when you said you were never coming back. I never meant the things I said to you. Your letters make it clear you believe that I hate you. 'Detest' is the word you use. Oh, my dearest child, if only – if *only* – I could put into words how much I love you, how much I care! I only wanted what was best for you . . .

The mist seems to be thickening. Darkness falls. Or is it my eyes? How drab and barren everything looks. Black clumps of earth, dry leaves, not a single flower in sight! Flowers – you loved picking flowers. Bluebells in spring. You'd pick a bunch of bluebells, hide them behind your back and then give them to me as a surprise. You would then shut your eyes and I knew you expected a kiss. Your sweet lovely face . . . No bluebells now – wrong

28

season – not a single splash of colour. Only last week the trees were flame-red, but nature's started dying. Decayed leaves everywhere – heaps – mounds. I don't like mounds, they remind me of graves. There's a smell in the air . . . something rotting . . . some dead animal . . . I don't feel too well –

I am being morbid and melodramatic, I know, but if I were to die, would you come back for my funeral? Put flowers on my coffin, shed a tear?

I haven't been able to sleep. It is as though I've been fed *Cannabis indica*. That's Indian hemp, hashish. I suppose you get a lot of that sort of thing where you are at the moment? Do you take any drugs? I am prone to all sorts of silly fancies . . . Paranoid . . . You see, I suspect Lucasta of putting something in my tea, of trying to sedate me. She fusses too much. She believes I am mortally ill, that I may pop off at any time. I find her attentions annoying, to say the least. I know she means well, but she does tend to overdo things. Perhaps it was a mistake marrying her. I should have devoted myself to you, body and soul – to *you*, dear child. I should have tried to understand you better.

There is a heaviness about my heart. Pain in my left arm. Lead and ice. Lucasta tells me it's no good investing so much feeling in you, but it's like ordering the sun not to set in the evening. The other day she called my love for you a 'galloping gangrene of the soul'. She doesn't understand a thing. Jealous, I suppose. She says my love for you will kill me eventually. She'll never succeed in putting me off you, never. I only need to shut my eyes and I see you – the way you were as a child – a halcyon creature – a circle of golden summer round you. So lovely, so warm, so *bright* . . . I must stop. You never liked me when I went on. Sodden with a sick kind of self-pitying sentimentality, I can hear you say!

Your letters. I cannot get your letters out of my head. I can recall every single word you wrote. I find it imposs-ible to believe you've done any of those things. Shall I tell you what? I think you made it all up in order to punish your foolish old father for what he said to you that day. Well, I deserve to be punished for being unable to control myself. Perhaps I deserve to suffer.

They do something called 'anger management' nowadays. Some nonsense. I'm too proud to do anything about my moods, you see. I can't express my feelings properly. I was furious when you refused to do as I told you. Please, forgive me. I can't help loving you. Is that such a terrible thing? All I wish for is that you should come back – make up with me – *ut amem et foveam* – allow me to love and cherish you once more – get married to the right boy – lead a good life – a *normal* life.

I dreamt you came back the other night. I felt so happy, so relieved. I fell to my knees and asked you for forgiveness. You kissed me and allowed me to kiss you. It was a reconciliation scene on the grand scale.

What a thick black cloud that is. As black as a tar-barrel. I think it has wings! How fast it comes. It looks like some monstrous crow.

I refuse to believe that you – *that you are about to marry an Indian gangster*. That's what you wrote in your last letter. *Roman is a cool guy who collects automated weapons and kukris – the curved knives favoured for decapitation.* You made that up, didn't you? You can't possibly marry an Indian gangster. Such a preposterous idea. I absolutely refuse to believe the other things you wrote either, in your earlier letters.

I have been engaged in transactional relationships for some time now. There is no economic reason to be moral. I have been trading sex for money. I am expensive and high maintenance. A night's 'work' buys me a Louis Vuitton bag.

You couldn't really have worked as a professional call girl, could you?

Trading sex for money. Nonsense. I can't believe it. I can't. I *can't* –

* * *

30

Lord Justice Leighton gasped and the silver-topped cane slipped from his gloved hand. It's true of course, he thought. He knew it was true, the news of the forthcoming nuptials with the gangster. In his latest report over the phone, Knight had told him that his daughter now went round with a young Indian whose name people in the streets of Goa whispered with awe and fear. A young man who was extremely, *murderously* jealous of Ria. Those had been Knight's exact words. Apparently Knight had witnessed a row between the two. Then the rest must be true too – what Ria had written about acting in a film. *A blue movie*, she had called it in the American manner.

He shut his eyes. The caress of the mist through his hair seemed human and caused him to shiver.

You slut. You unprincipled whore. To have descended to the very depths of Gomorrah. Trading sex for money. Was that really what you wanted? To fuck in front of a camera? First with men, then with other sluts as well? While being watched? You wrote as though you'd enjoyed every moment of it. How can you do this to me? Is that your gratitude, for everything I have done for you?

Lord Justice Leighton's right hand went up to his chest. There it was again. The pain. Lead and ice. Only now it was sharper, much sharper than the other day. Like a knife cutting through him. He found it difficult to breathe.

Ria, he whispered. *Ria.*

He kept his back against the oak. Dazed and numb. He looked round. There was a man with a dog. Not too far. Would he see him? It was so dark, or were his eyes failing? He put up his left hand. He opened his mouth but no sound came out. Perhaps the man would notice him if he moved away from the tree? He took a tentative step to the right, waved his arms and suddenly pitched forward.

He fell into a heap of dry leaves. The rotting smell in his nostrils was overpowering. Was that it? Was that it? Was that the end? Death. Contrary to what Henry James said, there was nothing distinguished about it. It wasn't how he'd imagined it. To die like a dog. Like one of Iris's dogs.

31

How ridiculous. Lucasta'd be upset. Had he signed his new will? Lucasta actually loved him. Shame that he no longer wanted her love.

He tried to raise his head. How dark it was. Was he going to die without seeing Ria? The pain came again – quick and sharp as that of fire – excruciating. No sensation whatever in his left arm – a chilling numbness was wrapping itself about his heart, creeping into it. He gasped as he felt something like a taut wire snap. The next moment the monstrous crow descended upon him . . .

Lord Justice Leighton didn't see the man and the dog start walking fast in his direction. Nor did he see his wife and his sister who were following at a run.

'There he is, there he is,' Lucasta reiterated and she pointed with her forefinger. 'He will be all right. He will be all right . . . Toby! We're coming, darling! You will be all right!'

Iris Mason-Stubbs's hands flailed ineffectively in the air as she stumbled over a tree root. She had already managed to lose her glasses. With her wild hair and round eyes she brought to mind the White Queen in *Alice*. As it happened it was she who arrived first and kneeled beside her brother's body.

'Oh dear. My poor Lucasta,' Iris said after a pause. 'He is dead.'

4

The Bone Collector

Thousands of miles away, in Goa, Sarla Songhera was roasting a whole chicken in her oven. She kept opening the oven door and poking at the chicken with a fork. She was impatient. The chicken was neither too big nor too small but of moderate size – exactly as the *kala iilam* had instructed. She had got up at dawn and wrung its neck herself. Eventually the chicken was ready and, putting it on a plate, she carried it across her fully modernized kitchen to the table beside the window.

She proceeded to eat. She needed to consume every piece, every scrap of flesh, very fast. Her eyes remained dull but her teeth chomped away in an energetic manner and she tore at the chicken with her bare hands. Her fingers with their long red-painted nails – not unlike Kali's lolling tongue in the black statuette on her shelf – glistened in the sun. It looked as though she ate greedily but in fact she hardly noticed what the chicken tasted like; that was not the point of it. She tried not to think of anything, that had been the other instruction. Following the instructions was of paramount importance. She did her best to 'empty' her mind, she tried to think of a blank wall, but she found it difficult. Thoughts and images kept intruding. Those two – entwined. She was a seething cauldron of resentment, of jealousy and of frustration. She was filled with a sense of hurt, so deep she couldn't breathe. When she finished eating, she broke up the chicken's skeleton, again with her bare hands. That was easy. *Snap, snap.* For some reason she laughed.

She then put the bones on a platter (a silver one, with 'Harrods' engraved on the bottom), which she placed outside, on a small table on her balcony. Three days in the sun, she had been instructed, but she had no patience. She didn't think that part of it really mattered. What mattered was her belief in what she was doing, in the results she would be able to witness soon – and her belief was strong.

Sarla sat down in a peacock chair made of rattan and waited, gazing at the bones fixedly all the while. Every now and then she reached out and touched them with the tips of her fingers. She kept waving the flies away. The heat was intense, but her brow was cold with sweat. Her raven-black hair soon felt as though someone had set it on fire, but she decided not to put on a scarf or a hat. That slut, with her long golden-brown hair and enticing ways – a *professional* slut, Sarla had heard it whispered – an English girl called Ria, whom Roman desired more than anything in the world.

Sarla had had a wig made, exactly the same style and colour as Ria's hair. She had gone all the way to Delhi for it. The wig had cost a fortune. Sometimes Sarla put it on, covered her face with peach-coloured liquid foundation, applied bright red lipstick to her mouth and plenty of mascara to her eyelashes and imagined she was Ria. Well, unless her mirror was a liar, the resemblance was uncanny.

Perhaps one day she should go to Ria's bungalow, get into the bedroom and put on the gossamer-like silk dress she had seen Ria wear once – it was slashed to the navel. She would make her face up. She would then lie in the bed and wait for Roman. Her thighs were too dark, she hated her thighs, but perhaps she could cover them in peachy make-up too? Now, if she made herself up properly and wore the wig the *whole time*, Roman would never know it was her. Roman would think it was Ria! He would kiss her tenderly – passionately – fold her in his arms – make love

34

to her. But first she must make sure Ria was not coming back. *Yes.* They wouldn't want Ria barging into the bedroom and disturbing them, would they?

It took the bones less than half an hour to become really dry – as dry as, well, as a bone – wasn't that what the English said? A funny way of putting it. The English – they had a lot to answer for, Sarla thought grimly. Roman was in love with the English. Carrying the platter back inside the flat, she tipped its contents on the highly polished floor. She had pushed all the chairs (imitation Sheraton) out of the way and rolled up the carpet (an original Axminster). She had a beautiful house. What she didn't have was love.

She was ready and eager to start. High time! She felt excited, full of hope. She kicked the ornate slippers off her feet, pulled up her sari and put on the wellington boots. They were brand new and reflected the sun. She had never worn them before. They had been a present from her husband. Roman had bestowed on her a number of useless presents before they had parted. English things – a porcelain cow creamer, which had been insensitive of him, given their religion, but then he'd never had any respect for their religion – a pair of big shining garden cutters, what the English called 'secateurs' – a set of silver fish knives – a set of silver fruit knives. As though she'd have any use for a fruit knife! She had pretended to like them; she'd gasped in admiration; she had wanted to please him. She had been hungry for his kisses. The boots were olive-green, with black rubber soles, and looked incongruous next to her red-and-gold sari.

She remained still for about a minute, concentrating on what she was about to do next. She thought of the instructions the *kala iilam* had given her.

Whip yourself up into a frenzy of anger and the vilest of detestations. Allow all the hatred of the world to penetrate your body and spread fast, like the poison of a krait. She pushed back her long black hair and shut her eyes. A krait, she'd nearly stepped on a krait once, in the back garden. She had flattened its head with a stone. That was what she'd like to do to that slut. She might still do it if this thing didn't work ... *Concentrate* ... She groaned. She had seen them ... those two ... embracing ... rolling in bed ... whispering dirty words into each other's ears ... lovey-dovey ... Tears started rolling down Sarla's fat sallow face and her lips quivered, then her monstrously bloated body shook.

She saw terrible things happening to Ria: it was as though a film was being played before her eyes. (*Not* the kind of film she normally watched; it was highly doubtful whether the Bollywood dream factory would ever produce such a film.) She saw Ria engulfed by flames – torn to pieces by two tigers – stung by a krait, her body swelling and turning black – strangled by a woman who looked like the Queen of England – poisoned by gas as she lay in her bed – drowning in the ocean while swimming, her corpse washed up on the beach, covered in seaweed – caught in a wood-cutting machine, her body mangled, mutilated beyond recognition ... Envisioning her wishes, the witch doctor had told Sarla, would add great potency to the hex.

Be thinking of all this while doing this hex and when it says, 'With these bones I now do crush,' take a hammer or use feet and crush the chicken's bones to powder. Feet is better.

Sarla spoke.

> *'Bones of anger, bones to dust,*
> *Full of fury, revenge is just.*
> *I scatter these bones, these bones of rage.*
> *Capture my enemy – into the cage!*
> *I see my enemy before me now,*
> *I bind her, crush her, bring her low.'*

It was at that point that she stepped across the chicken's bones with her booted feet.

> *'With these bones I now do crush,*
> *Make her turn to dust!*
> *Torment, fire, out of control,*
> *With this hex I curse her soul!'*

36

Sarla was gratified to hear the crunching sounds from under her feet. She went on stomping – faster and faster – *faster* – as fast as her weight allowed. Soon she was breathing stertorously. Sweat poured down her face.

Her eyes had glazed over. 'You scarcely know my name, let alone what it stands for,' she said in English in a voice that did not sound like hers. 'It stands for Despair, Bewilderment, Futility, Degradation and Premeditated Murder.'

Then it was all over. She was done. The bones had been transformed to powder, almost. She was not aware that she had spoken at all. She swept them up and placed them in a bag. She was going to sprinkle them later around Ria's bungalow first, that was where Roman and Ria met, then around Coconut Grove, in case Ria moved in with Roman. I hate him too, Sarla said, her eyes filling with tears. I want him dead.

The procedure, she had been told, might have to be repeated if it didn't work the first time. And if it didn't work the second time or the third time, well, she would have to think of some other way of getting rid of Ria. Actually, she didn't want Roman to die. She wanted him – back.

'Only her!' Sarla raised her voice. She shook the bag with the powdered bones. And once more she addressed the spirits, which, she felt sure, were all around her, 'Do you hear? *Only her.*'

She felt a sudden sharp pain, just above the collarbone. So sharp, it made her gasp. She had the funny feeling that one of the shadowy figures she had seen earlier on, the 'Queen of England', had plunged a fruit knife into her throat.

5

Another Country

'*Miss Darcy has that priceless gift, part Ancient Mariner, part Scheherazade, that keeps the reader turning the pages,*' Major Payne read out. 'That's good, isn't it? They do love your stuff.'

'I don't know. They seem to,' Antonia said over her cup of coffee. Her new book had come out the week before.

'What do you mean, "seem to"? They love your stuff. Listen to this. *The plot is subtly pitched between unfathomable and coherent: at first there are only questions without answers, and then gradually information is given away – but only by minute degrees.* That's praise of the most undiluted kind.'

'Look at the bottom – they call the denouement "somewhat outlandish".'

'Most readers love outlandish denouements.'

'Do they?'

'Aunt Nellie loves outlandish denouements, don't you, darling?'

'I adore outlandish denouements,' Lady Grylls said absently. 'So what do you think, Hughie?'

He went on reading. '*Miss Darcy deals with the familiar country house set-up in a refreshing and exhilarating way.*'

'So what do you think, Hughie? Good idea, eh?'

'Oh, I don't know.' Payne looked up. 'We can't just up and go, darling. You don't really expect us to make a snap decision about that sort of thing.' Over the last five

38

minutes Payne had been dividing his attention between his wife and his aunt. 'You make it sound as though Goa is Hampstead Heath.'

'Planes, you seem to be forgetting, are the magic carpets *de nos jours*. Besides, Charlotte is my oldest friend. I wouldn't say my dearest friend, she was never that, but she is one of the very few still round. She was the mistress of somebody I knew quite well, who's dead now. She writes most persuasively. See for yourself.' Lady Grylls tossed the letter across the breakfast table.

Major Payne felt obliged to put *The Times* to one side. There was a pause. 'She says foreign travel broadens the mind. She says she'll take care of our travel expenses and we'll get the second best bedroom at the house. She says we won't have to spend a penny. A freebie, eh? Does she mean that?'

'Of course she means it. Charlotte's got pots of money, doesn't know what to do with it. Guy left her well provided for, beyond the dreams of avarice. At one time Guy's family owned most of Northumberland.'

'Mrs Depleche. I believe I remember her. Face like a hawk?'

'More like a vulture now.' Lady Grylls guffawed. 'She's got all her marbles, mind, so you don't have to worry on that count.'

Antonia asked Lady Grylls whether she wanted any more toast.

'Yes, one more slice, my dear. I'll have it with your excellent strawberry jam. Fancy you making your own jam. I thought no one living in London did these days. One doesn't expect it of writers in particular.'

It was an extremely cold day in early February. Although the central heating couldn't be turned up any higher, the dining room felt chilly. Lady Grylls had two shawls around her shoulders, a blanket across her knees and mittens on her hands, but she had never once complained. She had been staying at their house in Hampstead since December. Although the cataract operation had been a success, she still wore the piratical purple patch across her left eye and read with the aid of an enormous tortoiseshell-rimmed magnifying glass. Both patch and glass were used for effect, rather than out of any actual necessity, Antonia suspected. Chalfont Park was undergoing major repair work and they had pressed her to stay until things were back to normal once more.

'She says the view from the house is stupendous. She says it's going to be hot in Goa, but only tolerably so,' Payne went on. 'It's still the tourist season. In March it starts getting really hot and that goes on until June. After that comes the rainy season, which lasts three months.'

'That's one of the few things that worry Charlotte – the rainy season. Three months without stopping. What would she do when it rains for three months? Stanbury says she can watch old Cagney films on DVD. She has a thing about gangsters. She's buying this house. She's thinking of – what's that horrid word they use? – *relocating* to Goa.'

'Place called Coconut Grove. Built in the hacienda style. Beautiful terraces overlooking the sea. Golden beaches. Sapphire skies.' Payne's eyes remained on the letter. 'She's buying it from someone called . . . Roman Songhera. Who, it turns out, is the grandson of her late husband's Indian orderly. She says Roman's come up in the world and is now the uncrowned king of Goa. Golly. She's been to India before, hasn't she?'

'She has. Guy Depleche was one of Dickie Mountbatten's aides-de-camp in the last days of the Raj. When was it? Ages ago. 1946?' Lady Grylls paused reminiscently. 'D'you realize I remember the time when almost every nation of the world seemed to be governed by a Grand Old Man? There was Churchill in Britain, Eisenhower in the United States, Adenauer in West Germany, Nehru in India and so on. Isn't that extraordinary?'

'I wonder what happened to that race of larger-than-life statesmen . . . Nine o'clock. Shall we listen to the news?'

'No,' Lady Grylls said emphatically.

Major Payne helped himself to more coffee. '*I remember, I remember*. This can be made into a game, you know. Shall we play it?'

'No, Hugh, please. We can't play games at breakfast,' Antonia said.

'Why not? Organized games are fun at any time of day. It would also give you time to make up your minds.' Lady Grylls turned towards her nephew. 'What are the rules?'

'No rules.'

'Every game has rules.'

'This one hasn't, darling. No, no prizes either. It's all very simple. You just throw your mind as far back as you can and tell us what you remember. The more random the memory, the better. Would you like me to go first?' Payne fixed his eyes on the ceiling. 'I remember the yeti. I remember when alien abductions were all the rage. I remember feeling particularly disturbed by Betty and Barney Hill who drew pictures of aliens under hypnosis.'

'My dear?' Lady Grylls looked at Antonia.

'I am not playing.'

'I wish you weren't such a spoilsport.'

'I remember hating organized games when I was a child,' Antonia said.

'I remember being given codeine cough syrup when I was about six or seven,' Payne said. 'I remember spending days submerged in a pretty powerfully altered state of consciousness.'

'I remember snorting cocaine,' Lady Grylls said.

'I remember Sonya Dufrette's doll in the river,' Antonia said.

'*That's* the spirit, my dear. I remember my father-in-law employing a boy to loosen the collars of his intoxicated gentlemen guests.'

'I remember when not a year passed without some dance craze,' Payne said.

'I remember a joke.' Lady Grylls took a sip of coffee. '*Apart from that, Mrs Lincoln, how did you enjoy the play?*'

Despite herself, Antonia laughed.

41

'I remember getting stuck in the middle of a singularly tedious passage of Cicero's *De Senectute* at school. I remember hearing, at various times of my early life, the reputedly authentic story of a lorry transporting strips of corrugated iron, one of which slips off behind and decapitates a motorcyclist.'

Lady Grylls stared back at her nephew. 'I expect he fell off the bike?'

'As a matter of fact he didn't. The motorcycle was travelling at great speed and it continued to keep pace with the lorry. The lorry driver, paralysed by the sight of a headless rider, not to mention the stream of blood, lost control of the driving wheel and collided with another vehicle. He was instantly killed himself.'

Antonia expressed the opinion that that was nothing more than an urban legend.

'Odd things *do* happen, my dear. I remember Charlotte telling me about her first party at Government House in Delhi when all the memsahibs were given pillow-slips and instructed to put their feet in. Charlotte got it into her head it was some sort of Hindu ritual, but it turned out it was for protection against mosquitoes since it was the mosquito season. Too Somerset Maugham for words.'

'How long did she stay in India?'

'A year or two. Guy was considerably older than Charlotte. She was eighteen when she married him and terribly innocent to begin with. He was at least fifty. Edwina took her in hand and introduced her to some high-caste Indian men. That was at the height of Edwina's affair with Nehru, you know. Well, Dickie was most certainly queer. Guy wasn't, but he was getting on, men did age fast in those days, and anyhow all his energies went into playing polo and collecting butterflies. Charlotte hinted at an "ice-box honeymoon", though they did manage to produce a son.'

'Whatever made Mrs Depleche think of us?' Antonia asked.

'I did. Charlotte wrote to me over Christmas and said how she dreaded the idea of travelling on her own, or with Stanbury, and how she couldn't get anyone decent to go with her, so I told her how clever the two of you are and how splendid to be with when one is abroad.'

'I don't think we've been abroad together, have we?' Payne frowned.

'Charlotte was awfully impressed. She'd rather have you than Stanbury, of whom she takes a fearfully dim view ... Stanbury's her grandson, yes, didn't I say? He's something in advertising and seems terribly keen on Charlotte buying this property in Goa. It will be his holiday home one day. He's married to a weather girl, Charlotte says – a platinum blonde – apparently she's often on the box. Charlotte takes a fearfully dim view of her too.'

There was a pause.

'She's thinking of leaving on the twelfth of February. Twelve days from now.' Payne shot a quizzical glance at Antonia.

Antonia's feet felt as cold as ice and, at the moment at least, the prospect of a flight to a hot climate wasn't too repellent. 'I don't know,' she said.

'It's all settled then. Charlotte would be terribly pleased. I'll write to her at once.' Lady Grylls nodded. 'The plane journey lasts for ever, apparently, but all you need to do is sit next to Charlotte and keep her amused. Chat to her, play a game or two. Anything to do with gangsters or sex will do as a topic. Don't let her drink too much or flirt with the stewards – *that* could be tedious. She can be a malignant old cat where women are concerned, so she may not really take to you, my dear,' Lady Grylls turned to Antonia, 'but don't let that bother you. She'll adore Hugh.'

'Lucky Hugh.'

'It won't be anything personal, you must understand, it's just that Charlotte prefers men to women. She told me once – Charlotte's *histoires* are endless – that she'd had affairs with a married man, with a ladies' man, with a man's man, with a bad lot, with a good shot, with someone

43

who was queer but was terribly drunk, with a lovable shit – and with a gentleman jockey.'

'There were probably only three men. The good shot could easily have been a bad lot, a man's man and also a married man,' Payne mused. 'The gentleman jockey could have been a ladies' man *and* a lovable shit.'

'Ladies' men are almost invariably lovable shits,' Lady Grylls said. 'You'll need to get your jabs as soon as possible. Malaria, cholera, snakebite and so on. Once you get to Goa, you won't have to lift a finger.'

Payne gave the letter another glance. 'The house apparently has every *confort moderne*. Each marble bathroom features three basins labelled "Teeth", "Hands" and "Face". The most advanced sewage system.'

'Plumbing nowadays costs the earth.' Lady Grylls heaved a heavy sigh. 'We are talking the kind of money that'd buy me a nice little house in St John's Wood. I'd have come with you like a shot, Charlotte did invite me, but I'll have to be getting back, isn't that a bore? I can just see you – sitting on the terrace under striped awnings with scalloped frills, knocking down gin and bitters. It isn't,' Lady Grylls went on, 'as though you are about to get involved in some mysterious death, is it?'

'How do you know?' Antonia said. 'We might.' I shouldn't provoke Fate, she thought.

'We always seem to get involved in mysterious deaths.' Major Payne frowned. 'Isn't that odd?'

6

Belle de Jour

Along the beguilingly balmy Betalbatim beach Ria walked, under a blazing sun. Unusually, there were a lot of people around her, a real crowd. That didn't bother her, but something else did. For the last couple of minutes she had been aware that someone was following her. With the tail of her eye she saw it was a man. When she started walking faster, so did he. When she slowed down, he did too. What *did* he want?

Looking over her shoulder, she saw that it was her father.

Well, he didn't look like her father at all, not the way she remembered him. Their last confrontation had taken place a year and a half before, on the very day she left England. Then her father had filled her with terror as well as with the hysterical desire to laugh aloud. Ashen face twisted in impotent rage, old and wrinkled, something simian about him, tufts of white hair standing on end. Roaring like a bull and emitting sparks – nearly detonating with rage. Now he looked different: much younger, darker, taller and more handsome – not unlike Roman, in fact. There was a little smile on his lips. She didn't see his mouth open, yet she heard his voice.

You shouldn't be afraid of me any more. I am dead. It is all over.

Ria swung round and began to run in sudden blind

panic, but her progress had become difficult. The people round her had grown in number and she had to push them out of her way. Her feet sank deep into the sand, which seemed to have turned the consistency of treacle. Her heart was racing and she was gasping for breath. When she felt a tap on her shoulder, she gave a cry –

She opened her eyes.

It was morning and the room was full of bright light. The sun played on the platinum cufflinks which Roman had left behind the night before and made them glitter. Ria lay in her bed, the ridiculously regal bed Roman had had specially made for her, a four-poster, with carved pillars and a canopy. Her heart was still beating fast, as though she had really been running. She glanced at the gilded clock on her bedside table. Ten to eight. The electrically operated curtains moved in the breeze. As usual, the night before she had left her windows open. She could see part of the palm tree that grew outside. For a couple of moments she lay very still.

What was that poem they had taught her at school?

> Dismiss the dreams that sore affright
> Phantasmagoria of the night . . .

Yes, quite. 'It's only a dream,' she said aloud. 'My father is dead.' As though to convince herself she rose on her elbow and, reaching out, opened the bedside table drawer and took out the letter.

Your father died of a pulmonary embolism, that's what the doctor said, her aunt had written. *He collapsed in the woods, where we found him, and was taken to hospital. He died soon after without regaining consciousness. The funeral was rather a grand affair, but I won't bore you with details. I don't for a moment imagine that this news will cause you any great grief or sadness. I know how you felt about your father. I am perfectly aware of the fact that it was because of him you left England, but perhaps now you could find it in your heart to forgive him?*

Ria – whose real name was Marigold – looked up. She smiled. Dear Aunt Iris. Face like a friendly sheep. What

46

was it she'd heard her father say once? That Aunt Iris was as hopeless as the Poles and the Irish – she liked to tell you what you wanted to hear, but was ineffectual and untrustworthy. Ria was sure her aunt hadn't cared much for her brother either . . .

She dropped the letter. Well, that was that. Her father was dead. The ogre was six foot under. She was never going back to England. They didn't have to stay in Goa either. In fact, there would be no question of their staying in Goa. She couldn't stand the place. The dirt, the poverty, the stray dogs, the hungry crows, the cripples, the children from the orphanage with their 'sponsorship' forms, the impossibly hot spices they seemed to put into every kind of food, the – well, everything.

East meets West? It hadn't worked for Jemima and Imran – nor for Diana and Dodi. One relationship had ended in divorce, the other, well, in death. As soon as they were married, they'd leave. Yes. She'd never have to see Roman's wife again. Roman's wife somehow embodied all that to Ria's way of thinking was wrong with India. Her name was Sarla, and she and Roman lived separately. Ria had seen Sarla only three or four times, but that had been enough.

She remembered the second time. It had been very odd. Ria had seen Sarla from her window, walking up the path, a voluminous bag in her hand. She had been afraid that Sarla was going to make a nuisance of herself, that she might create a scene, attack her even – but Sarla hadn't rung the front door bell – all she had done was empty the bag on the ground underneath Ria's sitting-room window. The bag seemed to contain some kind of greyish powder. On another occasion she'd woken up from her siesta and thought she'd seen Sarla's face at the bedroom window, staring at her. She had been frightened out of her wits and cried out, but by the time she'd got out of bed, the face had disappeared. Had that been a dream? On that occasion Sarla's hair had been exactly like hers – long, golden-brown. Perhaps it was a dream.

Pay no attention, Roman had said. She is mad. I've told her she's a dead woman if she tries to touch you. I'll get

47

her fitted for a tight jacket in a narrow room with soft walls, he'd added for good measure. Ria smiled. She liked him when he talked like an American gangster. Each time she saw Sarla, Ria experienced a shrinking, creeping sensation – exactly like when she had seen her first cobra at Kilhar's market . . . or her first female scorpion, plump with poison, four babies on her back, crawling along the kitchen window sill . . .

Each time Roman suggested she have a bodyguard, she said a firm no. Someone spying on her, reporting everything she did to Roman? No, thank you very much. She had made it absolutely clear to Roman that she didn't want to stay in India. With Roman's money, they could live anywhere in the world. Somewhere warm. Spain or Italy would be her first choice, but she wouldn't mind the South of France either. Thanks to his Portuguese blood, Roman could easily be taken for a denizen of any of these countries. When she had first met him in Dubai, she had thought he was Italian.

Ria sat up in bed, brought her knees up to her chin and contemplated her reflection in the mirror on the wall opposite. 'Mrs Roman Songhera,' she said aloud. There were mirrors everywhere, even on the ceiling above the bed. That was the way Roman liked it.

She examined herself critically. Well, even at this early hour, even after her nightmare, she looked good – no, *stunning*. An oval face, high cheekbones kissed by the sun, almond-shaped eyes, smooth supple neck, thick golden-brown hair that owed nothing to chemistry and everything to nature that had been too generous, perfectly shaped breasts that were tantalizingly outlined through her Brooks Brothers pyjamas. Ria pushed her bare leg through the silk sheets and stretched it out before her, like a ballerina. So long – so smooth . . .

It wasn't surprising that Roman was mad about her. 'Crazy' was the word he used. Sometimes he spoke like an American, which she liked better than when he put on his stuffy English accent. 'I am crazy about you. I can't get you out of my mind,' he had told her the night before, between kisses. 'When I am not with you, I don't feel right. I get restless, anxious, depressed. I can't settle down to doing anything important. I keep seeing you. You are inside my head. My life is dominated by my desire for you. I desire you all the time. Do you understand? *All the time.*'

Ria's hand went up to her cleavage and she smiled again, a slow, lazy smile.

I can't get you out of my mind. Her father had written something on those lines in one of his letters. Roman was as obsessed with her as her father had been, now wasn't that freaky? People did do crazy things when they were obsessed with someone . . .

Roman had said he'd kill his wife. Would he really do it? Well, he sounded as though he meant it – if Sarla refused to divorce him, if she tried to make any trouble between them. There was no question of him doing it in person of course. He'd have Sarla bumped off. He could do it, easily. Everybody listened to him. He had the local police eating out of his hand. It wasn't without a reason that he was known as the king of Goa.

She had dreamt that she was being followed. Funnily enough the other day she had had the feeling that someone *was* following her. She had been in the market place. She hadn't seen the person but the feeling had been there all right. Somebody's eyes boring into her. She thought it was a man. Well, it had to be a man. Was it possible that Roman was having her followed? Did Roman suspect that she might be seeing somebody else? She had caught him watching her speculatively on a number of occasions.

Did Roman know about –? Superstitiously Ria tried not to think of the boy's name. She wasn't 'seeing' him. She had 'seen' him *once*. Still, Roman was pathologically jealous. She didn't want to think what he might do if he got to hear about it. She shouldn't have done it. It was interesting the way her father had been transformed into Roman, but then that was the illogicality of dreams. Was her subconscious trying to warn her about Roman?

7

The Shadow

The moment he had stepped off the plane he was enveloped in a surge of stifling hot air which might have sprung from some steam room. Blistering heat. He remembered his thoughts: *I am moving towards dissolution.*

On the minibus, as they drove away from the airport, he felt ill, feverish, drained of all energy. Dozing off, he dreamt he was on board a ship. At first all seemed to be well, the most marvellous indigo sea, but then the ship started shaking and suddenly they found themselves invaded by hairy apelike creatures with hungry burning eyes. The creatures swarmed about the deck and started gnawing the ropes and cables with their sharp teeth. He saw the mast toppling, coming towards him – he tried to jump out of its way and woke up with a violent start.

It had taken him several moments to remember where he was and why. He had stared out of the dusty minibus window at the angry, orange-red sky. The air was full of dust; it made him cough. Most of the people on the bus wore turbans and they spoke in a language he could not understand. He felt so disoriented, for a moment he convinced himself this was another dream. But of course it wasn't a dream. He found himself wondering how normal, ordinary people spent their lives.

The minibus had stopped at a petrol station that looked like a shack. He thought of getting off and stretching his legs, but decided against it. He couldn't believe how desolate everything looked. An alien landscape of great menace, at least that was how he saw it.

He continued gazing out of the window. He saw a little bird get caught in a curtain of creepers across the brick wall adjoining the shack, its wings beating helplessly. The next moment a copper-coloured snake appeared from somewhere – such a large head – he could see its forked tongue flick in and out from where he sat! The snake slithered fast. Aware of its approach the bird made one last futile effort to disentangle itself –

He had looked away. His ears had rung with the bird's desperate chirruping. He had heard some of his fellow passengers laugh and whistle.

Thank God they had driven away.

It had come as a shock to see her in the hotel foyer, sitting in one of the leather chairs, wearing a snuff-coloured tropical suit, drinking tea and looking through a three-month-old copy of *Country Life*. The ground moved under his feet with a dancing sway and it had suddenly felt dark and extremely close, as though an old-fashioned photographer's black hood had been drawn over his head. He had stood and stared. He had been rendered speechless.

At first he thought she was a mirage conjured up by the heat, but the next minute she had opened her mouth and spoken to him. She had managed to track him down. She'd booked in at the same hotel. Well, where else? This seemed to be the only decent place around. She patted the sofa beside her and asked him to sit down. Would he have some tea? She told him not to be agitated – his face was too red – it was bad for him – he should keep calm in this appalling heat. Before he knew what she was doing, she reached out for his wrist and checked his pulse. She had brought his medicine, she said. Was he aware he'd left his medicine behind? He said he didn't need any medicine. He felt better without it! He glared at her. He asked her what she thought she was doing. Why had she followed him? Who the hell did she think she was? His bloody shadow? Couldn't she leave him alone – *ever*?

She had remained unruffled. Not in the least discomfited. She was good in a crisis. Well, he had to hand it to her. She had nerves of steel. She feared for him, she said – for his health and safety. Roman Songhera wouldn't be happy if he knew what he was planning to do, would he? She seemed convinced his mission was doomed to fail. Something in her voice made it clear to him that she *wanted* it to fail. She looked so terribly smug and self-righteous. She was not quite human. She was right about that filthy wop, though. Roman Songhera *was* dangerous.

She meant to take good care of him, she said. He might not realize it but he needed her.

He told her she was an infernal nuisance. He didn't want her here. He wished she could go away. He said he didn't trust her. He hated her. He reminded her how she had urged him to adopt a resigned and a non-emotional attitude and become reconciled to his 'loss'. Well, he refused to become reconciled to his 'loss', so there! She gave an indulgent smile and patted his hand. She had already ordered more tea. China tea. Extremely refreshing, she said. The kind of tea one got at Brown's. We *are* at Brown's, he pointed out. She made a moue – well, *yes* – not quite the real thing, though, was it?

She produced a pill and instructed him to put it under his tongue. He grumbled but did as asked. It was easier that way. He didn't have the energy to argue. He shut his eyes. He felt her hand on his forehead. Her hand was cool and dry. He felt calmer. He told her he didn't want her to interfere in his affairs. Don't try to stop me, he said. I wouldn't dream of it, she said. He looked at her suspiciously. He was sure she was humouring him now.

There was another English couple in the foyer. He listened to their conversation absently.

'There was an advertisement at Reception,' the woman

was saying. 'One could have one's very own personal guru, apparently.'

'What should I want with a guru?' the man grumbled.

'A personal guru helps you meditate and purify your inner self, so that you can look inwards and find peace and tranquillity.'

'I'd rather have a gin than a guru!' Laughing, the man snapped his fingers. 'Waiter!'

He held his eyes tightly shut, trying to persuade himself that when he opened them, she'd be gone. We are in this together, he heard her say. You need me. I will do *everything* to help you. It isn't so bad here, actually. If one stuck to the hotel and didn't mind the smells, one could imagine one was in England. Besides, the place is not without beauty. It is the violet hour now – that's what they call it – *look*.

Reluctantly he looked. She was right about that too, blast her. He had to admit she was often right. The place was not without beauty. Indeed. The late afternoon sun was filtering through the jacaranda trees, casting sublime purple shadows on the terrace. He heard her cancel his single room and book a suite for the two of them . . .

Tomorrow. He'd go tomorrow. No point delaying.

He *had* to see her.

He had a bad feeling about it.

8

When a Stranger Calls

Pulmonary embolism . . .

Ria reached out and picked up her aunt's letter once again. As though she cared! Why did some people insist on quoting post-mortem results in obscure medical terminology? On second thoughts, it was good to know the precise phrase – she found that reassuring – it made her father's death *real*. Well, this meant she wouldn't be writing any more letters. She sighed. She'd miss that. The letters had become a part of her life. The game was over. She felt disappointed – empty. A great sadness swept over her. How funny. She suddenly felt tearful. She wanted to howl. What the fuck was wrong with her? Withdrawal symptoms?

What else had her aunt written? Nothing much. It wasn't a particularly cordial letter. It made no mention of Lucasta. Poor old Lucasta – forever babbling about bulbs. Lucasta must have been distraught. She had doted on her father. Her life had revolved around him. Apparently Lucasta had been in love with Ria's father all her life. She'd get the house and everything else, Ria supposed. Well, good luck to her. Ria didn't really care. Uncle Henry had come up with the suggestion that Lucasta had actually poisoned Ria's mother while nursing her, so that she could get into Toby's bed. Uncle Henry was funny. Ria had rather liked him and from the way she'd caught him looking at her, she had no doubt he liked her too, though in a somewhat different way –

She smiled. Did she have a one-track mind? Was sex at the bottom of *everything*?

Had her father and Lucasta ever had any sex? It seemed an impossible thought. No, one simply couldn't think of Lucasta in those terms. That marriage, like most late ones, was probably still unconsummated. Then another idea struck her. Could her father have actually lusted after *her*, Ria? That kind of thing did happen. Her father had dressed it all up in high morality and ethics and paternal love and concern for her welfare and good intentions and so on, but of course that was the kind of thing Lord Justice Leighton *would* do. Well, that would explain his obsession with her – the way he'd slapped her face – didn't they say that violence was sublimated carnal desire?

That poem – she couldn't get it out of her head.

> *Confound my carnal enemy,*
> *Let my flesh not corrupted be –*

Let my flesh not corrupted be. A little too late for that. She hadn't had her orange juice. Leaping out of bed, she walked bare-footed across the room. It was a lovely room – all white – the most luxurious deep-pile white carpet – white modern furniture, which had come from Sweden – everything exactly as she liked it. She walked out into the hall. She twiddled her fingers in greeting at her radiant reflection in the oval silver-framed mirror that hung on the wall. She went into the sitting room and turned on the radio. There was an Italian music station she adored. *Ciao Amore*. Of course they would be playing love songs today. St Valentine's. What a bore.

The kitchen was also white and fully fitted. *New Millennium* in snappy chrome letters shimmered on each cupboard as well as across the double-width fridge. Air-conditioning. Every possible gadget. A smoothie maker. A shining espresso machine. Kopi Luwak coffee. The most expensive coffee in the world, apparently. A pound of KL coffee cost three hundred dollars, Roman had informed her. Imports from Italy, Germany, the USA. Roman hadn't stinted himself. One had to give him credit for that. A woman came and cleaned every day. 'Anything you want. All you need to do is tell me,' Roman had said.

She poured herself a glass of orange juice. Florida oranges. Roman too had orange juice in the morning. Sometimes when he was with her, they sat side by side, drinking orange juice out of tall crystal glasses. Sometimes they talked but more and more often they sat in companionable silence. As though they'd been married for ages. Darby and Joan. How depressing.

Was orange juice all they had in common? What else was there? Well, they hated Sarla and loved sex – they were good at it. Both had enjoyed the drag revue at Le Carousel in Paris. Both loved girls – funnily enough Roman didn't mind her being with other girls – he liked to watch, though he said that once they were married that would have to stop. (He *was* funny.) Both had a weakness for expensive jewellery – Roman more than her, in fact – the way he decorated himself, like the maharajas of old, or like a tart. (It had made him angry, when she had said that – Roman didn't have much of a sense of humour. He hated it when she teased him.) Both liked expensive scent. What else? They loved the sea. They went swimming together. Both enjoyed smoking hashish every now and then. (One of Roman's ventures was the selling of hash and he used a customized Cartier cigarette case for his marijuana roll-ups.) Anything else? Well, they loved dancing. Was that a good enough foundation for a lasting relationship? For a lifetime together? She was twenty-four, Roman twenty-nine. They could have fifty-five years together.

Ria took a rice cake out of a jar, spread it lightly with manuka honey and bit into it thoughtfully. Fifty-five years with Roman? She feared she'd be bored. They didn't have much to say to one another, really. She'd already started finding him tedious, if she had to be perfectly honest.

Roman liked to talk about his enemies, what he'd done to them, what he wanted to do to them, or he told her how much he wished he could get to one of the Queen's garden parties, or he boasted that he could buy himself a barony complete with a castle in Scotland, if he wished – an English solicitor had already explained to him the procedure in some detail.

A garden party. There would be a garden party at Coconut Grove later today, in honour of the old hag who had come from England. She was buying Coconut Grove from Roman. Ria was expected to put in an appearance at some point. Roman was terribly keen on her doing so. He wanted her to make a good impression. He insisted that she wear her floral dress and pearls, her Alice band and white elbow-length gloves, like some perfectly groomed deb out of an early 1950s *Vogue* cover. Quite different from an earlier fantasy of his. Ria smiled, remembering. Wouldn't it be fun if she were to appear at the garden party wearing the black bustier, garter belt, fishnet stockings and snakeskin stiletto heels?

Roman wanted the old hag to like her – the Honourable Mrs Depleche. He said he hoped Ria and Mrs Depleche would be 'friends'. He seemed to envisage Mrs Depleche in the part of Ria's chaperone. The elderly duenna and the young ward. Totally pointless, inexpressibly bizarre. Roman seemed to hanker after some kind of aristocratic Arcadia. The truth was that he was twitchy about social status, which, exasperatingly, eluded his otherwise cocksure purchasing power. She meant of course social status in the 'English' sense. She kept telling him England was completely different from what he imagined it to be, but he didn't seem to believe her. Well, he got all his ideas about English high society from 'society' novels of the 1920s and 1930s – he'd found a boxful of those somewhere – the kind of trashy novelettes shop-girls had read once.

She didn't feel the slightest inclination to grace Roman's garden party. She didn't feel like meeting any English people, particularly not the kind of English people who might know her father. 'Marigold Leighton? I wonder now – aren't you poor Toby's gel? We heard something. I am sure we got it all wrong. Fancy bumping into you here, of all places ...' No, she definitely did not want to go – but Roman would be furious if she didn't. They'd have a row. She couldn't bear the thought of another row.

Ria sighed. To think that when they had first met, she had considered him the best specimen of his kind – exciting, vigorous, dangerously sexy. Unlike any other man she had been with. She'd considered Roman the very personification of va-va-voom. Full of testosterone-fuelled bounce. She'd had a name for him: Tigger! (She remembered how she'd always said she'd marry Tigger.) Sadly, the novelty had worn off. He had revealed himself as petty and petulant, possessive, given to violent jealous rages – same as her father, in fact. He had also started putting on weight and was no longer anything like Tigger – and, goodness, he talked so much rubbish. Still, he had money. Money *was* important. If she played her cards well, she could have it both ways. She could have – *fun*. She needed to be extremely careful though –

That boy would be there, she suddenly realized – at the party. She held her breath. He'd be serving the drinks or proffering canapés. Now, was that a good thing or a bad thing? Part of her wanted to see him – very much – another part said, no, that would be total madness – he might give himself away – in fact he was *bound* to give himself away, the silly young fool – the way he gazed and gawped at her! Roman or his henchmen would be sure to notice. Sometimes Roman 'noticed' things that weren't there. He was paranoid. He didn't like it when she smiled at people. He'd already accused her of 'flirting'. He didn't trust her. *I gave commands, Then all smiles stopped*. Ria shivered. She'd actually found 'My Last Duchess' wonderfully creepy when they did it at school.

Her phone rang and she picked it up.

She heard a sharp intake of breath and knew at once who it was. Talk of the devil! That silly young fool – how had he managed to get hold of her phone number? Suddenly she panicked – could Roman have had the phone tapped? Could Roman, or one of his men, be listening in? He wouldn't go as far as that, would he?

'I told you not to call, didn't I,' she whispered.

'Ria – please –'

'It was a mistake, I told you. A big mistake. I don't want to see you again. Not as long as I live.'

'Please – can I come and –? I want to give you something. It's St Valentine's Day – I *must* see you!'

'No.'

'I *will* come –'

'Don't you dare!'

She slammed down the receiver. Her heart was once more beating fast. She felt as though she were walking on the edge of a precipice. She hoped Roman would never know about it. Roman would kill him if he knew – she had no doubt about it. He'd kill *her*.

The love-lorn puppy! But what a sweet smile. She rather liked the way he talked. He was not a real waiter. Ria believed she was the only one who knew his secret. She admitted to herself she was flattered by his ardour. She should never have done it. Never. Valentine's Day. For some reason she thought of the massacre rather than of roses and violets and love. She was sick and tired of love. *Ciao Amore*. Nothing but trouble. She hoped Roman would never know about 'Bond' either. She *had* been a naughty girl. She needed to start behaving. 'Bond' had been nothing but a whim – she hadn't even fancied him that much – she had been in his taxi – she had been extremely bored, it had also amused her, that was the *only* reason she had invited him in.

That dream . . . Meeting her father on the beach . . . She still felt shaken up by it.

It was some twenty minutes later that she heard her front door bell ring. She put down her cup of coffee. Who could it be? She looked through the window.

There was a stranger standing there. A man.

9

The Mysterious Commission

Julian Knight tried not to drink on the morning of the fourteenth but found it difficult. He knew perfectly well what would happen and he dreaded it. By nine o'clock his hands would start shaking. Sweat would break out all over his body and that would be followed by a creepy-crawly kind of sensation. Withdrawal symptoms – it happened every time he failed to have his usual 'intake'. He invariably started the day with a Kingfisher, the cheap local beer, for which he had acquired a taste – his fridge was stacked with Kingfisher bottles. He went on to drink whisky, then moved on to brandy, then back to Kingfisher, then –

Not today. Today he had to make a good impression.

The phone call had come late the night before, only moments after he had finished the bottle of Napoleon brandy. The voice had been loud and clear. A woman's voice. A very English voice. As it happened, Julian had been in a morbidly mawkish mood – it always happened on the eve of St Valentine's. Bloody St Valentine's – how it brought back memories. He'd been thinking of Carolyn, his former wife. When he heard the woman's voice, his heart missed a beat. For a wild moment he imagined it was his wife who was ringing him from England. He thought she might have undergone a change of heart, that she wanted them to get back together again, that she had decided to give him another chance.

60

It was five years since they'd got divorced. *Five years.* How time flew. His wife had said she was leaving him because of his drink problem while he was convinced he had started drinking *because* of his suspicion that she was preparing to leave him for another man. A suspicion that had proved only too correct. Now, which one had come first? Which was the truth? He couldn't say. The past was fast becoming a blur.

The woman had told him who she was and then explained why she was phoning. His mind had been a complete blank. Her name had meant nothing to him. Her tone was superior, peremptory; he didn't like it at all. *What was she talking about?* He shouldn't have drunk so much. Eventually her words had sunk in and at the same time he recognized the name. So *that* was who she was. Fancy now. He had never had any dealings with *her* before. At first he thought she was employing the royal 'we', but then she told him they were both in Goa. That surprised him, though of course it was none of his business where they went or what they did. The only thing that mattered was that he was going to be paid for his services. As soon as she mentioned money, he had pulled himself together and concentrated. It was a simple enough request. Of course, madam, he said. No problem, madam. I would be delighted to be of service.

She phoned again at eight o'clock in the morning. Where *was* he? They were waiting for him. She sounded impatient, cross. He might have been her servant. Was he on his way? Yes, yes, he said – coming – sorry – will be with you in five minutes. He had already got out of bed, bleary-eyed, his face like that of a drowned man, if his cracked mirror was to be trusted. He didn't feel like going *anywhere.* He felt like slipping back into bed, curling up and resuming his sleep. Still, they were paying him – and action was better than inaction. A commission provided him with a purpose. It gave his day a structure. It made him *try* not to drink.

He reached for his notebook. It was bound in soft reddish-brown leather and had a picture of an Arthurian sword on the front cover. He had written his name inside the sword, vertically: KNIGHT. His little joke. That was some time ago. Quite some time. He no longer made jokes.

The notebook contained all his reports. He leafed through it. Funny requests, some of his clients had. No, he didn't think he could kill anyone, no matter how high the fee. For one thing, he wouldn't be able to do it properly – he couldn't shoot, stab or strangle anybody – his hands shook too much. (He had already refused to release a poisonous snake into a bedroom.)

Would he commit perjury for a fee? Not even if the money was good? No – *never*. He might have been a much richer man if he'd been less scrupulous. One might not think it of him, but he had his principles. Knight by name, knight by nature. He went on turning the pages of his diary. He used capital letters because his hand was so often unsteady, he couldn't decipher his own handwriting. A paper cutting fluttered out from between the notebook's pages. He caught it before it reached the floor and saw it was a three-year-old *Times* article.

If there is a problem group, it is lone men aged fifty-plus, who are more likely to suffer health problems such as alcoholism, panic attacks, suicidal thoughts and depression.

Well, yes. All correct. Lonely, boozy, emotionally volatile and, when he wasn't drinking, more than faintly depressed, desperate in fact, that was him to a T. He drank to allay his sadness and fear of life. Still, he managed to do his job properly. His clients were happy with his services. So far only Madame Scarpetta had been difficult. She'd refused to believe her husband was having an affair with an Englishwoman and said he'd got it all wrong. Mrs Agrawal on the other hand had had no problem accepting the outlandish nature of her husband's passion and had started filing for divorce.

Actually, he needed no reminders of the kind of person he had become, so he crumpled up the paper cutting and dropped it on the floor. The floor was covered with things he no longer needed. He wished his hands didn't shake so! He went into the bathroom. Was there a cure for him? He had attended a service at the local Catholic church the previous Sunday and prayed for a miracle. He had felt encouraged by the sermon, but his optimism had lasted only a short time, and been replaced by his usual dark despair. What was else was there? Alcoholics Anonymous – rehab? The point was he couldn't be bothered to seek treatment. He'd have to return to England. Although he found Goa isolated and backward, he felt reluctant to leave it. *No.* England would be worse. He would rather stay here till he died. How about suicide?

He paused, the razor gleaming in his hand. His face in the bathroom mirror was deeply tanned, yet pale.

'Hello. My name is Julian Knight,' he said to his reflection. 'And who are *you*?'

Sometimes he talked to his reflection as to a stranger. Was he losing his mind?

There was something on his chin – dark drops – blood? Yes. Must have cut himself while shaving. He knew the colour of blood was red but of course he could neither see nor recognize red. He gave a twisted smile. He was denied the beauty of rubies, roses and rainbows. He was born that way – colour-blind – well, that was the least of his troubles!

One of the worst features of his nervous breakdown had been the conviction, coming in flashes every now and then, that he was not real any longer; that his body and his inner self had moved apart, the first walking or talking in everyday life like an articulate dummy, while the brain remained in another place. Sometimes he felt as though he were dead already and seeing his body move . . .

Julian Knight put on his panama and his dark glasses. *En avant*, he murmured. He went out. Eight thirty and already so hot. There was going to be a solar eclipse at about eleven, that's what they said on the news – a partial one – it would only last five minutes. He felt vague

63

stirrings of anxiety. He didn't like the idea of darkness at such an hour. He knew he wouldn't be able to bring himself to look up at the sky. His anxiety spells were becoming worse; they were particularly bad in the early hours of morning. He felt cold and clammy and started mopping his face with his handkerchief. He was dying for a drink, that was the trouble, but he knew that would have to wait. Business first.

Out in the street he bumped into his Chinese landlord who said something to him, but Julian didn't respond. He was concentrating on his feet. Left right, left right. He wanted to make sure he was walking in the right direction. He carried his left shoulder slightly lower than the right and glided somewhat. He was a familiar figure in the streets of Kilhar. Some people smiled when they saw him, others tut-tutted and shook their heads.

Left right.

He had no idea he was on his way to a murder.

After he left them, Julian Knight walked fast down Fernandez Avenue and bought two bottles of Kingfisher beer from the kiosk at the corner. Well, *now* he could drink. He finished the first in six seconds. His eyes shut and he gave a deep sigh, his enjoyment was so intense. He opened the second bottle. Drinking more slowly, he made his way to the beach. The beggars didn't bother to approach him – they knew he'd have no time for them. The ocean looked smooth. There were several fishing boats in the distance. Shakeel's Sea Shack was only a minute away. Reaching it, he bought two more Kingfishers and a small bottle of Portuguese rum. He sat down at one of the little wooden tables and opened his third Kingfisher.

His mobile phone rang half an hour later. By now he was feeling extremely mellow, the way he liked it. It was her again. Another request. He thought she sounded odd. He was ready to swear someone was sobbing in the background. Would he be able to ...? He listened

64

dispassionately and said he would try. The money they were offering was good – much better than any of the rates he charged for his services. Again, cash on delivery – that suited him down to the ground too – cashing cheques in Kilhar could be extremely tricky.

He managed to obtain a pass to Roman Songhera's party with comparative ease and comparatively cheaply, by bribing one of the guards. That, he had discovered, was the manner in which most difficulties were resolved in India. There was always a way round every seeming impossibility. He also contrived to learn details of the gathering.

The gathering – a 'garden party' in the English style – was going to take place at Coconut Grove at five o'clock in the evening. Roman Songhera would be there in person. Roman Songhera was entertaining some high-ranking English visitors. An Honourable lady, a Mrs Depleche, and her friends, a married couple of the name of Pyne or Payne. It was the head waiter at Coconut Grove who provided Julian Knight with the guest list; it cost Julian a further five thousand rupees. He reflected that Roman Songhera, powerful as he was, had in fact feet of clay. Roman instilled terror but not the tiniest drop of loyalty. Feared, loathed and despised, yes, respected, no – not in the least. One of these days, like Humpty Dumpty, Roman Songhera was going to have a great fall.

Julian wondered about the kind of drinks they'd be serving at the Coconut Grove party. He had heard the head waiter refer to cocktails with rather exotic names. Ice-cold cocktails. Julian's mouth started watering. He felt his hand rummaging inside his pocket, scooping up change.

He bought another bottle of Kingfisher.

10

The Garden Party

'Terrorism and cricket, that's right.'

'I said *tourism* – not terrorism.' Major Payne raised his voice. Mrs Depleche, he suspected, was a bit deaf. '*Tourism* and cricket.'

'So you did, Hugh. I am being naughty,' Mrs Depleche confessed with a cackle. 'One shouldn't say such things, I know. The locals might kick me out or have me beheaded or something. I quite agree with you. Their only salvation. Yes. *Yes.* Poor benighted country. Lovely house and all that, but things aren't much different from when I was here last all those years ago, really. Still, they can't *all* be waiters and cricketers, can they? Or can they? I suppose some of them could be rent boys – don't you think? We seem to have got the finest specimens here.' She meant the waiters.

'Perhaps some of them are – in their off-hours,' Major Payne said.

The waiters were hurrying about on the sun-drenched terrace, handing round drinks. They all sported toast-golden tans and wore red boots with upturned toes, black baggy trousers and green and highly ornate tunics, bearing name tags. They had the grace of dancers. Ganymede himself couldn't foot it more featly, Payne thought. They tended to overdo the prancing a bit, though. Judging by their names – Manolo, Marcello, Faustino, Felicio and so on – they were all of Portuguese extraction.

'*Love is the sweetest thing*,' Mrs Depleche hummed. 'You don't fancy any of them?'

'No. I know it's extremely boring of me, but one either does,' Major Payne said, 'or one doesn't.'

'How interesting . . .'

'There's more to life than sex, Charlotte.'

'*Is* there?'

Mrs Depleche was tall, with a ramrod back, and she was dressed in a long dress of pale blue silk, with two strings of pearls at her throat and some more wound round her left wrist in a chunky tangle. In addition she wore a sola topi, whose brim almost touched the bridge of her beaky nose. She had a pair of diamond-encrusted opera glasses hanging round her neck. Major Payne saw her raise the glasses to her eyes and subject the waiters to a hawk-like scrutiny.

He looked round. Coconut Grove, frequently described as a 'jewel of a house', was built on a cliff overlooking the ocean, with terraced gardens hanging as in a theatre set. There were baskets of red roses everywhere, their heavy scent wafting through the heat-laden air. Heart-shaped balloons in all the colours of the rainbow and streamers fashioned as Cupid's darts fluttered above their heads in the light breeze.

The song that was being transmitted through the loud-speakers was 'Love is the Sweetest Thing'. Earlier on they had been treated to 'Les Yeux d'Amour', which of course was the French version of 'The Look of Love'. (Major Payne and Mrs Depleche hadn't been able to agree which James Bond film it came from.) The welcome party given in their honour had a St Valentine's theme. It had been their host's idea. At nine o'clock in the evening they were going to be treated to a 'spectacular' firework display on the beach below. Mysteriously, their host hadn't appeared yet . . .

'I do feel the stirrings of romance . . . *Such* poppets . . . I know I am being deliriously silly. Shall I tell you what they remind me of? I don't think you'd ever guess.'

'The genie from Aladdin? *Sans* the yatagan.'

'Yes! How clever of you! Would they fulfil all my wishes?'

'If you paid them, they might.' I shouldn't give her ideas, Payne thought at once.

'Would have been dangerous if they did have yatagans. Nervous guests might not like it.'

'Would have interfered with their waiting too. Actually, their garb has nothing to do with Goa or India. They are dressed up like Turks at the time of the Ottoman Empire.' Major Payne's head might have started feeling as light and inconsequential as one of these ridiculous balloons, but his sense of reality and knowledge of history – for which he had got a first at Oxford – hadn't abandoned him yet.

'Dear Roman has a penchant for the picturesque, if not for the carnivalesque, have you noticed?'

'I have noticed. I never imagined historical accuracy was his strong suit.'

She adored the balloons, Mrs Depleche went on. And the cocktails had such splendidly seductive names. Perhaps there were too many colours? The colours made her feel a little dizzy. She wasn't drinking too much, was she? Hugh must tell her if he thought she was. Stanbury insisted she drank like a fish, but she had grave doubts about Stanbury's judgement. Now she had rather a weakness for Roman, she couldn't quite say why. Had Hugh seen Roman's signature? So splendidly baroque – a calligraphic *chef d'oeuvre*, really – all curlicues, loops and flourishes!

'How very interesting.'

Mrs Depleche gave him a sideways glance and said she had the feeling Hugh didn't care much for Roman.

'No, not much,' Payne admitted.

Well, she might live to regret it, but it had been her misfortune to fall for flamboyant men – Mrs Depleche transferred her gaze from Major Payne to some distant object on the horizon – for men *that went too far*. It had brought her nothing but tears. She was *not* a happy woman. What was it they said? Your company determines your conduct, your conduct determines your character, and – what was it?'

'Your character determines your destiny?'

How true! Her last great passion had been a man called Glazebrook. Did Hugh know Glazebrook by any chance? Glazebrook had been an extremely distinguished military man. Glazebrook had had a number of endearing foibles, some of them far from innocent. He'd had a moustache. No? How very odd. She understood Hugh had met Antonia at the Military Club? Well, people did meet at the most peculiar places. A great friend of hers had met her future husband in Belgrave Square. Perhaps Antonia had been in the army herself? Some women had most distinguished military careers, or so she had always been given to understand . . . Where *was* Roman? A fine host he was, failing to appear like this!

Mrs Depleche sipped her cocktail, then pointed with her opera glasses. 'That boy, by the potted palm . . . So terribly subdued, but *such* a pretty face.'

'He has the kind of outrageously innocent look that appeals to elderly women.'

'Looks sad. Why is he so sad? Can't bear to see pretty boys looking so sad.'

'Perhaps his lady love has left him? Always the saddest when it happens on St Valentine's Day.'

'Let's drink to St Valentine, shall we?' Mrs Depleche snapped her fingers and called out raffishly to a passing waiter: 'Another Mumbai Mule, Marcello, and go easy on the crushed ice, there's a good chap.' There were twenty different cocktails on offer. Mumbai Mule, she had declared, was the one that gave you a definite 'kick'. 'To think I could have gone through life without ever tasting a Mumbai Mule.' She pointed to Payne's glass. 'What's yours called?'

'Scorpino.'

'What's in it?'

'I'd say – I'd say it contains lemon sorbet, cream, Cointreau and Kalashnikov vodka.'

69

'Sounds heaven. Isn't Kalashnikov a Russian machine gun? Years ago I used to do target practice. I do intend to try every single cocktail on the list, you know. So far I've had – let me see – three.'

'Five.'

'Widow's Wink. Black Russian. Shirley Temple. Bahama Mama. Mumbai Mule ... Yes, five. You are quite right. What an observant boy you are.' She patted his arm.

'This Mumbai Mule is your sixth cocktail.'

'This is such fun. I am enjoying myself enormously. To think that only last month I convinced myself that I'd finally reached the age of disenchantment. It was pelting with rain in Wiltshire, I was feeling utterly unstrung, so I sat down and added a note to my will, what I believe is called a "codicil", saying I didn't want a Christian funeral, rather, when I snuff it, throw my body to the dogs at a meet. I'd had all sorts of worries. The house in Eaton Square, Stanbury, death duties, my teeth. Well, I've had several marriage proposals since then, so everything hasn't been doom and gloom.'

'You've had marriage proposals?' Major Payne cocked an eyebrow. She was seventy-five, if a day.

'Several, yes. One or two extremely promising ones. Ah, look at the sea!' Mrs Depleche pointed. 'Just look at it. Too perfect for words. The sky is so cloudless and such an intense blue. It's like a – a – Can you think of something? Your aunt said you were terribly clever.'

'I am sometimes described as "astutely analytical" ... The sky is like a paladin's mantle. The sun stands absolute in its heaven.'

Of all the desultory conversations, Payne thought. We could go on like this for ever. Time seemed to have stood still. He almost wished something could happen. *'Fear no more the heat o' the sun,'* he cried, wagging his forefinger at Mrs Depleche's sola topi. Now why did I do that, he wondered.

She frowned. 'D'you write too? I thought your wife was the writer.'

'That's *Cymbeline*, actually.' By jingo, I am tipsy, he thought.

Mrs Depleche informed him that her sola topi was one of great antiquity – she had first worn it in India sixty years before. She had been a prim miss who had wandered from the sedate salons of *Sense and Sensibility* straight into the louche alcoves of *Les Liaisons Dangereuses*. She wasn't in the least literary, Mrs Depleche pointed out, but she did get the odd inspiration, after a drink or two.

Payne tried to see her as fresh-faced, pink-and-white and parasol-twirling, and failed. Soft and demure and uncorrupted? Quite impossible to imagine.

'What's this wonderful game you've been playing? Your aunt told me about it. *I remember, I remember*? Let me see. I remember my first Mumbai Mule.'

'Too recent,' Payne said.

'I remember the solar eclipse this morning.'

'Too recent.'

'Don't they say that a solar eclipse is a bad omen? I remember my first footman mainly because I did *not* have an affair with him. I remember the owl – that's when one of the novice guns shot an owl.'

'There's no need to explain.'

'I remember being much married.'

'You can't remember being much married, Charlotte. You *are* much married.'

This is the kind of brittle whimsy that passes for wit among members of jet-sets, Major Payne thought as Mrs Depleche cackled. Five minutes of their relentlessly droll conversation was bound to drive any sane person to distraction. He suddenly felt depressed. He wondered how long it would be before things started to really pall. It was only their second day. The sun showed no signs of weakening . . .

'I remember when my life was a frenzied dance and feast of pleasure. I remember attending a Second Childhood party. Would you like me to go on?'

'No,' Major Payne said.

71

Mrs Depleche gave a delighted croak. 'Your aunt was right. No one could live up to your smart repartees. You are the best company I've ever had. I think I will leave all my money to you.'

'Nonsense, Charlotte. You can't possibly do any such thing.' Payne looked worried. 'What about your grandson?'

'Ha. You don't think Stanbury deserves a penny, do you? Where did your clever wife disappear? You haven't had a tiff, have you?'

'*Pas du tout.*'

'Clever women can be the devil, but then you too are clever, so it doesn't really matter, I suppose.'

'Antonia is not used to the heat – wanted to sit near the fountain for a bit.' Major Payne shaded his eyes. 'I think – I think she's sitting inside the folly.' He strained to catch a glimpse of his wife. The folly was shrouded by brilliant scarlet and maroon bougainvillea.

'That floral georgette she's wearing . . .' Mrs Depleche's diamond-encrusted opera glasses glinted like a dragonfly in the sun as she adjusted them to her eyes. 'I am sure it's an original Vionnet. Goodness. *She's writing.*' Antonia might have been playing the harp or standing on her head, she sounded so surprised. 'Plotting her next book, no doubt?'

'Well, ideas come to Antonia in the most unusual circumstances.'

'I love reading other people's jottings, but *only* if they are indiscreet. She doesn't think there's going to be a murder here, does she? Now then, if there were a murder, who d'you suppose would be the victim?'

'You,' Payne said promptly. 'The killer would turn out to be your grandson.'

'Stanbury? But he isn't here!'

'He is. He'll have arrived secretly. He'll appear in a minute dressed up as a waiter or a visiting maharaja and he'll manage to hand you a poisoned cocktail.'

'Look at that lunatic – just look at him!' Mrs Depleche cried, pointing. 'Nearly fell into the fountain. What an idiot! He's holding a glass!'

'Not his first, that much is clear.'

'Blind drunk!' Mrs Depleche cackled.

'Could be lethal in this heat.'

The man was tall and stooped a little. He wore a sun-bleached jacket, a panama hat and dark glasses. A reddish-brown book protruded from his jacket pocket . . .

They watched him stagger shambolically across the sleek green lawn. He held his left shoulder higher than his right and he had a curious gliding walk – a bit like the actor Alastair Sim, Payne reflected. He gave the impression of being disorientated . . . Something desperate about him . . . Was the fellow a lunatic or merely sozzled? He displayed the dipso's unnerving indifference to what others might think of him. He was heading in the direction of the folly. Hope he won't bother Antonia, Payne thought.

'The fountain's a mini replica of the one at Castle Howard,' Mrs Depleche said. 'Did you see the teddy bear on Roman's desk?'

Payne said he had. 'It's got a Harrods label.'

'What an observant boy you are. Roman gets all his stuff from England. He's mad about England, you may have noticed? He would give anything to be able to call himself Lord Brideshead or something. He is a romantic, I suppose.'

He is an egregious ass, Payne thought, though he didn't say so.

'He's got an English girlfriend, apparently. He promised to introduce her to us. I hope her Englishness is not her only virtue.' The next moment Mrs Depleche flourished her opera glasses by way of a greeting. 'Ah Roman, my boy. Where have you been hiding? We were just admiring your fountain. However do you manage to get everything so right?'

11

Murder is Easy

The first death was yet to be discovered, but the second couldn't have been more public.

It had taken place some six hours before the garden party at Coconut Grove, at the time of the partial solar eclipse.

The body lay on the main street of Kilhar for at least five minutes before somebody thought of dragging it on to the pavement. The hawkers stopped shouting their wares and people gathered around, some of them holding pieces of smoked glass, through which they had been gazing at the sky, and pointed to the blood, which was seeping from a wound in the head. Flies and hornets buzzed above. A dog came over, sniffed at the blood and dipped its tongue in it. Another dog joined it – then a third. No one made any real effort to shoo the dogs away. A shop assistant eventually threw a foul-smelling piece of tarpaulin over the body, but so casually that an arm and part of the head remained exposed. Some people started walking away, others lingered. A one-legged man on crutches bent over, ostensibly to pull the tarpaulin over the head and the arm, but when he straightened up, he was holding a wristwatch. He quickly pushed the watch into his trouser pocket. No one appeared to notice the theft.

Twenty-five minutes later a police car arrived. There were three uniformed policemen in it. One of them unveiled the corpse and frowned down at its face. He put questions to the men in the crowd but got only shrugs and shaking of heads. No one admitted to knowing the victim. One man then came forward and said that he had actually seen the accident.

The death had been caused by a speeding car. The car hadn't stopped. It had been grey in colour – or maybe white, in need of a wash. No, the man hadn't taken note of the registration number. Had there been anyone with the victim? Yes – a woman. A local woman in a sari, her face concealed by a red scarf. They had been walking side by side, she and the victim. Now the witness couldn't swear to this but he imagined the woman gave the man a shove just as the car approached, causing him to stagger and fall in front of it. The woman had then run off. She had vanished in the crowd. It had all happened very quickly.

Could the witness describe the woman? Tall – big hands – pale gold sari – red scarf – the face was veiled. The witness couldn't *swear* that the woman had actually pushed the man, no. It all happened very quickly, he repeated. She'd moved in a funny way, not really like any of the local women. In what way funny? The witness couldn't say. Was it possible that 'she' had actually been a 'he'? A man? The witness shrugged. He had no way of knowing. It was possible, yes. The police officers shook their heads. One of them lit a cigarette. The other spat on the ground, then he too lit a cigarette. Eventually they let the witness go.

An ambulance arrived and two paramedics carrying a stretcher went up to the body. After exchanging a couple of words with the policemen, they placed the body on the stretcher, which they carried back to the ambulance.

One of the policemen observed that Kilhar was a terrible place for accidents and his colleague agreed. The first policeman then said that his mother-in-law was becoming too big for her boots and having her in the house was driving him mad, the mornings were particularly bad and he had problems sleeping; one of these days he wouldn't be responsible for his actions, he said. The second police-man said that the new brothel was not what it was cracked up to be, he didn't think he'd go again. Eventually the two policemen departed and the crowd dispersed. The dogs stayed a while longer, licking at the blood on the pavement.

In a couple of minutes there was no sign that anything untoward had ever taken place in the street.

12

The Public Enemy

Remember you are just an extra in everyone else's play. That saying of Franklin Delano Roosevelt's popped into Major Payne's head as he watched their host swagger towards them across the terrace. The throng of local dignitaries and their wives and the couple of English expatriates who had been invited to greet Mrs Depleche parted at his advent. Payne was put in mind of the bizarrely curdled appearance of the Red Sea when divided by Moses in the film of *The Ten Commandments*.

Roman Songhera was a well-set-up, olive-skinned young man with a florid face and sensuous lips. He had drooping eyelids, thick lashes, and somewhat restless light-brown eyes. His appearance was less colourful than that of his waiters, but nearly as theatrical. He was dressed, monochromatically, in white: a double-breasted suit with broad lapels, one of which was adorned by a black gardenia, a gleaming white shirt with a buttoned-down collar, and a white turban that was crossed from each side of his head very symmetrically in such a way that it came to a peak at the top of the forehead where there shone a large ruby. His pointed patent-leather shoes were also white.

'He only wears the turban for my sake. I have a thing about men in turbans,' Mrs Depleche whispered. 'He hates what they call "ethnic" dress, poor darling, but would do *anything* to get me to buy the house.'

Their host looked as anachronistically quaint as the unicorns and damsels sporting on a medieval tapestry. He brought to mind a stage conjurer from the heyday of the English music hall, Payne decided. However, the ruby gave every impression of being the real thing. Roman Songhera's platinum tie-pin, gold cufflinks, and Rolex watch seemed genuine too.

But it was the sight of Roman's striped tie that caused Major Payne's eyebrows to go up. It was an Old Harrovian tie. How silly of the fellow to put on an OH tie for the visit of the one person who, better than anybody else in the world, knew that his background wasn't exactly exalted – that he was the grandson of an Indian orderly and the son of a grocer from Kashmir – and that the big money had come from his – now estranged – wife Sarla. Mrs Depleche had told them the story on the plane.

Sarla Songhera, it appeared, had won a fortune on the lottery. The Sublime Subcontinent Lottery – the Incomparable Mother India Pools – some such name. Several billion billion *billion* rupees. Or was it trillion? Some such mad figure. It amounted to less than one and a half million pounds, if that, according to Major Payne's vague estimate, but by Goan standards that was fabulous wealth – what sultans and maharajas, if not exactly the Queen of England, had in their coffers.

'High time!' Mrs Depleche croaked.

Roman's eyes were bloodshot and he seemed to find it hard to concentrate. Something appeared to be weighing on his mind. Still, he managed to play the gracious host. He put on what Mrs Depleche had affectionately referred to as 'Roman's society nonsense'. Bowing his head slightly, his right hand fiddling with his cufflink in a manner reminiscent of Prince Charles's famous nervous tic, he said, 'I do apologize, Charlotte. Major Payne. Not the done thing, I know. Something cropped up. Untoward as well as unavoidable, alas. Terrible bore. Too dreary for words to start explaining.'

'Where's your mysterious English girlfriend?' Mrs Depleche asked. 'You promised to introduce her to us.'

'I fear she's indisposed.' Roman paused. 'Bad tummy – awful bore.'

Songhera's voice struck Major Payne as peculiarly familiar. He frowned, then it came to him. Golly, he sounds like me, almost. I wouldn't say 'indisposed', though, would I? *Only* as a joke. I'll never say 'awful bore' again, as long as I live. Songhera seems to have a mynah's ear for accents . . . Am I being a crashing snob?

'Oh, what a shame.' Mrs Depleche tut-tutted. 'I'd been so looking forward to meeting her. Never mind. I hope she'll be better soon.'

Roman asked them if they were having a good time – did they have everything they wanted? If they didn't, they only needed to tell him. He informed them that he was considering buying two peacocks for the garden, then suggested that they try the ice cream – apparently there was a thirty-*ninth* flavour on offer now – a jelabis ice cream – gorgeous sticky golden balls dripping with rose-water syrup. Couldn't he tempt them? It was awfully good. They could have jelabis ice cream with hot wafers. A dish fit to lure Zeus away from Olympus, Payne murmured, but he declined nevertheless.

'How about Eton mess? My chef makes perfect Eton mess.'

'I went to Harrow, actually,' said Payne.

'I am not allowed any pudding,' Mrs Depleche said. 'Something to do with my sugar levels.'

'Such wet blankets!' Roman shook his head in mock despair. He then said he wanted to propose a toast. Shooting out his cuffs, he picked up a cocktail glass from a tray and held it aloft. 'Sorry, Charlotte, I should have done this earlier. Terribly remiss of me. Welcome to Coconut Grove. I hope it will be as good a home to you as it has been to me.'

Mrs Depleche laughed. 'Not so fast, Roman. It's a splendid place but I haven't said yes yet, you know.'

'I am sure it is only a question of time before you do. Major Payne, I am thinking of organizing a polo tournament here. The trouble is that my chaps don't quite know the ropes. I understand that you are a seasoned polo player and I very much hope you would be able to advise me.'

'I'd be happy to, my dear fellow,' Payne responded in part. 'I can hardly wait to see your stables.' His enthusiasm on this count was unfeigned – he liked horses. 'Perhaps you could instruct one of your grooms to show them to me?'

'I will show you my stables personally.'

'You are too kind. I look forward to it.'

'The pleasure will be entirely mine.'

'What about your crocs? When will you show us your crocs? As far as I am concerned, crocs come before horses,' Mrs Depleche declared extravagantly. 'Roman's got a croc farm a stone's throw from here,' she explained to Payne.

'How terribly amusing,' Payne said. A croc farm was one of the most grotesque things he could imagine. I could kick this young man in twenty-one different positions and still feel half-starved, he thought.

'Apparently the muggers disport themselves in a decorative lake of sorts. They become snappy at feeding time,' Mrs Depleche explained with relish. 'The spectacle can take on apocalyptic overtones when, in the general excitement, a servant falls into the lake – or is pushed in, isn't that what you said, Roman?'

'We do that kind of thing only as a special treat for VIP visitors.' Roman gave a bow. Payne's eyes narrowed. A jolly tasteless sort of joke – still, the fellow seemed to have a sense of humour of sorts – or *could* he be serious?

'When are we going then?'

'Tomorrow morning after breakfast?'

'I can't wait. I've been mad about crocs ever since I got my first alligator-skin pumps,' Mrs Depleche said. 'What time is the firework display tonight?'

Their host didn't answer. He was staring down at his cufflinks as though in dismay. Payne was put in mind of the mother in the poem whose face takes on a 'distressing error in form'. Well, Songhera's cufflinks were wrong all right – they didn't match his tie-pin – they should have been platinum, not gold. Songhera was clearly the kind of chap who minded terribly about perpetrating a sartorial faux pas.

'Do excuse me, such a bore.' Roman took out his mobile phone as a buzzing sound was heard. He seemed to have received a message. He stood stock-still, reading it, his lower lip stuck out. He scowled. He went pale . . .

There was a pause. Something jolly unsettling seemed to have happened. Major Payne struck a match and put it to his pipe. Was Interpol after him? Or had Songhera's English girlfriend run off with his main rival perhaps, if indeed he had a rival? Payne remembered his thought earlier on about being an extra in someone else's play.

What *was* Songhera's play?

13

Witness for the Prosecution

RS's kingdom is the kind of place where anything can happen. RS presents an interesting study. Histrionic, vain as a peacock, given to bombastic declarations, busy playing the grand seigneur. He is treated like a god – one of those capricious, rather wilful Indian gods. He seems to expect it. A preening, pouting solipsist, he cuts a ridiculous figure, but he is in fact a dangerous bully. He punched one of the waiters last night because the poor boy had been looking at him 'insolently'.

Antonia found that she couldn't concentrate on her diary. Her eyes kept straying towards the man who had sat on the bench opposite her. A tall, gaunt Englishman in his sixties – his left shoulder slightly higher than the right – he couldn't be anything but English. He was dressed in a light grey suit that had seen better days, and wearing a white panama, not unlike the one her husband had on at this very moment, only grubbier. The man's face was unevenly tanned. He held his left hand clenched in a fist, so tight that his knuckles had gone white. He seemed in the grip of some powerful emotion. The panama was pulled down on his forehead and he wore large dark glasses. (Was he trying to conceal his face?) He was holding a notebook, kept twisting it between his fingers. The notebook was bound in soft reddish-brown leather and brought to mind an old-fashioned Boy Scout's diary – it had the picture of a sword on the cover. Was it really a diary?

A fellow diarist. Antonia was naturally drawn to people who kept diaries. She watched the man open the notebook and start writing in it. She felt the irresistible urge to know what it was he was writing. A totally irrational urge. None of her business. It might not even be a diary . . .

His hand shook. He wrote as though his life depended on it. He was using capital letters, she could tell from the way his hand moved. It seemed to her he didn't trust himself to use joined-up writing. The tip of his tongue protruded between his lips. Drops of sweat glistened on his face, which was mottled, with an unhealthy greenish pallor about it. The man's lips trembled and he started muttering to himself.

He had joined Antonia in the folly some five minutes previously. She had nodded to him but he had hardly taken any notice of her. He had a dazed air about him. Like a man who'd had a bad shock? Was she imagining it? It might be the heat – or he might have had too much to drink. Or, Antonia decided, he might be in the early stages of Huntington's disease. (She was fascinated by multiple possibilities.) There was the twitching mouth, the spasmodic movements of the arms, the sweating. It was a genetic disorder that started mysteriously in mid-life and progressed to insanity. The man seemed the right age. She had done research on Huntington's disease for a novel. She might be wrong of course.

They were playing 'Killing Me Softly' now. (With your smile?) She cast a glance towards the terrace. Roman Songhera was standing not far from her husband and Mrs Depleche, talking urgently to a man the size of a wardrobe – one of his minders, no doubt. She saw that her fellow diarist (if indeed that *was* a diary) was gazing in the same direction and she was startled by his expression. It was a blend of – of great distress, acute misery, loathing and fear. Antonia thought she could read people's faces correctly. She might be mistaken. Well, if one had to make a fool of oneself, one might as well do it inside the folly, as Hugh was likely to say. She mustn't stare. Terribly ill-mannered!

83

She bent her head over her diary once more, but now she found it impossible to write a word.

'Excuse me,' she heard her fellow diarist's tentative voice. (Why did she keep calling him 'her fellow diarist'? The reddish book was probably not a diary at all.)

Antonia smiled, her polite social smile. 'Yes?'

'I – I'm sorry to bother you like this . . .'

A very English voice. Somewhat breathless. 'No bother at all,' she said brightly.

'You're not a friend of Roman Songhera's, are you?'

'What if I am? Actually no, I am not. I hardly know him.'

He swallowed. 'What – what about the others? The old lady and the man. They are English, aren't they?'

'Yes. Well, the man's my husband. He is most certainly not Roman's friend –'

'Roman Songhera is an extremely dangerous individual. He is a psychopath. He –' The man broke off. 'This is a matter of life and death. I need to talk to you.' He rose abruptly. 'May I sit next to you?'

Was he mad? Why did they always meet people like that? Antonia drew back slightly, but she decided to risk it. She was curious. 'If you like.'

The man still held his left hand in a fist. His wristwatch appeared to have stopped at one o'clock.

'Something happened earlier today. It was – horrible! It's about Roman Songhera's English girlfriend. Her name is Marigold, but everybody calls her Ria. Her father's asked me to trail her.' The man spoke haltingly, breathlessly. 'I haven't heard from him for some time – he lives in England – no one answers their phone, but I've been going on with the job – he commissioned me.'

'Commissioned you?'

'Yes. My name is Julian Knight. I am a policeman – used to be. You look as though you don't believe me! You think I'm mad, don't you?'

'I do believe you,' Antonia reassured him.

'I'm – a bit drunk. I needed to – to steady my nerves – after what I saw. It was horrible. I was sick. You *must* believe me. You are my only chance. They might come for me any moment!'

'Who might come for you?'

He looked round and lowered his voice. 'Songhera's men. It would be no good talking to the police. The local police are all in Roman Songhera's pocket. They'd do anything he said. *Anything*. They are corrupt – same as the local politicians – too scared of him. Roman specializes in contract killings. His men are everywhere. He gets his men to do all sorts of things. But this was completely different. This time he did it himself –'

'*What did he do?*'

'He killed Ria. I saw him. I was there when it happened.'

This is a trick, Antonia thought. I am being set up. Hugh and Mrs Depleche are behind it. Mrs Depleche doesn't like me. She suggested it because of the kind of story I write and Hugh went along with the plan. She wants to make me look a fool. This is an actor specially hired for the purpose –

The man was speaking. 'There'd be a cover-up. Or the body'd just disappear. Perhaps it's disappeared already. They can make it look as though the death never happened. Or as though it were some sort of accident. I'm telling you, he – Roman Songhera – can do *anything*. I won't be able to hide or run away. They'll get me – he's got his spies everywhere.' The man was becoming quite agitated. 'There's nowhere for me to hide here. It was madness, coming here, into the lair of the beast, but I heard there'd be someone from the British High Commission – from Delhi. I thought they might be able to help me – have the matter properly investigated – give me protection. D'you know when they are coming?'

'I have no idea,' Antonia said. 'I don't know about anyone from the High Commission. Can't you phone them?'

'I tried, but didn't get a connection. The line was down – that sort of thing happens all the time here – or maybe it was Roman Songhera who made it happen!' Suddenly the man reached out and clutched at her arm. 'Would you help me? *Please.*' His voice quavered. It seemed as though he was about to burst into tears.

'What – what do you want me to do?'

No, he wasn't an actor. His distress was quite genuine. His face glistened with sweat. There was a whitish stripe across his forehead. His lips were trembling. His hands were pale pink, like monkey's paws. The long hand of his watch had moved to five past one. So his watch hadn't stopped after all. And his left hand continued to be clenched in a fist. The silly things she noticed! He was shaking. Poor man. What a terrible situation!

'I am in great danger. You *must* believe me. If Roman knew there'd been a witness – that I saw him kill his girl-friend – he'd kill me too! He wouldn't hesitate a moment. They were having an argument – shouting at each other. She – she'd done something she shouldn't. I think he saw her with another man, or it was reported to him. I didn't get the exact details. He is extremely jealous. Suddenly he flipped – went mad. It was dreadful. I keep seeing it – what he did.'

'What did he do?'

As though on cue, a blood-red balloon floated into the folly and lodged itself near the ceiling. Antonia and the man looked up at it at the same time. She saw him shudder.

'Was there . . .?'

'No, not much,' he whispered. 'Just a trickle from her mouth. But that was *later* – when it was all over. It looked like a scarlet ribbon . . . She shouldn't have made him angry. He went for her – like a raging bull. He gripped her by the throat. He banged her head against the wooden bedpost – it was a four-poster bed. There was a crack.' The man pressed his knuckles against his mouth. 'I wanted to intervene, but I was scared – paralysed – scared out of my wits. I'll never forgive myself. I keep hearing that crack.

86

She didn't utter a sound. Her body went limp. When he let go of her, she fell across the bed.'

'Are you sure she was dead?' Antonia asked after a moment's pause.

'I am sure. I've seen dead people. I *know*. I think he broke her neck. Must have. I saw her eyes. She lay very still – her eyes open – staring. He then reached out – closed them – that's when blood came out of her mouth. He started crying – howling – it suddenly hit him, I think. Then – then his mobile phone rang. He got up – ran out – didn't look back.'

Antonia frowned. 'Where did all this happen?'

'At Ria's bungalow. In the bedroom. I was – outside. Looking through the bedroom window.'

'What were you doing there?'

'I've been following her. I told you. Her father's been paying me. I've been writing reports for him. He – Lord Justice Leighton – wanted to know *everything*. What she did, where she went, the people she met. Old Leighton wanted to know everything about her relationship with Roman Songhera. He loved her very much. He was extremely worried. She did things she shouldn't.' The next moment the man groaned. 'Oh God. Is that "Love for Sale"?' He meant the tune that was being played.

'I think so. Yes.' Antonia looked at him curiously. 'That's not what she did, is it?'

He gave a little nod. His lips trembled. He dabbed at his forehead with a tissue. Something like a sob escaped his lips and he covered his mouth. He leant forward. Antonia thought he looked on the verge of collapse.

A voice came from the direction of the terrace. 'Mr Knight? Julian Knight? Is there anyone called Julian Knight here? Mr Julian Knight is wanted on the telephone.'

It was one of the young waiters who was calling. The man dropped the tissue and sat very still.

'They are calling you,' Antonia said.

'Yes.'

'Mr Knight? A phone call for Mr Knight.'

'There couldn't be a phone call for me,' he whispered. 'No one knows that I am here.'

'Are you sure?'

'Of course I'm sure. I told no one I was coming to Coconut Grove. There's no one to tell.'

'You have no family – friends?'

'No. No one here.'

The waiter had walked down the few stone steps that led from the terrace to the lawn and was approaching them. The man leant towards Antonia once more. 'I gate-crashed. I bribed one of the guards, that's how I got my pass. If Roman Songhera knew, he'd –' He broke off. 'Perhaps he *does* know!'

'Mr Julian Knight?' They heard the waiter's voice again.

'I don't even know your name,' the man said.

'Antonia. Antonia Darcy.'

He seemed to come to a decision. 'Take this,' he said, pushing the reddish-brown notebook into her hands. His fingers came into momentary contact with hers; they felt cold and clammy. 'You look like a wise and decent woman. Take good care of it, would you? I wrote it all down. What I saw.'

His left hand continued to be clenched in a fist. Was he holding something in it?

'In case something happens to me. If – if I don't come back. If I were to – disappear. I'm not mad. You don't understand. Get someone from the High Commission. Tell them –'

'Mr Julian Knight?' The waiter was standing outside the folly, looking up at Antonia's companion.

The man ducked his head and stared like an animal that couldn't make up its mind whether to bolt or not. 'Yes? What is it?'

(Couldn't he have said he was *not* Julian Knight? Couldn't he have refused to go – made a scene – shouted that he was being kidnapped – that there had been a murder? All these ideas were to occur to Antonia later, after he had gone. Why did good ideas always come when it was too late?)

'A phone call for you, sir. They said it was urgent. The telephone in the vestibule.'

'Who is it? Did the caller give a name?'

'No, sir. No name.'

'Man or woman?' He was sweating really badly now. His hands were shaking. His face had turned the colour of a dead fish.

'A lady, sir, I think. I am not sure.' The name tag on the waiter's chest gave his name as Patricio. 'I was only told to say it was urgent.'

'Urgent . . .' The man rose to his feet. He didn't look at Antonia. He held his left hand clenched in a fist across his chest, in the manner of one taking some kind of a formal oath, which seemed strangely appropriate. Knight by name, knight by nature?

Antonia watched him shamble wearily across the lawn. She expected him to turn his head and cast one last imploring glance at her over his shoulder, but he didn't. He looked oddly resigned. He walked with his head and shoulders slightly bowed. Like a lamb to the slaughter, she thought, telling herself at once not to be absurd. What could possibly happen to him?

She glanced at her watch. Sixteen minutes past six. She discovered she was clutching at the reddish-brown notebook with both her hands. After a moment's thought she placed it inside her own diary. She cast a furtive glance round. No, no one was watching her.

Well, Julian Knight's paranoia seemed to be infectious.

14

Never Come Back

Antonia sat very still and waited for him to come back, which she told herself he would do before long. She smoothed out her dress and looked down at the subdued splash of peonies, the full-blown roses and ivy – a sort of William Morris print swooning after a pink gin, as Hugh had put it. She then watched two wasps buzz over the empty glass Julian Knight had left on the bench. They were so large, she could see their black and yellow stripes quite clearly. She tried to remain calm. She told herself she needed to keep an open mind, to neither believe nor disbelieve the incredible story she had heard. Don't jump to any conclusions, she ordered herself.

Stay cool.

Easier to say than to do – especially in this heat.

She tried to arrange her thoughts in a rational manner. Julian Knight was probably an alcoholic. She had smelled alcohol the moment he had staggered into the folly. His hands had been shaking. His left hand must be worse than his right, hence the fist. He had been a funny colour. Alcoholics were often delusional. They saw things, which weren't there – giant lizards, armies of spiders, talking bears or, for that matter, English girls having their necks snapped.

He hadn't actually lisped or slurred. He had spoken quite clearly. And he had given specific names, which added verisimilitude to his fantastic tale: Marigold Leighton, Lord Justice Leighton. These names could be checked easily. What if his muddled account of the murder was, after all, the truth? Julian Knight had called Roman a 'psychopath'. That Antonia could well believe. She glanced down at what *she* had written about Roman in *her* diary. Yes. Roman could have killed his English girlfriend all right . . .

Julian Knight had been frightened but also extremely upset. Antonia had had the distinct impression he had been *grieving* for the girl. Curious, that. Had he known Marigold Leighton better than he made out? Could he have been in love with her? These things did happen. What was it he had been holding in his clenched hand? Was it something he had picked up at the scene of the crime? Something that proved Roman Songhera's guilt beyond any reasonable doubt? Some small object, it had to be. Why hadn't he given it to her? Too preoccupied, so he had forgotten all about it? Julian Knight must have entered the bedroom moments after Roman left. So he didn't tell her the *whole* story –

Antonia bit her lip. There I go again, she thought.

On the plane Mrs Depleche had told Antonia, 'I haven't read any of your detective stories, but I bet you are the kind of woman who lets her imagination run riot.' Mrs Depleche had had three neat scotches and had been holding forth in a voice more suited to chiding clumsy beaters on the grouse moor. 'If I ever decided to commit a crime, my dear, I'd use you in some way. *I'd take advantage of your imagination.*'

There had been a hush in their part of the plane. Everybody seemed to have been listening – including the two air hostesses! Antonia had seen a man take his earphones out and crane his neck in their direction, so that he could hear better! Earlier on Mrs Depleche had talked about Coconut Grove and what a jolly good time they had in store of them . . .

Well, Mrs Depleche was right – Antonia's imagination was as much a curse as it was a blessing. On at least one memorable occasion it had caused her to make a complete ass of herself . . .

The song being played on the loudspeakers was 'Out of Nowhere'. Appropriate, in a funny kind of way. In the song it was love – all the songs today were about love – but it was murder she had on her mind. Murder had come out of nowhere and hit her on the nose. In this garden that looked like a miracle out of the Arabian Nights, with its hedges of flowering cacti and dazzling banks of azaleas – a stone's throw from the emerald-green sea – under the golden globe of the sun . . . On the very first day of their holiday she was getting involved in murder . . . yet again!

No conclusions, she reminded herself.

The air round her shimmered. She felt drowsy and a little confused. Well, they had exchanged a world that was recognizable and rational for one that seemed surreal and unknowable. At the moment England seemed as distant as the moon. They were at Roman Songhera's mercy. Julian Knight wanted to speak to somebody at the British High Commission. Would the British High Commission be able to help him? Antonia had no idea how these things worked. Well, the British could bring the affair to the attention of the Indian government, she supposed – if that indeed was what happened in such cases – but first they would have to accept Julian Knight's story as bona fide. Which they probably wouldn't. Julian Knight wouldn't be considered a trustworthy witness.

Antonia looked at her watch. Ten minutes. She saw the hand move. Eleven minutes. Eleven minutes *and* ten seconds . . . So slow . . . Julian Knight's watch wouldn't be much good to him since it was five hours behind. How hot it was. Antonia yawned. Her eyes shut, then opened again. She didn't feel like thinking about anything important. She felt rather odd, actually, in a muzzy state . . . She wasn't used to the heat . . . Once more she glanced across at the empty cocktail glass Julian Knight had left behind, then at the crumpled tissue on the floor, as though to convince herself that Julian Knight hadn't been a figment of her over-heated imagination. How grubby the tissue was – brown with dust and sweat. Urgh. Julian Knight's notebook wasn't a mirage either – it was inside her diary.

He had been real enough. He had been witness to murder. Or so he claimed.

Where *was* he? Still on the phone? Or had he gone to get himself a drink? Had he perhaps forgotten that he had entrusted his notebook to her? She looked across at the terrace –

There he was, at long last, coming down the steps! Antonia jumped to her feet. What a relief. He seemed all right. Thank God!

No, it wasn't him. Another man in a panama hat was walking across the lawn towards her. Her husband. Hugh was holding a small tray with a tall glass of what looked like orange juice on it. He had wrapped a crisp white napkin around it.

She was glad to see him. Hugh would probably know what should be done.

Coming up the steps, Major Payne entered the folly and kissed his wife. 'This is the longest and laziest afternoon I have ever been through in my entire life. Everything seems to be standing still. That is what eternity must be like. And of course one can't help thoughts of love. *We would sit down and think which way to walk and pass our long love's day.*'

'I am neither your mistress, nor am I coy,' Antonia said. 'For some reason I've never liked Marvell.'

'*Ah, to have a wife worthy of being a mistress!*'

'Is that Marvell again?'

'Casanova, actually. You do look ravishing in your Vionnet dress. Charlotte was green with envy. She said she felt like coming over and ripping it off your body.'

'You are drunk.'

'*Pas du tout*. Do have a sip of mango juice – it's freshly squeezed.'

Antonia drank thirstily. Ice cubes tinkled inside the glass.

'Love is in the air,' Payne said. That, as it happened, was the song they had started playing. 'Are you all right? You strike me as a bit subdued. We were getting worried about you. Charlotte feared you might have had sunstroke.'

'She doesn't really like me, does she?'

'She said you were clever. Did you know Songhera had a croc farm?'

'*Crocodiles*? How awful.' They wouldn't feed Julian Knight to the crocs, would they? Once dropped in the lake, the body would disappear in seconds. Antonia pulled herself together. 'Hugh, did you see the man who was here? He went back to the house about fifteen minutes ago. Did you see which way he went?'

'Tall chap in a panama? Old Zebra Face? Yes. I saw him. As a matter of fact, he bumped into me – don't think he apologized – staggered blindly out into the hall. Earlier on he nearly fell into the fountain. Too much to drink. Did he bother you? He didn't make a pass at you, did he?'

'Did you see anyone follow him into the hall? Roman – or any of Roman's bodyguards?'

'Should they have done? I don't think I saw anyone follow him. Songhera wasn't there. He's had to go somewhere urgently. He seems to have a lot on his mind –'

'He never returned to the terrace, did he?'

'Songhera?'

'No,' Antonia said impatiently. 'Julian Knight. That's the man's name.'

'I don't think so. He never came back.'

'He never came back,' she echoed. 'I don't suppose you heard anything – commotion of some kind – someone crying for help?'

'Should I have done? You do say the oddest things. Incidentally, you've caught the sun a bit and it's made you look particularly lovely. May I kiss you?'

'Oh, I should have gone with him!' Antonia cried. 'Why didn't I think of it? They wouldn't have dared touch him with me there.'

'What are you talking about?'

'That man – Julian Knight – told me a most extraordinary story. He said he'd witnessed Roman Songhera kill his English girlfriend. A girl called Marigold Leighton.'

15

Evil Under the Sun

'Dear old thing,' Payne said. 'The fellow was blotto.'

'He did strike me as genuinely distressed and frightened.'

'Well, a brain that's been pickled in a variety of spirits can conjure up fearful monsters that are as good as real ones. Is that his glass? Jolly treacherous things, cocktails. One can get quite drunk without becoming aware of it.'

Antonia pursed her lips. 'I can see *that*.'

'I'm not drunk, only, as the poet put it, a trifle exalted. You don't want me to prove it to you, do you? *Flamboyant feminist polemicists flummox male fiends.* You thought that was easy? *Swedish psychotherapists summering in Sardinia.*'

She sighed. 'How unfortunate that my husband should be drunk at a time when I need him most. How many cocktails did you have?'

'One or two. All right, three. Can't remember. Not as many as the Honourable Charlotte anyhow. She's sleeping it off in one of the hammocks at the back.'

'Is she really? You mean she left the party?'

'No. Joking. Actually she's in her element. She's chatting up one of the *serviteurs*. Chap called Camillo. A waiter *très triste.*'

'Will you be serious?'

'You started telling me something about that chap, Julian Knight. It seems he came up with the most extra-ordinary allegation about our host, correct? Now then, I'd like you to tell me all about it,' Payne said slowly, 'omitting no detail, however slight.'

With a sigh, Antonia did. There was a pause.

'Remarkable. You did say something odd, though.' He drew a thoughtful forefinger across his jaw. 'How can Songhera be the law – and at the same time be above it?'

'Hugh, don't be exasperating. You should get some strong black coffee into you.'

'That's a dangerous-looking sword.' He pointed to the picture on the reddish-brown notebook, which Antonia had taken out of her diary. '*Knight*. One must assume that Knight's distant ancestors were knights. Second names are frequently indicators of occupation or of some personal characteristic.'

'Actually, you are being a major pain.'

'I don't suppose you realize what a sublimely funny thing you just said? Is that an example of what is known as "spontaneous wit" – or was it completely unintentional? Odd things, names,' Major Payne went on. 'If Julian Knight had been a Swede his name would have been something like "Gyllensvard" – *vaard* being Swedish for "sword". *And* he is engaged on a quest – a perilous quest. That's so *apt*.'

'Oh God, we are wasting time. You are drunk. You are gibbering inconsequentially and your eyes look funny. You *must* have some coffee.'

'I'm not gibbering inconsequentially. That was a horrible thing to say. I am deeply hurt. It's too hot for coffee anyhow. I'm sure I'd be sick if I had the tiniest sip. Did you say Knight wrote an account of the murder in that notebook?'

'I won't discuss anything with you till you've had some coffee!'

'You are being hysterical now. A cup of proper coffee in a copper coffee pot. If I'd been drunk,' Payne pointed out, 'I wouldn't have been able to say this either. Oh, very well, I'll ask one of Songhera's Turks to bring me a cup of coffee.'

'Let's go and see if we can find him,' Antonia said. 'I'm getting really worried. I hope I'm not making a fool of myself.'

'You couldn't make a fool of yourself if you tried,' Payne said gallantly.

They left the folly and started walking across the lawn.

'He's probably at the house,' Antonia said.

But he wasn't.

The English gentleman, they learnt from the imposing bearded and turbaned servant who seemed to be in charge of the hall, had been there, yes. The English gentleman had spoken on the telephone some twenty minutes before, but he left the premises immediately after. Left, yes. He had walked out of Coconut Grove. The Indian pointed towards the front door. No, he had never seen the English gentleman before. The English gentleman – a Mr Knight – had been in a state of some considerable agitation. He had put down the telephone and waved his arms in a wild manner. The Indian demonstrated with such zeal, he nearly knocked the telephone off the desk. Antonia was annoyed – she was not in the mood for histrionics – she was sure the servant was exaggerating.

Mr Knight had asked for Miss Antonia Darcy most specifically, that had been earlier on, that was when he arrived. Antonia stared at him incredulously. How could Knight have known about her? The Indian shrugged and said that he had directed Mr Knight to the folly where he had seen madam sitting. Who was it who had wanted Mr Knight on the phone? No name had been given. It had sounded like an Indian voice. Man or woman? Antonia insisted. A woman with a deep voice, the servant thought; it might have been a gentleman, yes – he couldn't say for certain.

The Paynes lingered for a couple of moments, wondering what to do. The hall was a busy place. A van stopped in the sand-covered drive outside and men in blue overalls brought in baskets of flowers – they were directed towards the terrace. The flowers were followed by cases of champagne (Château Latour 1980), arriving at the same time as shining metal containers with ice cream and caviar. Two long rolled-up carpets were brought in, one of a Persian design, the other white and deep-piled. 'Storeroom!' The turbaned concierge waved them majestically towards the swinging doors on the left, where, Antonia imagined, the storerooms were. More cases, this time of Rémy Martin cognac. The next two deliveries consisted of some multi-coloured cushions and a dozen red, yellow and black oblong boxes with FIREWORKS written on them.

Going back to the terrace, Major Payne stopped one of the waiters and asked for some black coffee. He turned back to Antonia. 'The Brahmin might have been instructed to feed us whoppers. All part of the conspiracy and so on. Is that what you think?'

'I don't know. Well, yes, that's what I think.'

'On the other hand, people do get emergency phone calls in the middle of parties –'

'Which so unsettle them that they dash off, leaving behind their highly personal diaries? Julian Knight told me no one could possibly know he was at Coconut Grove.'

'Well, it does look as though the phone call was a ruse to get him inside the house. And then – what? A knock on the head? Did they bundle him into a car and spirit him away to the croc farm?'

'The thought did occur to me,' Antonia said with a shudder. 'I don't think things like that happen in real life, do they?'

'I am not sure ... What an extraordinary business ... The point is, as things are, we can't do much about it ... Where the hell has Charlotte gone? I hope she hasn't been abducted too.' Payne stood looking round. 'How about reading Knight's diary?'

'Now we can. Yes. Not here, though.'

'Most certainly not here. We need privacy and seclusion. Shall we toddle back to the folly – or to our room? Our room would be better. I need to take a couple of aspirins. I'm afraid my head feels like somebody else's – Ah, that must be my coffee! Thank you so much, Faustino.' Payne took a sip and stared down at the cup. 'Gosh. Authentic Rose Pompadour. No stains or chipping. How ludicrously pretentious. Suggests an artificial nature, a love of the flowery and the unreal. I don't think I'll ever come to share Charlotte's affection for our host.' His hand went up to his forehead. 'I have a bad headache, old thing, did I say?'

'Oh, really?'

'It ill becomes you to be so woundingly sarcastic . . . Bloody cocktails . . . I won't touch another cocktail as long as I live. Do let's go.'

'Won't they think it antisocial of us if we were just to sneak off? The party's not over yet.'

'Nobody knows us here.' Payne took another sip of coffee. 'I can't see our host anywhere. The local sahibs are a bit shy. Earlier on one chap talked to me about cricket and his mem told me they always had tea at Fortnum's when in London. Another mem asked me if I had met Songhera's girlfriend and looked relieved when I said I hadn't yet had the pleasure. I wonder why. That has been the extent of my "social interaction", as modern jargon would have it.'

'From something Julian Knight said, I gathered Roman Songhera's girlfriend might have been a lady of easy virtue.'

'You don't say. And I imagined Charlotte was the only one around. Where *has* Charlotte disappeared to? I'm worried that she might be engaged in doing something not particularly dignified.'

'There she is,' Antonia said as she saw that lady walking towards them.

'You'd never believe this, but I heard the most extraordinary story. Exactly your cup of tea, my dear,' Mrs Depleche told Antonia. 'It's simply crying out to be made into a detective novel. *Evil Under the Sun*. That's a clever title, don't you think?'

'It's already been used.'

'I've been talking to that poor boy, Camillo. He's actually of the *noblesse*, would you believe it? Conquistador blood, if that indeed is what they are called, but fallen on bad times, that's the reason why he is "in service". But definitely one of us. There was instant understanding and sympathy between us, a mental force and communication that could be felt as palpably as – what was it the sage said? – as the body gives out heat?'

Payne's eyebrows went up. 'Oh yes? Is that what the sage said?'

'He said I reminded him of his Portuguese grandmother – Donna Alba di Salvadoris, some such name, which is not exactly complimentary, but it explains why he made me his confidante. The poor boy is terribly unhappy – as well as horribly frightened. He thinks he is going mad.' Mrs Depleche paused dramatically. 'You see, he has had the misfortune to fall in love with a gal whose boyfriend is one of the most dangerous men in Goa. Watch out, Hugh – you're spilling coffee!'

'Did he tell you the man's name?'

'No, no names, my dear. It's all very mysterious, awfully romantic and unutterably sad. You must promise to tell no one. Camillo had been with this gal only once – an English gal, incidentally – and then she told him it was all a mistake and that it had to stop. That devastated him for he is head over heels in love with her. He said he couldn't imagine his life without her. Said he'd kill himself, silly young fool. They talked on the phone this morning, as a matter of fact –'

'What time, did he say?'

'I think he said it was "early". She told him she didn't want to see him but it's Valentine's Day and he felt he'd die if he didn't see her, he had a present for her, petits fours, something of the sort, one of those circular gold boxes with ribbons, no doubt, so he decided to go to her place, even though he knew perfectly well it might land both of them in trouble. The gal has a little house not far from here, apparently. The usual bijou residence, I imagine. I've always had sympathy with kept women. I've never been one, mind – quite the reverse in fact.' Mrs Depleche frowned. 'What would the masculine equivalent be, I wonder. Where *would* kept men live? Any ideas, Hugh?'

'Albany? Or do you want me to coin a phrase?'

'Camillo went to see his lady love at midday. He heard the Catholic church bell chime twelve as he rang her front door bell. Nobody answered. He rang again – he thought he heard a noise inside – he turned the door handle. The door opened and he walked in. And now comes the spooky part – you promise you won't breathe a word to anyone? Ah, there comes Roman! Handsome as ever. Looks a bit pale, but I think it suits him. I'm sure he'd be extremely interested to hear the story. Would you mind terribly if I started again?'

'Sorry, Charlotte – I need to go to our room. I'm afraid I don't feel very well,' Antonia said. She tugged at her husband's sleeve. 'Hugh, would you come with me?'

'You should wear a hat.' Mrs Depleche wagged her forefinger at her. 'The sun here can kill you. Do wait a minute. It's the spookiest tale you've ever heard. Roman used to love mystery stories when he was a boy. He liked English mysteries best. I wonder whether he's read any of yours, Antonia. You aren't terribly famous, I know, but you never know. Roman, my boy, d'you remember the mysteries you used to read as a boy?'

Their host was now standing beside them.

'Yes. I thought Nancy Drew was jolly clever. I was potty about Nancy Drew.' Roman spoke in a distracted manner. He was extremely pale and heavy-eyed. 'The Famous Five were jolly clever too. Have you been talking about mysteries?' He didn't sound particularly interested. His mobile phone was in his hand and he kept glancing down at it.

'We have. Well, one particular mystery. You'd never believe this but one of your young Turks –' The next moment Mrs Depleche cried, 'Hugh, watch out – Antonia!'

Antonia had swooned. There was a mighty crash as she clutched at a passing waiter and caused him to drop his tray laden with cocktail glasses on the alabaster terrace floor. Payne managed to catch her before she fell.

'I did say she had to be careful with the sun,' Mrs Depleche observed in triumphant tones. 'She's not used to it and she's not wearing a hat. Clever women are frequently impractical. Bluestockings and so on. A hat's an absolute must in this part of the world. Back in '45 I used to wear a spine-pad at my back as well.'

16

The Knight's Tale

'That wasn't a bad stunt. The very best in diversionary tactics. You should be on stage,' Major Payne said, 'You possess all the guile Eve passed on from the Serpent.'

'Stop talking like a book,' Antonia said.

'Isn't life rendered meaningful or sensible *only* within a literary culture? All right. Let me put it another way. What you did was, in the memorable words of Roman Songhera, jolly clever.'

'I couldn't think of anything else. Apart from throttling Mrs Depleche! Poor lovelorn Camillo would have been in mortal danger if Roman had learnt he and Ria had had an affair. Roman wouldn't hesitate to have him killed too!'

'We haven't got any evidence yet that he's killed *anyone* . . . We do seem to get ourselves let in for rather peculiar situations, don't we?' Payne went on ruefully.

It was some twenty minutes later and they were in their room. Antonia was sitting in her bed and, in case someone were suddenly to enter, she was holding an icepack to her forehead in the time-honoured manner of people affected by sunstroke. On her bedside table, in a broad silver dish, lay a much bigger cube of ice, which a servant had brought in. Payne was lounging in an armchair close by. He was in his shirtsleeves and was sipping his second cup of black coffee. His headache had gone and he was feeling a new man, he had declared.

'You don't think Mrs Depleche will start telling him the story again when she gets a second chance?' Antonia asked anxiously.

'Highly unlikely. She's jolly scatty. She's probably forgotten all about it.'

'Where is she now?'

'She was on the terrace, talking to the Gilmours.' Payne had gone back to retrieve his pipe. 'She was telling them how much she had fancied Jinnah, the founding father of Pakistan. Apparently she met him in 1943, in Hampstead of all places. He was quite Anglicized and sported Savile Row suits, heavily starched shirts and two-tone suede shoes. He had a Bentley and a chauffeur called Bradley and, as though that were not enough, he kept a West Highland terrier called Mop. He was embarrassingly unfamiliar with Islamic methods of prayer, or so Charlotte claimed.'

'I suppose I am being paranoid, but do you think Roman will ask her to finish her story?'

'Highly unlikely. I don't think he was paying any attention. He looked as though he had a lot on his mind.'

'I noticed. Well, so he would – if he really did kill his girlfriend! Beneath all that veneer Roman is nothing more than a common or garden thug.'

'Interestingly enough, the cult of the Thugees actually arose, came to fruition and flourished somewhere round here. It was a nineteenth-century cult of assassins who saw it as their holy mission to harvest bodies for the bloodthirsty goddess Kali . . . What's the matter now?'

Antonia's eyes were fixed on the lowboy with its lion-paw feet and brass handles shaped like snarling lions. She then looked across at the copy of Galland's *Les Mille et Une Nuits, Contes Arabes* – up at the rotating fan in the middle of the ceiling – down at the bowl of fruit on her highly polished bedside table.

'Is there perhaps anything you see, but I don't?' Payne asked.

Stretching out her hand, Antonia ran her fingers over the plump purple figs resting in their green leaves, the pomegranate and the pineapple. 'You don't think the room's bugged, do you?'

'Beware of the mike in the pineapple . . . Shall I run the bath?' Payne said languidly. 'That's what people do when they suspect somebody's eavesdropping on them.' He recrossed his legs and took another sip of coffee. 'The room isn't bugged.'

'How do you know?'

'I checked. That was one of the first things I did yesterday. You were having a bath. I know exactly where to look.' Payne had at one time worked for the Intelligence Service.

'Mrs Depleche said she was coming to the spooky part of the story. What was it Camillo found in Ria's bungalow? I don't think he found Ria's body,' Antonia mused. 'Mrs Depleche wouldn't have put it quite that way if he had.'

'No. You are right. Camillo thought he was going mad. If I have to venture a guess, I'd say that he found . . .'

Antonia lowered the icepack. 'Yes?'

'He found . . . *nothing*. The room was empty. What struck him at once was that it did not look like Ria's room at all. It was absolutely bare but for a desk beside the window, a filing cabinet in the corner and a calendar on the wall showing the now extinct New York Trade Center at night. On the desk there was a laptop and a calculator.'

'Had Camillo entered the wrong bungalow?'

'No. He had been to Ria's bungalow before. That was where they had made love. Camillo stood and gaped. Suddenly a tall, middle-aged man appeared. He was clean-shaven, his grey hair in a boyish crewcut, and he looked benevolent as only an American preacher can. He wore an off-white suit and a bow tie. He was holding a steaming cup of coffee in his hand. He smiled and asked Camillo whether he had come for his tickets. He spoke with a pronounced American accent –'

'What tickets?'

'Plane tickets. The American gentleman said that Las Vegas was most certainly the kind of place for a fine young man like Camillo to have a dandy time in. Camillo had made the right choice. When Camillo, in something of a daze, asked where Ria was, or Miss Marigold Leighton, the man appeared greatly puzzled. He shook his head and said that he was sorry, but he knew no person of that name. No, sir. But this is her bungalow, Camillo cried. No, sir, the American said. This was his office – had been for the past six months – he was the head representative of Tramsfeld Travels. With a little courtly bow, he introduced himself as Tom Tramsfeld the Third. In actual fact he was one of Songhera's agents.'

'You are making this up, aren't you?'

'Of course I'm making it up. How could I possibly have known what Camillo saw? I haven't spoken to the fellow yet.'

Antonia sighed. 'We are wasting time, Hugh.'

'It was Charlotte who put the idea into my head. She thought I too wrote. She was impressed by my turn of phrase. It made me wonder whether I could be as good with plot as well.' Payne frowned. 'My intention was to create a bizarre situation in a convincing enough manner. And I think I succeeded, wouldn't you say? You were riveted.'

'I was not riveted.'

'You were riveted. You are annoyed now because you fell for it, admit it.'

'*We are wasting time.*'

'You do seriously believe that Knight saw a murder and, as a consequence, was removed and eliminated?'

'As a matter of fact I do. He was extremely upset and I don't think it was because he'd consumed a vast quantity of alcohol. I don't think he was that drunk.'

'You can never tell with alcoholics. They are adept at maintaining a semblance of sobriety when they are in fact solidly sloshed. Perhaps he played a practical joke on you?'

'It wasn't a practical joke!'

'Very well. Let's read Knight's account, shall we?'

Antonia silently drew out the reddish-brown notebook from under her pillow.

'Are you angry with me?' Payne asked.

'No. Only annoyed.'

He put down his coffee cup. 'Would you like me to join you? Shall I slip into bed with you and put my arm around you? We could read the Knight's Tale together. I could put on my pyjamas. Get cosy –'

'I don't want us to get cosy. I will read and you will listen and comment.'

'Well, the Honourable Charlotte warned me. She said clever women were the devil. Perhaps she did have a point.'

'I am sure the Honourable Charlotte knows all about clever women. I never particularly liked Chaucer. Do you remember *The Knight's Tale* well?'

'I do.' Payne leant back and lit his pipe. 'A tale of courtly love and chivalric rivalries.'

'How sordid all this is. Julian Knight seems to have been working on several cases. A Mr Stanley of Stanley & Lommax – some kind of an Anglo-Indian import-export company – suspects his junior partner of appropriating funds and frequenting a gambling house. Mrs Agrawal – the wife of a local factory owner – believes her husband is the habitué of an all she-male bordello. Madame Scarpetta is convinced her husband is having an affair with a Mrs Gilmour.' Antonia looked up. 'I wonder if these are the same Gilmours who came to the party?'

'Bound to be. I suppose there's very little else to do in a place like this.' Payne yawned. 'Especially in the monsoon season. She-males. Good lord. Some people do live.'

The windows were open. A perfectly breathless evening had started descending outside, scented and warm. There were no stars, only a pink glow suggesting the sky had been permanently overheated. Antonia had expected an invasion of moths and the kind of horrid little things with hard bodies that dash themselves furiously at the lights – but, so far at least, none had appeared.

'In each case Knight is paid to trail someone and report back.' Antonia turned another page. 'Squalid amours. More squalid amours. I mean *really* squalid. The mind boggles. How could people do things like that?'

'Things like what?' Payne sat up. 'Do read it out. I'd like to hear all about the squalid amours.'

'Some pages are stained. Julian Knight seems to have spilled something.' Antonia's face twisted squeamishly as she sniffed at a page. *'Wine.'*

'How fascinating.' Payne sounded annoyed. 'Red or white? Or is it pink champagne?'

'Twelve, no, thirteen pages are devoted to Ria and her exploits ... *Ria, 24, leaves home after quarrel with father. Shanghai – Dubai – Goa.* She was first spotted in RS's company on the sixteenth of November. She met Roman in Dubai – introduced to him by someone called "Mihail" – info provided by RS's personal valet – four thousand rupees. *Old Leighton rather coy about exact nature of Ria's exotic perambulations, but valet's account leaves nothing to the imagination. Valet claims RS picked her up in foyer of the Balmoral Hotel in Dubai City, where LON congregate –'*

'What's LON? No, don't tell me. Ladies of the night?'

'Notorious picking ground. Any taste catered for. Shall I race ahead?'

'I'd rather you slowed down, actually. This is getting interesting.'

'Oh, here it is! He's dated it. *14th February. I may be dead when you are reading this. Please do something. This morning I witnessed the brutal killing of Marigold Leighton. You will find the body at 19 Fernandez Avenue –'*

'19 Fernandez Avenue?' Payne wrote the address down on a pad.

'If something happens to me, let it be known that Roman Songhera is a killer ... Well, that's it.' Antonia looked up. 'He has signed it JK. He uses big block capitals throughout.' She put the diary down. 'What shall we do?'

There was a pause. 'You are determined that we should do something? Well, as it happens, so am I.' Payne stroked his jaw. 'This is the course of action I propose. Pay a visit to 19 Fernandez Avenue and check if there's really a body there. My guess is that there won't be. Have a word with Camillo about his strange experience earlier today, though that can wait. Try to find Julian Knight. He might not be dead. It's possible that he's gone into hiding. Do we know where he lives?'

'His name and address are on page one . . . 203 Vindia Street, Kilhar.' Antonia paused as Payne wrote the address down. 'What's the time now?'

'Half past seven. It's got dark.'

'That's good. We won't be attracting attention.' Antonia slipped out of bed.

'We'll get a cab. I wonder if all local taxi drivers are Songhera's agents.'

'There'll be fireworks on the beach at nine.'

'I hate fireworks,' Payne said.

'The whole thing is totally mad. Sometimes I wonder if there's something wrong with us. We keep getting involved in bizarre situations.' Antonia put on her shoes, then stood in front of the mirror and patted her hair. She reached out for the bottle of Penhaligon's Bluebell, which she had brought with her from London. It was her favourite scent.

Payne asked her if she was nervous.

'Of course I am nervous. Is my face too red?'

Payne had put on his jacket. He kissed her. 'Not at all. Your headache gone?'

'I never had a headache. *You* did.'

'Look here, old thing – we must be careful,' Payne said.

Antonia suddenly sat back on the edge of the bed. 'Roman wouldn't like it if he caught us trying to prove he was a murderer. What shall we do if we do find Ria's body? Or, for that matter, Julian Knight's body?'

'We'd be in something of a fix. We could try reporting the matter to the police, though chances are we'd be

110

shopped to Songhera straight away. I don't know. We'll have to play it by ear. We could try to get in touch with the High Commission in Delhi, I suppose. Delhi's miles from here. God knows if our mobiles will work. The last time I checked, there was no network.'

'There's an internet room downstairs,' Antonia said.

'The internet was not working this morning, at least that's what the boy said. We seem to be completely cut off. Didn't Knight tell you he couldn't get through to the British High Commission?'

'He did. The line was down, apparently.'

'He had no mobile phone?'

'I have no idea. I didn't see a mobile. They wouldn't have rung up Coconut Grove and asked for him if he did have a mobile, would they?'

Major Payne said, 'The more I think about that phone call, the less I like it.'

17

Journey into Fear

They managed to leave the house without attracting too much attention. Antonia feared they might bump into Mrs Depleche but that lady was nowhere to be seen. Nor was their host. The bearded concierge sat behind his highly polished mahogany desk and he wished them a resounding, 'Good evening, sir. Good evening, madam! Kindly remember – fireworks at nine. It will be a spectacle you will not want to miss.'

Outside, the party was going on. Music and laughter and the popping of champagne corks came from the terrace and the garden, both of which were now illuminated by a profusion of Chinese lanterns and flickering firefly lights. English voices –

'Brown's, as in Dover Street in London. It does look like the real thing, yes. That's where English visitors usually congregate – unless they've decided to go native. It overlooks the sea – spectacular view – sometimes we go there for tea.'

It was a woman who had spoken. The adulterous Mrs Gilmour? Other English people seemed to have turned up for the firework party. How large exactly was the expat colony in Kilhar?

'There are some new arrivals. An ornithologist and a couple that had Home Counties written all over them. Quite respectable-looking. The husband was in a dreadful state – he was accusing his wife of cheating on him, that's what it sounded like. *It was you. You lied to me!* She was very much the *pas devant* type – trying to put her hand over his mouth. Actually, I'm not sure they were husband and wife –'

'The place is riddled with superannuated hippies, simply riddled,' a man was saying. 'Some of these chaps have been here since – you wouldn't believe this – 1967! One keeps bumping into them on the beach. They stagger about in headgear twisted and broken by long use, straw sticking from fraying rims, suitable only for donkeys to wear – like mad kings in Shakespeare's plays! *Peace, man –*'

Arm-in-arm, the Paynes walked briskly down the dimly lit drive. Coconut trees grew on both sides of it. The air was heavy with the heady aroma of mimosa and some other flowers Antonia did not recognize. Hugh's left hand was clenched into a fist, she noticed – as though he anticipated some form of attack. Neither of them spoke. Julian Knight had been holding something in his left hand – so tight that his knuckles had turned white. What *was* it? She would never rest till she found out. She looked up. The moon was out – full moon – enormous – blood-red – sinister.

She consulted her watch. It took them exactly a minute to reach the electronically operated gates. Antonia glanced over her shoulder once, then a second time. She had imagined the bearded servant's hand had moved towards the phone on the desk. Had he informed his master or the chief of security that they had left the building? Well, nobody was following them. There was a guard standing by the gates, a powerfully built Indian in a white short-sleeved shirt and black, carefully pressed trousers. He gave them a good-natured smile and waved them through. Thank God! She sighed with relief. She had been convinced they would be intercepted, frog-marched back and put under house arrest.

They saw several cabs further down the street, their drivers standing about, smoking and talking.

113

They got into the first one. 'Fernandez Avenue,' Payne said. 'You know it?'

'Yes, sir,' the young driver replied in English. He had long raven-black hair, which he wore in a pony tail. 'Fernandez Avenue is very near. Very nice street. Very nice peoples.'

'Do many English people live there?'

'Rich peoples. Some English ladies and gentlemen live in Fernandez Avenue. Yes. Some Portuguese peoples too. Very nice clean place. Very nice houses. Real class. Very safe place.'

They had been plunged into total darkness and were driving at a breakneck speed along an extremely bumpy road. There wasn't another car following them, was there? No. The driver took a turn – they felt the helpless swing of the skid – then another bump! Antonia clutched at her husband's hand.

Major Payne cleared his throat. 'A bit too fast, old chap?'

'I like speed. Speed is good. I like fast cars!' The driver laughed. 'James Bond!'

'Have you been frightfully busy this afternoon?'

'Busy, sir? Yes. I am very busy today. Not all time, no.' He glanced at Payne over his shoulder, causing Antonia to wince.

'Watch out!' she cried as the car leapt upwards.

The driver laughed again. 'James Bond,' he said again. 'James Bond has new car every time. *Every time.* I want to write letter to James Bond.'

'You can't. He's a fictional character,' Payne said.

'I can write in English!' Once more the driver glanced over his shoulder.

'Hugh,' Antonia said warningly.

'James Bond most famous English gentleman in the world!'

'You think so? Not David Beckham? Well, you are right. David Beckham is one of nature's gentlemen, but hardly what you'd call "the real thing" ... I suppose you could send your letter to James Bond care of the Pinewood

114

Studios in London. There's bound to be somebody there who'll answer it. They may even have a specially designated employee who takes care of that sort of thing –'

'*Hugh.*'

Payne asked if by any chance the driver had seen an English gentleman walk out of Coconut Grove. 'About – um – an hour and a half ago?'

The driver waved his hand. 'I see many English gentlemans today. On the beach, on the market and on nice restaurants. Goa is a very popular place.' Suddenly the car slowed down. 'This is Fernandez Avenue. What number, sir?'

'Number 19.'

'Ah, number 19.'

'You know it?' Antonia asked.

'I know number 19. I go sometimes, yes. A very nice English lady live at number 19. Very young, very beautiful. No, not today. Today I go other places. James Bond has new girlfriend every time.' The driver sighed. '*Every time.*'

'Bond girls tend to get killed, don't they?'

Hugh should stop provoking him, Antonia thought, but the driver laughed. 'I like killing!'

'You do?'

Fernandez Avenue had some street lamps, but they only emitted the palest of glows. A ghostly road . . .

'The English lady at number 19 is Roman Songhera's girlfriend, isn't she?'

'Yes, sir,' the driver said after a pause.

'You know Roman Songhera?'

'Everybody know Mr Songhera.'

'Did Roman Songhera come to number 19 today, do you happen to know?'

'No, sir.'

'You mean he didn't or that you don't know?'

'No, sir.'

'What car does Roman Songhera drive?' Payne persisted.

'Two car. BMW M6 Coupé. Aston Martin DB9. And he has a Suzuki Bandit 1200S motorbike . . . This is number 19.' The driver pointed.

'You don't happen to know which of the James Bonds "The Look of Love" is from, old boy, do you? A friend of mine and I were having an argument about it,' Major Payne said as he was paying him. 'You know the one?' He hummed a couple of bars.

'*Casino Royale*,' the driver said.

'Of course. That silly old one – *not* the new one. Thank you so much. I don't suppose you approve of a blond Bond? You strike me as a purist.'

'Hugh,' Antonia warned again.

'Le Chiffre and that infamous torture scene. Must tell Charlotte,' Major Payne murmured as he helped Antonia out of the cab.

He thought the fee the cab driver asked quite exorbitant. 'Notice how monosyllabic and subdued the chap became the moment I brought Songhera into the conversation?'

18

The Mirror Cracked

They stood looking at number 19. 'Not exactly what one imagines a courtesan's *casa* to be,' Payne said. 'But then what *does* a courtesan's *casa* look like?'

'We might be in Bognor Regis.'

'Or in good old Broadstairs.'

It was a neat white bungalow, indeed of the kind one saw at the English seaside – highly respectable – freshly painted – green shutters – a pleasant little garden in front – a trim beech tree – no unruly palms. At the moment all the windows were lit and had been left open – thin silk curtains fluttered in the light evening breeze. Lively music was coming from inside. An Italian song. It struck the only exotic note. 'Una Lacrima Sul Viso'.

'Is that Bobby Solo?' Payne murmured. As they walked up the path towards the front door, he observed that everything seemed to be fine. Ria seemed to be entertaining. She seemed to have recovered from her bad tummy.

'She is supposed to be at Coconut Grove, Hugh. You said Roman looked very worried. This doesn't make sense,' Antonia said.

'It doesn't, you are right. This is rather spooky, actually.'

They rang the front door bell several times, then knocked. When they got no reply, Payne tried the handle. The door opened and they entered. The music became louder. 'Hello!' Payne called out. 'Miss Leighton?'

No answer came. They stood and looked round.

The hall was brightly illuminated. They saw open doors and caught a glimpse of the rooms behind them. There appeared to be four rooms. Only one door was closed. Antonia's eyes fixed on it. The bedroom? She was aware of her heart starting to beat fast. Everything was white – the floors, the walls, the furniture, the rugs, the chest beside the bedroom door. The whiteness created an impression of spaciousness and light. It also made the air feel cooler somehow.

Payne wondered whether the choice of white held any special meaning. The obvious association was with 'coolness' . . . A cool girl . . . There was also the Snow Queen . . . Was Ria trying to strike a balance between being a lust object and an ice maiden? Or perhaps she intended it as an ironic statement – white also stood for innocence and purity.

Antonia was sniffing the air. A scent? Something old-fashioned and stately – not what one would have associated with a young girl of Ria's persuasion, but then Ria might have got a kick out of playing different parts.

'Badly pulverized petits fours.' Payne had picked up a red, black and gold box from the floor. It looked as though someone's heavy foot had trodden on the box and caused it to burst open and spill out its contents. '*Madame Landru, Geneva. The best quality chocolate, marzipan, almonds and nougat,*' he read out.

'Camillo's Valentine gift?'

'Yes. Must be. What *was* it he saw?' Payne placed the squashed box on a side table.

'The mirror – somebody's broken the mirror.' Antonia pointed.

The hall mirror had hung on the wall opposite the closed door, but it now lay on the floor. There was a crack running across it.

'Camillo might have pushed it off the wall as he fled from whatever horrors he witnessed. Or it may have fallen off of its own accord. Mirrors sometimes do, inexplicably. According to the ancient superstition, when that happens a seven-year curse follows.'

'The hook's here.' Antonia was standing beside the wall. She tried the hook with her forefinger. 'There's something caught on it. What's this? Looks like white hairs.'

'Ria might have been visited by some malignant old crone,' Payne said. 'The Wicked Witch of the East? Or she might have had a fight with some client of venerable age. She might have found his demands too much on the *outré* side.'

Antonia shook her head. 'Don't you ever get tired of saying silly things?'

Payne stood peering at the hairs. 'These are not human hairs. It is some animal. A goat? This is getting stranger by the minute.' Turning round, he bent over the white rug in the middle of the hall. He ran his hand over its surface. 'No, this is too short.'

They looked into each room in turn. Sitting room, dining room, kitchen – all gleaming white, spotlessly clean and in perfect order. Only the radio in the sitting room was blaring away – some Italian station, by the sound of it – *Buona sera, signorina, buona sera –*

Payne turned it off.

Then they stood outside the closed door.

It was the bedroom, as they knew it would be.

Antonia's hand had gone up to her throat. What kind of stormy petrels were they? Wherever they went, murder and mayhem seemed to follow. It had been said that certain events attract certain people, but it might be the other way round – certain people attracted certain events . . .

The bedroom, however, was empty. There was no sign of Ria, dead or alive. Perversely, Antonia felt a twinge of disappointment.

Standing side by side, they took stock of their surroundings.

A rosewood four-poster bed carved to perfection. Two pale cream satin chairs. A rather striking antique dressing table. The clock that stood on the table was all pink enamel and gilt amoretti, and beside it lay a book whose cover bore the picture of an imperious beauty with almond-shaped eyes. *The Dream of the Red Chamber*. Antonia could never resist the sight of a book, so she picked it up and read the blurb. The story of an *ernai* – the pinnacle of Chinese courtesans – who had become a favoured consort of the Chinese Emperor and been so richly rewarded for her services that she managed to provide financial support for three generations of her family.

Well, Ria didn't need to support any of *her* family. The Leightons, Antonia imagined, were extremely well off. Why exactly did girls like Ria become prostitutes? That should be the real mystery.

'That's the devil of a lot of mirrors!' Payne was looking at the ceiling. 'Wouldn't you like to have mirrors like that on our bedroom ceiling in Hampstead?'

'No,' said Antonia.

He frowned. 'Why has the bed been pushed to one side? A whacking big four-poster . . .'

'The maid – while hoovering?' Antonia ran her finger across a side table and discovered it was covered in dust. 'No. The room hasn't been cleaned today.'

Payne opened the wardrobe and peered inside. 'Haute couture. Prada stilettos. Some rather outlandish outfits. Gosh. Quite outrageous, in fact. Enough to make a bishop kick a hole in a stained-glass window. Designed to beguile and entice rather than to clothe. Wouldn't you like to take a peek?'

'Not particularly.'

'What a little Puritan you are.'

'I am not a little Puritan. All right, let me see.' She joined him beside the wardrobe. 'Wow.'

'You don't have to humour me.'

Ria couldn't still be plying her trade behind Roman's back, could she? Antonia wondered aloud if perhaps Ria had kept these garments as mementoes of her colourful past career. 'Garments' being a courtesy title since the idea behind them was clearly to *reveal*.

'Perhaps Songhera likes her to dress up,' Payne said.

Antonia's attention was drawn to a black bustier, which had been ripped apart. *The clothes of the dead won't wear long – they fret for the person who owned them.* So claimed another ancient superstition. 'We'd have some serious explaining to do if Ria suddenly came back,' she said.

'Pray that *Songhera* doesn't suddenly turn up!'

The bed was unmade. 'Silk sheets ... The wasteful extravagance of it all ... Is she a brunette?' Payne had detached a black hair from one of the two pillows.

'No idea. It might be Roman's.'

'Too long.'

'His hair might be long under the turban. Sikhs keep their hair long, don't they? Is he a Sikh? Or a Hindu?'

'He is an ass. *The Asinine Assassin*. That's the play Ionesco never wrote,' Payne said. 'The Honourable Charlotte should be more discriminating in her choice of friends, really. A woman of her standing shouldn't be con-sorting with thugs.'

Antonia examined each one of the bed's four pillars. 'No blood. Well, Julian Knight said there wasn't any blood.'

'There wouldn't be if her neck was broken or if she suffered an internal haemorrhage.'

'Solid wood – extremely hard. Would it be enough to cause death, though? I suppose it all depends on Roman's strength and the fragility of Ria's skull,' Antonia mused. 'Julian Knight said he heard a crack.'

'Couldn't she have been merely concussed? She might have come to eventually and walked off.'

'Julian Knight was positive that she was killed. Her eyes remained open, apparently. It was Roman who closed them.'

Major Payne stood examining the array of objects that lay on the right-hand bedside table. A pair of pendant ear-rings, a make-up kit, a bottle of nail varnish remover, a

121

Penguin paperback. *Andersen's Fairy Tales*. How interesting. One always assumed hookers were pragmatic, hard-boiled and cynical. He couldn't quite envisage Ria reading fairy tales at bedtime. Hard to imagine her identifying with, say, the ultra-fastidious princess who had been given a sleepless night by a pea placed under a pile of mattresses.

What was that? A single sheet of mauve-coloured writing paper lying across the pillow. He picked it up and smoothed it out. It was a letter. He glanced at the bottom first, then read it through.

'How normal and reassuring that she should have an affectionate aunt called Iris who lives in Cambridgeshire,' he observed. 'Ria's father died last November . . . He died of a pulmonary embolism . . . The funeral was a "grand affair" . . . They didn't get on.' Payne looked up. 'Maybe her father's the reason she turned out the way she did? Martinets' children frequently develop dissident personalities, haven't you noticed?'

'Should we be touching things like that?'

'We should have been wearing gloves, you are absolutely right. Too late now. You don't suppose we will be arrested on suspicion of murder, do you?' He didn't seem particularly concerned. 'That might provide you with spectacular publicity for your new novel.'

'We may be doing the local police a grave injustice. It would serve us right if they suddenly burst into the room and ordered us to hold our hands up.'

'Is the aunt Ria's only next of kin? Did Ria have no mother? Was she an only child? How frustrating not to know anything about her previous life.' Payne pulled out the bedside table drawer. 'Hello. What have we got here?'

'What's that?'

He had taken out a bundle of letters held together with two rubber bands. Detaching the top one, he read out, *'Noon's Folly Cottage, Noon's Folly, nr Ayot St Lawrence, Hertfordshire.* Noon's Folly. How quaint. D'you think "noon" is a corruption of "nun"? One *can* imagine a nun committing a folly . . . *My dearest girl, I love you more than*

122

words can express. A love letter, by Jove. *Your loving father.* Well, not quite. What's the matter now?'

'I do feel uncomfortable about reading people's letters.'

'Decent folk don't do that sort of thing? You are right, they don't. Well, it's a low job searching people's rooms and we are low hounds to do it, but the circumstances, you must admit, are quite exceptional. It's not as though we are motivated by vulgar curiosity.' Payne went on examining the letters. *'Your loving father . . . I would give anything to have you back . . . Your loving father . . . Don't you think you've been punishing me for too long? Have I been sentenced to a life of misery and pain? Please, my child, come back. Your loving father.'* Payne looked up. 'All the letters are from her father.'

'So I gathered. Poor man. He probably died of a broken heart.'

'He writes like a man possessed . . . Does anyone still live at Noon's Folly, I wonder? There's a phone number. Who knows? It may be up to us to break the awful news to Ria's next of kin.'

'We don't know yet if she is really dead.'

'Actually I would be interested in reading all the letters. We may get a better picture of Ria.' Payne stuffed the bundle into his pocket.

'If a British citizen were to die in Goa, the British High Commission would be notified first, correct? Then the High Commission would contact the relatives in England,' Antonia said thoughtfully. 'But what happens if a British citizen disappears and no one realizes they have? We've got no evidence Ria's dead, so that consideration may be a bit premature –' She broke off. 'What are you doing?'

Payne was kneeling beside the four-poster. He appeared to be examining one of its four legs. 'Did you say premature? I wouldn't say premature, no.'

'What do you mean?'

He rose slowly to his feet. He was holding something between his thumb and forefinger. 'Prepare for a shock.' He showed her his finding.

'White hairs?' Antonia squinted. 'They look the same as the ones on the hook!'

'They *are* the same. They were stuck to the very base of the leg – where it had pressed into the carpet.'

'There is no carpet. The floor is bare.'

'The carpet's been removed. They *needed* the carpet.' Payne stood looking at Antonia. 'Don't you see?'

'Oh, my God. Is that how they . . .'

Payne went into a silent pantomime. He pretended to be rolling up a carpet. He slung it across his right shoulder, then, staggering under its imaginary weight, lumbered in the direction of the bedroom door. Straightening up, he spoke: 'My guess is there were two of them. As they started crossing the hall, one end of the carpet pushed against the mirror, causing it to fall and smash on the floor. One of them trod on the petits fours which Camillo had dropped on the floor earlier on. I imagine they were acting on Songhera's orders.'

'Yes. He told them to go and collect the body. They placed the body on the carpet and rolled her up in it . . . So Roman did kill her!'

'Did they take her to the croc farm, I wonder?'

A vision rose before Antonia's eyes. Something they had seen earlier in the afternoon – at Coconut Grove – in the hall – two men in overalls being waved by the turbaned concierge towards the swinging doors. The men had shouted in an agitated manner. They had been carrying two carpets –

One of the carpets had been Persian – *the other white and with a deep pile.*

The Persian carpet was clearly a decoy. To distract attention from the white one.

'No, not to the croc farm. They took the body to Coconut Grove,' Antonia said. 'Remember the men with the carpets?'

Payne stared at her. 'Men with carpets? By Jove, yes! Songhera's goons!'

'That's what Roman must have told them to do. She is there now, Hugh. At Coconut Grove. *She is there now.*'

124

'Yes. Unless we're making complete fools of ourselves and she's having the time of her life with a new boyfriend somewhere. No, I don't think we are. She isn't having the time of her life.' Payne's expression was grim. 'She's inside the deep freeze. Next to the ice cream and the caviar. They wouldn't be taking risks in this hot weather.'

19

Indo-Chine

'One ignores the ancient and dangerous power of carnal love at one's peril. Think the *Oresteia*. Think *Othello*. Think *Carmen*. The betrayed lover's psyche must be a terrible place.' Major Payne shook his head. 'One finds nothing there but wild primitive irrationality, blind misery and obsessive craziness. Songhera chose to walk down an ancient and well-trodden path. He's not the first and, sadly, he won't be the last. Rage – violence – grief – overpowering sense of loss – howling emptiness. The sequence is always the same, depressingly predictable.'

'He did howl. That's what Julian Knight said.'

'Sex has laid waste to empires and launched a thousand ships.' Payne frowned. 'Didn't Elizabethan slang make "die" a synonym of climax? The power that founds dynasties is a strong voodoo.'

They had walked to the end of the road and were standing there looking out for taxis.

'Roman must have got wise as to Ria's affair with Camillo,' Antonia murmured.

'Or with somebody else. She seems to have been that sort of girl. You saw those outfits.'

A taxi appeared and Payne held up his hand.

'203 Vindia Street,' he told the driver. 'We might as well go the whole hog and see if we can find Knight.'

'Do you think we shall?'

'No. What's the time?'

'Half past eight. We'll be late for the fireworks.'

'The fireworks can go to hell,' said Payne. 'I have no idea what we'll do if we get saddled with two dead bodies. No idea at all. Apart from deriving the subliminal satisfaction that comes with being proven right.'

203 Vindia Street was a dingy building whose landlord, an elderly Chinese called Tang, spoke good English but seemed distracted. Tang held a long clay pipe in his hand and kept his thumb inside its bowl. He had run out of tobacco, he informed them, and there was no tobacco at the local shop or indeed at any other shop. Life in Kilhar was not easy. Tang shook his head. He would have to wait for a whole week now till he could have a smoke. No, he hadn't seen Mr Knight since early morning. He had seen Mr Knight in the street outside the house – Tang hitched up his right shoulder and gave a fair imitation of Julian Knight's gliding walk. It had been some time after eight o'clock. Mr Knight had been muttering to himself. He had appeared greatly preoccupied and hadn't responded to Tang's 'good morning'.

No, Mr Knight hadn't come back at any point of the day. Tang had sat with his friend, Mr Pereira, in the shop opposite the house, so he wouldn't have missed Mr Knight. Tang was absolutely sure of his facts. How was he going to manage without any tobacco? He was quite addicted to tobacco. What was that? Tang cupped his ear. The lady and the gentleman wanted to look round Mr Knight's flat? Tang seemed very much surprised by the request. Why should they want to do that?

'I am Julian's cousin,' Payne explained briskly. 'I just wanted to see how Julian lives. Is that so unusual?'

Cousin? From England? Tang pushed his forefinger into the pipe's empty bowl and frowned. Yes, it was unusual. Mr Knight had never been visited by members of his family before. *Never*. Only strangers visited him. And no one so far had asked to be shown Mr Knight's flat. Tang didn't know. Mr Knight might not like it.

'You come with us,' Payne said. 'You unlock the flat door and stand by. You watch us like the proverbial hawk. My wife and I just want to take a dekko. We won't be a minute. Incidentally, would you like to try my baccy?' He produced his tobacco pouch with a casual gesture. 'It's frightfully good.'

'You have tobacco?' Tang blinked.

'Three Nuns. Would you like to try it?' Payne unzipped the pouch and proffered it to Tang.

'You smoke pipe?'

'I most certainly do.'

'Three nuns? English tobacco?' Tang took a pinchful, sniffed at it, nodded and beamed. 'Smells good. Very good. I can have a smoke now?'

They watched Tang stuff his pipe. Payne handed him a Bryant & May box of matches. He gave Antonia a covert wink. For some reason she was put in mind of the First World War. British soldiers handing over cigarettes to enemy Hun ones on Christmas Day, during a temporary truce.

There was a pause. They awaited Tang's verdict. 'Good tobacco.' Tang nodded again between puffs and smiled. 'Very good tobacco. English nuns smoke a pipe, yes?'

'At some convents I imagine they do, though they risk the Mother Superior's birch,' Payne said gravely. 'I've got another packet in my suitcase. Sealed for freshness,' he added in casual tones.

The Chinaman looked at him. 'You have more English tobacco? The same three nuns?'

'The very same.' Would Mr Tang accept the tobacco, Payne went on, as a friendly gift from one pipe smoker to another? He would be happy to deliver the packet in person the following morning. He held the firm belief, Major Payne said, that pipe smokers the world over, irrespective of creed or political persuasion, should support each other.

* * *

Julian Knight's flat was the tiniest of bedsits. The interior was dark and drab, the predominant colour a kind of grubby beige. A musty smell hung on the hot, motionless air. The mess, Antonia thought as she stood looking round, was incredible, shocking. How could anyone live like that? Everywhere there were empty bottles. Wine, vodka, rum, whisky, gin, schnapps, orange peel liqueur, something called Kingfisher. Wine glasses, tumblers, sherry glasses and cups, some of them covered in mould, stood on every surface. A cockroach was trying desperately to climb out of a globular brandy glass. Antonia's face twisted squeamishly. Tins. Tattered cricket almanacs. A broken oil lamp. More bottles. A Carpenters LP: *This Masquerade*. A statuette of the Virgin and Child. A great number of cheap paperbacks. Antonia picked one up, holding it gingerly between her thumb and forefinger. *Amorous Nurses*. She opened it at random. *Dr Hamilton was gorgeous and efficient, a surgical whizz and the most handsome man she'd ever seen.*

Antonia glanced at the rest of the books. She would have expected a former policeman to read real-life crime or unsolved mysteries, if not detective stories, but all the paperbacks, astonishingly, proved to be American hospital romances. *The Tenderness of Doctors*. Not parodies, were they? *He Healed Her Heart*. No. They all seemed to be in dead earnest. One cover showed an intestinal-looking tree festooned with hospital equipment. If I carried this book round, everybody would be asking me what it was about, Antonia thought. One must be really desperate to read stuff like that.

Payne drew her attention to a photograph in a frame – a wedding group. The date was written out under it: May 1982. A broadly smiling bride and a bashful-looking groom. Was that Julian Knight? Antonia peered. Impossible to tell. She imagined she detected a resemblance in the curve of the mouth, but of course she couldn't swear to it. The fresh-faced young man in the morning coat and the topper couldn't have looked more different from the sweating twitching creature in the grubby panama and dark glasses who had buttonholed her in the folly. Old Zebra Face. Why had Hugh called him that? Because of the white stripe on his forehead? Julian Knight had been a bad colour. Mottled complexion. He had kept mopping his face. With a little shudder Antonia recalled the stained tissue Julian Knight had dropped inside the folly . . .

Payne had walked across to a small rickety writing table and opened a drawer. Antonia smiled at Tang who was standing in the doorway, smoking in an absorbed manner. 'So hot, isn't it?' she said.

'Very good tobacco.' Tang nodded. 'Madam smoke?'

'No, I don't. What's that?' She raised her hand towards a thick blackish smudge on the ceiling, which was almost four feet in length and immediately above the narrow bed in the corner.

'Smoke stain. Opium. No, not Mr Knight. Mr Knight no smoke. My cousin. My cousin live in flat before Mr Knight. My cousin philosopher. What is Infinity? My cousin always ask. Always. Can you explain Infinity? Can you reach Infinity? My cousin want to know. Madam know?'

'Infinity? Goodness.' Antonia frowned. 'Um. They draw it as an 8 that was so tired, it simply had to lie down and take a nap, don't they? It's where parallel lines meet, or so they say – isn't it? What a strange sight *that* would be,' she murmured thoughtfully.

'If we ever were to reach Infinity,' Payne said, 'all the numbers would be abolished, but then it must mean that Time will be abolished as well and no one will ever use the expression "in years to come" and there'll be no need for Multiplication Tables, nor for Addition, Subtraction or Division either, and there'll be no break-fasts, dinners or teas, and – '

'And nobody will grow old but stay the same age?'

'Which will be fine if you are thirty-something but not so fine if you are eighty-something.'

'Wife finish husband sentence,' Tang said approvingly.

'My wife never finish my sentence. My wife difficult and stupid woman, but she cook well. Madam like flat?'

'It's comfortable enough, but it looks a bit mournful,' said Antonia diplomatically. 'Not a single bright colour!'

Tang pointed to his eyes. 'Blind. Attention. Madam not to move. Mouse.' He now pointed towards Antonia's feet. With a little cry she drew back. She watched in horror as Tang, without taking the pipe out of his mouth, grabbed a roll of newspapers and killed the mouse with a crisp sickening thwack.

Tang laughed. 'Madam like mice?'

'No!' It took Antonia a moment to recover her poise. 'What did you mean, "blind"?'

'Mr Knight blind. See no colour. Mr Knight tell me, Mr Tang, beauty of world lost on me!'

'Oh, you mean *colour*-blind? Really?' With the corner of her eye Antonia thought she saw Hugh take something out of the desk drawer and put it into his pocket.

'Yes. Blind. See no colour. Madam have children?'

'Yes.'

'How many?'

'I have a son.'

'I have fifteen son.'

'Thanks so much for letting us see Knight's flat.' Major Payne joined them. 'Cosy little place. Could do with a lick of paint and a spot of spring cleaning, though.'

'You bring more tobacco tomorrow morning, yes?'

'Absolutely, my dear fellow. Either in person or I'll employ the services of one of our tame Turks. Incidentally, Mr Tang, which of Knight's shoulders is higher, the right or the left?'

'Right,' Tang answered promptly.

'You sure it's the right?'

'Yes. Right. You call your cousin by second name?' Tang gave a sly smile.

'Sometimes I do. We are not terribly close,' Payne explained, unperturbed.

Soon after they went down the staircase, which creaked ominously, and out into the street.

'An observant old bird,' declared Payne. 'Am I right in thinking Monsignor Knox ruled against Chinamen? I mean in his famous Decalogue. No self-respecting detective story writer should include sinister Chinamen among the suspects and so on?'

'Tang is not a suspect.'

'How do you know? I had the distinct impression he was seething with sinister intentions.'

'He killed a mouse most adroitly,' Antonia said in a thoughtful voice.

'There you are. Tang is a merciless killer. Monsignor Knox meant the Fu Manchu type of course,' Payne went on ruminatively. 'Tall, lean and feline, with a brow as wide as Shakespeare's and a face like Satan's, close-shaven skull and long magnetic eyes of the true cat green and embodying the cruel cunning of the entire Easten race.'

'You shouldn't be saying things like that. What did you take from the desk?'

'Nothing much. A photo of Ria and her papa. Would be useful to know what she looked like. Want to see it?' Payne's hand went to his trouser pocket.

Antonia stood examining the photograph. 'How can you be sure it's Ria and her father?'

'It says so at the bottom – ML and OL.'

'So it does. Marigold Leighton. OL? Oh. Old Leighton ... Marigold looks bold and beautiful – wasn't that the title of that dreadful American soap opera your aunt raves about?'

'Ah. *The Bold and the Beautiful*. Aunt Nellie has seen thirty-eight episodes – and it is far from over, apparently. Ria's got oodles of SA,' Payne murmured. 'Oodles and oodles and oodles of SA. Don't look so disapproving. Old Leighton gives me the jitters. Something nightmarish about him.'

'He doesn't look very happy.'

'He looks the epitome of the petulant tyrant. Observe the proprietorial manner in which he clutches his daughter's arm. I imagine he loved Ria beyond reason, beyond rectitude and beyond pity. Perhaps he was a little in love with her . . . I do have a way with words, you must admit.'

'Pipe-smoking nuns risking the birch! Really, Hugh, that was the most idiotic thing I'd ever heard.' Antonia shook her head. 'You have given Tang a terribly distorted idea of what life at an English convent is like.'

Payne sighed. 'I keep thinking of Songhera's crocs, my love. I know it's awfully silly of me, but I can't help it. When I was a young boy I always felt great sympathy for poor Captain Hook. Now I *know* how he must have felt.'

'Roman wouldn't dare throw us to his crocs, would he?'

'He would certainly do so if he thought we were conspiring to get him, I have little doubt. Charlotte, too – and it would serve her right. Killing Ria might have tipped him straight into the mouth of madness. Ah, there's a taxi at last.' Payne held up his hand. 'Songhera could always claim he never laid eyes on us. The police station,' he told the taxi driver.

Antonia frowned. 'What was that thing about Julian Knight's right shoulder?'

20

A Man Lay Dead

The police station was small and even dingier than Julian Knight's abode. Major Payne wished the policeman behind the desk a good evening. 'Do you speak English?'

'I speak English.' The policeman smiled at them in a friendly enough manner.

'I am terribly worried about my cousin. A Mr Julian Knight. He resides in Kilhar but he seems to have vanished into thin air.'

'Your cousin is English?'

'Yes. He lives at 203 Vindia Street. We've been to all the hospitals and now we'd like to report him missing.'

'All hospitals?' The policeman laughed. 'Only one hospital in Kilhar! When did gentleman disappear?'

'Can't say exactly,' Payne proceeded with caution. 'He doesn't answer his mobile phone. He hasn't been seen by his landlord. We fear he might have been involved in some accident.'

'Accident? Many accidents happen here. Many, many accidents. This is very nice place, very nice beaches, but we have many accidents.' The policeman had opened a large black book and was looking through it. 'Today is . . . fourteenth of February. Your cousin drive car?'

'I don't think so.' Payne looked at Antonia who shrugged.

'We have three car crashes today, two fatal, and one man died later at hospital. Lady fell under train – cut in two. This is bad, very bad. Your cousin is lady?'

'No. A man.'

'We have four dead bodies today. Three ladies, one gentleman. One gas poisoning, probably suicide, one decapitation, one fatal stabbing. Gentleman hit by car.' The policeman made a slashing gesture across his forehead. 'Not very nice. We find card in pocket.' The policeman held up the card. 'Mr – *Julio Kugtilo* – this your cousin?'

'No.'

The policeman laughed. 'I make a mistake. Sorry. Light is bad. It is Mr Julian Knight, of . . . of Knightsbridge Investigating Agency. Your cousin is private investigator?'

'Yes . . . Good lord.'

'And his name is Julian Knight? This is very, very bad news. I am sorry, sir, but your cousin is dead. You want to see body?'

Payne felt blood rushing to his head. Dead! So they did get him after all. Why did he feel so shocked? Hadn't they written Knight off as one already lost to this world? Antonia had gone very pale. Knight had talked to her. Poor darling. She must be feeling responsible, guilty, though what the hell could she have done? The way Knight had staggered across the lawn. All those hospital romances. Poor blighter. Rotten business. One body had turned up, the other was waiting to be discovered. Was Ria in the deep freeze at Coconut Grove? If they were to discover her there, what *would* they do? As pretty a tangle as any fellow ever stumbled into, as Richard Hannay put it. At least Knight hadn't been fed to the crocs. Thank God for small mercies.

Payne heard Antonia ask where the body was.

'Over there – you see that door?' The policeman pointed matter-of-factly with his thumb. 'Wait. I tell someone to take you. Please note that your cousin has head injuries. Not too bad but not nice.'

* * *

135

'Oh, my God,' Antonia said. A great nauseous shiver had gone through her. She had been holding her handkerchief against her nose. The room was pervaded by a terrible foul smell. She was sure she could hear the buzzing of flies, though it might be her imagination. She was afraid she would be sick.

The body lay on a tin platform on wheels. It had been pulled out of what looked like an enormous gimcrack cupboard.

'This is Mr Knight, madam?'

'I don't know. I – I think so.'

She couldn't say for sure it was Julian Knight and yet it must be him. The light in the room was poor. Its source was a single electric bulb in a socket above the door, through which they had entered. Well, the dead man *looked* like Julian Knight. He wore the same jacket, or something very similar. What would be the point of a stranger's dead body being passed off as that of Julian Knight? She couldn't think of any reason. No, that wasn't true – she could think of a number of reasons, but this was neither the time nor the place for fanciful speculation. Antonia held her hand firmly cupped over her mouth. She hoped she wouldn't disgrace herself.

She tried to think rationally. This *was* Julian Knight. Julian Knight had been witness to murder and now he too had been killed. He had been silenced. Cause and effect. If they – Roman and his henchmen – knew that he'd given her his diary, which contained his eyewitness account of the murder, then she would be in danger – Hugh as well. Actually, she couldn't *swear* that the dead man lying in the tin tray before her was Julian Knight. Julian Knight, when she had met him, had worn a hat with a slouching brim and dark glasses. She hadn't been able to see his face properly. Still, who else could this man possibly be? Of course it was Julian Knight. When people died, they always looked different. Shrunken. Diminished. The dead man looked smaller than the one who had joined her in the folly, but death did diminish people . . .

There was a horrible livid indentation across his fore-head. A tyre mark? Julian Knight's cheeks were covered in dirt. Didn't they wash corpses? Julian Knight's short grey hair was sticky with congealed blood. The eyes were wide open. The left eye looked damaged – as though it had – Antonia glanced away quickly. The eye couldn't have fallen out, could it? Julian Knight's mouth was gaping pathetically, like that of a dead fish. The lips were blue. The face had in life been deep brown but was the colour of lead now. Julian Knight's hands lay limply beside his body, palm upwards. She looked at them curiously. No, nothing inside either of them. Both hands were empty. What *was* it he had held in his left hand? Was the object in his killers' possession now?

Payne touched her hand. 'Shall we go?'

She jumped. 'Yes!'

'Is there going to be an investigation?' Payne asked when they stood beside the desk once more.

'Investigation? What investigation?' The policeman on duty seemed greatly surprised by the suggestion. 'No, no investigation. This is accident.'

'Have you managed to catch the driver of the car that hit Julian?' Antonia asked.

'No catching. No one saw number plate. Lots of people in street, but everybody looking at the sun, you see. No sun this morning. The sun disappear. Very interesting.'

Payne nodded. 'The partial solar eclipse. Yes. It didn't last longer than five minutes.'

For some reason the policeman reacted as though he had been rebuked. 'Not enough policemen for investigation!' He waved his hand to emphasize the empty space around him.

'Where did the accident take place?' Payne persisted.

'In town. In main street. Your cousin cross street, then – *boum!*' The policeman beat his fist against the palm of his left hand.

'Was anyone with him, do you know?'

'No. Yes. Woman. Local woman. She is walking with your cousin when accident happened.' The policeman spread his hand across his face. 'Her face covered. She wears veil. Tall woman. She runs away.'

'She ran away? Really? A local woman, did you say? Somebody saw her?'

'Yes, madam. One man saw her. She is tall and she wear veil.'

'Aren't you looking for her?' Payne asked.

'No. Why look? She is not his wife. Wife doesn't run away when husband die,' the policeman said sententiously and he made a dismissive gesture. 'Not important.'

'What happens if no one claims a dead body here?' Antonia asked.

The policeman shrugged. 'We bury dead bodies. Very high temperatures – very hot. Not nice. English people? Yes, English people too. This is law. Law is very strict.'

'Is it?' Payne cocked an eyebrow.

'If no one says, this is my husband or my father or my brother or my cousin, we bury them. Why keep bodies, if no one want them? We have power cuts. Blackout. Electricity is very expensive. We can't keep bodies. Not nice . . . Now you take your cousin with you, yes?'

'We most certainly shall, but not at this very moment.'

'You bury your cousin in England?'

'We'll be back. Um. We need to get a car,' Payne reassured him.

This was a blatant lie and for a moment he felt guilty, but then he reflected that Knight was past caring. Poor lonely blighter. What difference did it make where they buried him? *The earth is the earth is the earth.* There was a poem about it. Some people had funny ideas about burials. At one time Charlotte had wanted her dead body to be thrown to the dogs at a meet. And didn't the actress Sarah Miles have her playwright husband buried in her back garden? No, it didn't matter a hang where one's mortal remains were laid to rest. *All flesh is grass.* It was where the soul went that counted. Had Knight had any religious

138

beliefs? The statuette of the Virgin and the Child had been wedged between two of those tatty hospital romances. Knight's former colleagues at Scotland Yard would probably never know he had died. Or his former wife. (Who was the woman who'd run away? Had she had any reason to run away?) Did Knight have any children? Would anyone *care* he'd died and been buried in Goa?

Payne was feeling light-headed. Dizzy and quite upset, actually. A tight knot in his throat. Too long in the sun. Too much to drink. Bloody cocktails. Never again. Dog tired. Then this business. Rotting flesh. Nasty pong. All too much! And it was not over yet. They needed to find Ria. They were about to put their theory to the test – check the deep freeze at Coconut Grove. What if they were caught red-handed and Songhera turned nasty? The crocs! Payne dabbed at his forehead with his handkerchief.

They walked out into the night. It was still very warm, yet Antonia started shivering. Payne put his arm around her. Neither of them spoke. They heard distant explosions and the sky was suddenly ablaze with crimson – like a splash of blood – several splashes of blood – then golden yellow.

It was five minutes past nine o'clock and the firework display at Coconut Grove had started.

21

Murder as a Fine Art

'A riddle wrapped in a mystery inside an enigma. Churchill actually said that about Soviet Russia. What I mean, my love, is that it is all a little bit too much. It's not the complexities I object to, actually, but the roller-coaster rate at which things have been happening. Hardly any time for stock-taking, wouldn't you agree?'

A roller-coaster, yes. Antonia admitted to feeling disoriented as well as a little nauseous.

'I am sure that if this were one of your books, you'd want to pace things better, wouldn't you? '

'My editor might suggest it. I may also decide to revise the scene in the police station.' Antonia scrunched up her face. 'Do morgues at Goan police stations really resemble vile-smelling Third World butcher's shops?'

'That one did . . . This *is* the Third World.'

'I think most people enjoy fast-moving plots, no matter how improbable. Even the most sophisticated reader likes things to *happen*. Most readers prefer action to, say, discourses on the nature of evil or intricate descriptions of the weather. What else is there to write about? Do readers like analyses of the investigators' tortured love lives?'

'Some crime writers do go off at incredible tangents, I've noticed, describing in meticulous detail things that have nothing to do with the murder plot. I must say I have little patience with self-indulgent bores. Self-indulgent

bores should be on the High Executioner's Little List.'
Payne held up his forefinger. 'Those who ramble on about
gourmet food, the Book of Common Prayer, cats and dogs,
opera, church architecture and so on. Talking of tortured
love lives, did Dalgliesh marry Emma in the end?'

'I have no idea. I always thought that such an *unlikely*
sort of romance. So much to-ing and fro-ing. And it's all
so ponderous and gloomy.'

'The trouble with certain *grandes dames* is that they
would insist on being taken *au grand sérieux*. Being considered capable purveyors of escapist entertainment is
simply not enough for them.'

'If I were writing this up, I would have Ria alive rather
than dead,' Antonia said suddenly.

Payne looked at her. 'You would? How very interesting.
Ria is not in the deep freeze at CG?'

'No. That – that would be too obvious. The assumption
about Ria's being dead would turn out to be entirely
fallacious. I rather like the idea of the amateur tecs getting
it all wrong. The amateur tecs have been goaded into a
trap. Julian Knight has lied about witnessing Ria's murder.
He has had a good reason for it.'

'Go on.'

'Julian Knight's intention was to implicate Roman
Songhera. He saw Roman as his rival –'

'Rival? Do you mean Knight was in love with Ria?'

'Yes. Madly in love. Julian Knight had been stalking Ria
as part of his job – he had been observing her closely –
recording her every move – noting down the way she
dressed, the scent she wore and so on – and he became
obsessed with her. He decided he couldn't live without her.'

'Enchanted and enchained, eh? Like the chap in *Vertigo*?'

'This is what happens. Julian Knight pays Ria a visit. He
turns up on her doorstep and declares his love for her.
She stares at him. She has actually noticed him following
her. A pathetic Wurzel Gummidge of a man. Not at all
dangerous-looking. Actually the whole thing is an incredible hoot. She bites her lip. She is amused. She likes men

141

to fall in love with her. She takes a perverse pleasure in leading men on. She is rotten to the heart. She is in a particularly skittish mood that day. She says she is greatly flattered. She invites him in. She offers him a drink. She pretends to reciprocate his ardour –'

'She allows him to crush his mouth to hers?' Payne suggested.

'Possibly. She then suggests they meet again. Tells him to feel free to call on her again, very soon. Julian Knight takes her at her word. He arrives at the bungalow the very next day. He's brought her a bunch of flowers – but now she stares at him blankly. She is annoyed – bored with the whole thing – no, she's forgotten who he is! He is unkempt, looks incredibly wrinkled and reeks of drink. His leer repels her. She doesn't let him in. She pushes him away. When he reminds her of his feelings for her and of her promises, she laughs. She lets him know what she really thinks of him. In the end she admits it was all a game. He'd better scram, she says, or he'd be a dead man if Roman came and found him here. He knows who Roman Songhera is, of course? She then slams the door. Julian Knight staggers back. He is stunned – mortified – distraught –'

'The episode unhinges him somewhat?'

'It does. It unhinges him considerably. Julian Knight is a troubled man and now his first urge is to kill himself, but then – then he finds himself planning Ria's murder. He does it with the utmost care and the most scrupulous attention to detail. He is an ex-policeman-turned-private-detective, so he knows how to set about it. The murder will be pinned on Roman Songhera – his love rival! He himself will play the part of the witness to the murder. After he kills Ria, he will disappear, perhaps make it look as though he has committed suicide? But he needs some-one who will listen to him first, someone who will take his allegation seriously. He gatecrashes Roman Songhera's garden party and settles on me –' Antonia broke off. 'Does any of this make sense?'

142

Major Payne nodded. 'It was a friend of Knight's who phoned CG and asked to speak to him. Knight had put him up to it. All part of the plan. Or Knight paid one of the locals to make the call ... So Knight told you he had witnessed the murder *before* he actually went on to commit it?'

'That's correct. After he left Coconut Grove, he went to Ria's bungalow. He managed to sneak in. Either Ria had forgotten to lock the front door or he had a skeleton key in his pocket.' Antonia's eyes narrowed. 'He finds Ria in the bedroom. He pushes her on the bed – holds her down – grips her legs with his knees – puts his hands around her throat – starts strangling her. Ria struggles – as it happens, she is stronger than him – she claws his eyes. As he screams and pulls back, she reaches out and picks up something heavy from her bedside table.'

'An ormolu clock? An onyx vase? A copper candlestick?'

'Some such object, yes. She hits him across the temple with it. Then she hits him a second time. He goes limp. She pushes him off the bed. He falls on the floor and lies motionless. There is no blood. She prods him with her foot. He doesn't move. She checks his pulse and doesn't find it. He is dead. She has killed him. She is not particularly perturbed. She picks up the phone – Dear me, Hugh, I don't believe we are doing this!'

'I don't see anything wrong with indulging our wild and vivid imaginations in a gallop over wholly speculative courses, if that's what you mean.'

'You don't think it is irresponsible and childish of us?'

'Not really. Shall I go on?' Payne pulled at his lip. 'Ria calls two of Roman's henchmen – tells them to come at once. When they do, she orders them to take away Julian Knight's body. They put the bedroom carpet to good use. They ask no questions. They load the body into the boot of their car and later dump it in the street. They make the death look like an accident. Perhaps, for good measure, they run their own car over the body. Then they pay some-one to give the police an eyewitness account, to say that

Knight was pushed under a speeding car by a veiled woman.'

There was a pause.

'Where's Ria now?' Antonia said.

'Hiding somewhere. Apparently Songhera has luxury villas all over the place. Or she may have left Goa. She may have gone to Europe where she will lie doggo till things calm down. She may be in Rome or in Paris. She may be shopping in the Place Vendôme at this very moment . . . So Knight is the one and only all-important victim, eh? His is the only murder worth investigating? This is awfully good.'

'What was it Camillo saw at the bungalow that shocked him so much?'

'Maybe – maybe he witnessed the struggle in the bedroom? Sorry, old thing.' Payne had yawned. 'It's been a long haul . . . What's the time in England now? Are we five hours ahead or five hours behind?'

'Five hours ahead. If we were in England, we'd be sitting in the garden, having tea. No, not in the garden – in England it would be freezing –' The next moment Antonia clutched at his arm. 'Hugh, I do believe this is important!'

'What is important? Having tea or the freezing English weather?'

'*Five hours ahead*. Ten minutes ago I imagined that the policeman said something which suggested – no, *proved* beyond doubt that Julian Knight's death was all wrong.'

'Proved beyond doubt?' He stared at her. 'What did the policeman say?'

'I haven't got the obscurest of inklings. Now I am talking like you!'

'I am sure I never say things like "obscurest of inklings".'

'You do. You often talk like a character in a book.'

'I think we might be having a joint nightmare,' Payne said. 'We should never have left Hampstead. Aunt Nellie had no business recommending us to the Honourable Charlotte. No business at all. To think that we might

144

actually end up in a decorative lake full of crocodiles. This is most definitely *not* my idea of a pleasant holiday.'

'You can say that again.'

'What was it you imagined? Think back. The policeman mentioned a veiled one. Is that it? A woman was seen with Knight at the time of the accident. A tall woman who might have been . . . a *man*? The veil that covers a multitude of sins,' Major Payne murmured. 'Is that it?'

'I don't know. A moment ago I thought I had it, but it's gone now. It may be nothing but a wild fancy. For some reason I keep thinking of the Carpenters record in Julian Knight's room. *This Masquerade*. I don't think it's got anything to do with the veiled woman. Or perhaps it has.' Antonia sighed. 'Well, as Charlotte said, I am the sort of woman who lets her imagination run riot.'

'I am sure Charlotte knows everything about riotous imaginations. You mustn't pay any attention to a word she says.' Payne sounded annoyed. 'Charlotte's role in this affair is to make the obligatory cameo gargoyle appearance, nothing more. Strictly for comic relief purposes. If this were one of your books,' he went on, 'how would you prevent the second body from being found too soon? Pacing's always important, isn't it?'

Well, she might have an 'interlude', Antonia said after a pause – a shortish chapter, in which the amateur detectives discussed the murders as though they were something out of a whodunit – a postmodern conversation piece of sorts. And that would be followed by some bizarre episode, which would prove to be terribly important to the investigation – or it would only *seem* terribly important, but would in fact simply distract the amateur detectives from solving the murders. It was only then that the second body would turn up.

'In the deep freeze?'

'I have no idea. Perhaps.'

'I suppose the reader would go on labouring in Cimmerian darkness a little longer – without having the obscurest of inklings as to what was really going on,' said

Payne. 'Though of course, faithful to the spirit of fair play, you'd have scrupulously laid a trail of clues pointing to the truth.'

'The truth yes, though not the *whole* truth.' Antonia gave a little smile. 'There's always one final twist, you know.'

22

The Holy Innocent

They had got out of the cab some way from Coconut Grove and for the past ten minutes had been walking alongside the beach towards the steps that led up to the house. The sand beneath their feet kept slowing them down. The firework display in the sky above, on the other hand, hadn't relented for a moment. A shower of rubies was followed by a bouquet of sapphires, a fountain of pearls, then a burst of diamonds.

It was as light as day. On their left lay the sea, vast, smooth, unbelievably calm. Somewhere far off on the horizon flickered the lights of ships. Close to the shore lay a yacht, the *Caspar*, with strangely striped funnels. 'Have we been seen?' Antonia was gazing nervously towards the terrace. They could hear music, laughter, delighted gasps and, again, the popping of champagne corks.

'If we haven't, we soon shall be. So what? Don't be paranoid. We went for a walk. Nothing wrong with that, is there? I don't think anyone suspects us of any involvement in the affair yet. If they'd seen the diary change hands in the folly, they'd already have tried to deprive you of it.'

Antonia said that perhaps Roman Songhera's men had been to their room in their absence and taken it. She groaned. She hadn't bothered to hide the diary properly – she should have but she hadn't – she'd simply pushed it under her pillow.

'It's here, actually,' Payne said and he showed her the diary. He had picked it up while she had been standing in front of the mirror and put it into his pocket, he explained. Antonia kissed him.

There were people on the beach – the men in charge of the firework display. As the Paynes approached the stone steps a figure came out of the shadows. It was one of Roman Songhera's guards. He wished them a good evening and moved aside to let them pass.

The throng on the terrace seemed to have multiplied and become denser. 'I can't see Charlotte anywhere,' Payne said. 'No Songhera either ... Shall we go and inspect the freezer?'

'Would she still be there?' Antonia whispered.

'I imagine so. It was a *crime passionnel*, so Songhera still loves Ria. He wouldn't want to be parted from her. He hasn't come to terms with her death. My guess is that he bitterly regrets what he did. He would be in the doldrums. He'd be distraught and inconsolable. He'd be overcome with grief, guilt and, very possibly, self-loathing. Chances are he'd be feeling suicidal.'

'He was voted most unpopular person number two. He kept torturing poor Louis by throwing him overboard at every opportunity to punish him for his "lazy self-entitlement".' A woman somewhere on their right was speaking amidst peals of laughter. 'He poured a bottle of syrup on Mrs Cox-Bisham's head and then locked Pamela in her cabin for the best part of the morning *and* he turned off the air-conditioning with the portholes shut tight! The outside temperature at the time had reached forty degrees Celsius. It was supposed to be a joke.'

'Who was most unpopular person number one?' a man asked. Antonia smelled the whiff of a superior cigar.

'Angela! You wouldn't believe this, but she was discovered in the engine room, trying to remove a vital part of the generator – of all the asinine and childish pranks!'

'That's typical of Angela. Angela will never grow up.'

'Never!'

148

'Sailing isn't what it used to be. Hi-tech carbon and Nomex machines crewed by thirty professionals bear no passing resemblance to the gentlemanly sailing boats of yesteryear. Except that both have a hull, masts, sails and winches.'

'Jet-setters,' Payne murmured with distaste. 'I think they are from that yacht we saw earlier on . . . *Caspar*.'

'Champagne, madam – sir?' One of the waiters was standing beside them, proffering a tray.

'No, thank you,' Payne said. 'I would like some soda water, actually. With lots of ice – and a dash of lemon.'

'Yes, thank you. Champagne would be lovely,' Antonia said. 'I need a drink.' She peered at the waiter's name tag.

'Here you are, madam.'

'Thank you, Manolo.' Antonia raised the frosted flute to her lips. The champagne was ice-cold and very dry.

More disembodied snatches of conversation floated over to their ears.

'It would never have worked. India would have become another Kenya. A precarious balance between post-colonial market-dominant minorities and tribally politicized local poor –'

'What soul? Rupert has no more soul than a steamed asparagus.'

'I say, Manolo,' Major Payne said, 'I'd like to have a word with one of your colleagues. What was his name now? Camillo. Any idea where he might be?'

Manolo nodded. 'I am afraid Camillo is not feeling very well, sir.'

'Is he still here?'

'Yes, sir –'

The next moment they were interrupted. 'Major Payne, I was looking for you.' A local dignitary had come up to them. Antonia was aware of her husband wincing slightly. The man was stocky and running to fat. His skin was the colour of caramel and he sported a pointed beard and a waxed moustache. His white tunic was ablaze with decorations and he wore a Nehru-style hat. His name on the

149

large and superior-looking name tag was long, unpro-
nounceable and, one imagined, extremely distinguished.
He bowed to Antonia. 'Major Payne, I meant to discuss a
certain matter with you, but then you disappeared. Go
away,' he told Manolo. 'Don't you see I am talking?'

Payne leant towards Manolo. 'Tell Camillo that I'd like
a word –'

'Major Payne, I saw a documentary about the First
World War a month or two ago and I must admit I was
really quite shocked.'

'The First World War was a fairly shocking event,' Payne
said absently. 'The end of the long Edwardian summer and
all that.'

'It was the way the British conducted themselves that
shocked me. You might say it gave me the ghastliest of
jolts.' The dignitary's manner was a blend of pomposity
and earnestness. 'We are talking about a time when the
British Empire was still at its apogee and, yet, the British
officer class were revealed as irresponsible, frivolous and
decadent.'

'You don't say.'

'I am sorry, Major Payne, I am perfectly aware that you
are an officer and a gentleman, but Field Marshal Haig
was shown directing the Battle of the Somme from the top
of a helter-skelter – while the mounting casualties were
being posted on a *cricket scoreboard*.'

'My dear fellow, I do believe you are labouring under
a –'

'And that was not all. Marshal Haig and his adjutants
and his soldiers, *they all broke into a song and dance*. They
sang about it being a lovely war.'

'*Oh, oh, oh, what a lovely war*?'

'Exactly. This was not one of those tendentious German
propaganda films either, I assure you. I happen to be
something of a military historian –' The dignitary broke off
at the approach of a slender figure in a fez and baggy
trousers. 'What do you want? Can't you see I am talking?
Go away.'

'Sir – you wanted to see me?'

'I don't want to see you. These house-boys! This is intolerable. No respect, no discipline. That's why we are where we are and this country will never prosper!' The dignitary shook his forefinger at the young man. 'You see, Major Payne, don't you? This is most definitely not on. I *must* have a word with Songhera. One thing I like about Songhera is the strict discipline he maintains among his staff –'

'Ah, Camillo. Good man,' Major Payne said. 'Decent of you to seek us out. Let's go somewhere where we won't be disturbed . . . So sorry,' Payne told the dignitary. 'We'll resume our interesting talk at some later hour, hope you won't mind awfully? Got to dash now.'

'The folly?' Antonia suggested.

The garden sparkled with firefly lights. Once more Antonia sat inside the folly, with Payne beside her. Camillo chose to remain standing. He was an extremely good-looking youth, Antonia thought, with impossibly regular features, skin as white as magnolia petals and wavy light-brown hair. His smile was sad, shy and sweet.

'Charlotte – our friend – started telling us about your strange experience at Miss Leighton's bungalow, but was interrupted,' Payne began without preamble. 'Would you mind telling us what happened?'

The young man gazed back at Payne. 'You – you know Ria?'

'We don't know her. We know a little *about* her.'

Camillo swallowed. He looked from Payne to Antonia. 'You are Roman Songhera's English visitors, aren't you?'

'Visitors, yes, friends, no. In fact we strongly disapprove of him, so don't you go imagining this is some sort of a trap. You are perfectly safe with us. We got entangled in this business entirely by accident.' Payne rubbed his temples. 'We don't know yet what exactly is going on, but we are determined to find out.'

'Are you detectives?'

'Not really, but we are good at – um – how shall I put it without appearing odd or conceited? Ferreting out secrets? Unravelling mysteries?'

'So you *are* detectives.'

Poor boy, Antonia thought. He looks totally out of his depth.

'Only in a manner of speaking. We don't get fees or expensive presents or anything of that sort. Sometimes I think we are too observant for our own good. Afraid I can't offer you any explanation that's more rational than that. Incidentally, I am Hugh Payne, and this is my wife Antonia. Look here, we haven't got much time. D'you mind telling us what you saw when you went into Ria's bungalow this morning?'

Camillo passed his hand across his face. 'Very well. I rang the bell. There was no answer. I tried the handle and the door opened. I went in. I heard music. Some Italian song. Then I heard a noise – it came from the bedroom. Someone laughing. A woman's voice. At first I thought it was Ria. I didn't know what to do. Then I heard the laugh again. It sounded mad. *Gloating*. I knew it couldn't be Ria. Ria has a lovely voice. I walked up to the bedroom door and pushed it open. I – I couldn't believe what I saw. It was terrible.'

'What did you see?'

Camillo swallowed. 'For a wild moment I imagined it was Ria. I thought that something had gone dreadfully wrong with her.'

'What do you mean?' Antonia asked.

'Her hair – the woman's hair was exactly like Ria's – golden-brown – long and shiny. But the rest of her was all wrong. Bloated – misshapen! It wasn't Ria. Of course it wasn't. The woman was dancing about Ria's bedroom with her hands in the air. She was laughing, smacking her lips, muttering to herself. Her face was covered in paint – the most frightful collage of shadows around her eyes – eyelashes like bat-wings, dripping with mascara –'

He doesn't talk like an ordinary house-boy, Antonia reflected.

'– blue shadows around the eyes. And she was wearing a black bustier, fishnet stockings and snakeskin high heels – also Ria's necklace. I knew it was Ria's necklace – I'd seen it before. It is very distinctive – large rubies. Her – the woman's – flesh was spilling out of the bustier – the bustier was too tight for her –'

'What did she do when she saw you?' Payne asked.

'She stopped dancing – gasped – covered her mouth in exaggerated surprise – peeped at me through her fingers. She then put her head to one side coquettishly, stared at me – she gave a suggestive smile – she beckoned at me. She held out her hands, palms upwards, and twiddled her fingers. She kept nodding and cooing and then – then she sat on the bed and patted the space beside her – with her other hand she touched her breasts. She flung her head back, shut her eyes and made a moaning sort of sound. It was awful – grotesque. I turned round – fled.'

Payne cleared his throat. 'You dropped the petits fours. Did you step on them as well?'

'I don't think so. I am not sure.'

'You have no idea who the woman is?'

'No idea at all. But this is not all.' Camillo ran his tongue across his lips. 'The really awful thing was that Ria was in the bedroom too.'

Payne and Antonia stared at him.

'What?'

'Ria was under the bed,' Camillo said firmly. He looked from one to the other. 'I know this sounds completely mad, but I don't think I imagined it. Ria was hiding under the bed. I – I suddenly saw her – her hair showing from under the other side of the bed. Her lovely golden-brown hair. I didn't see her face but I am sure it was Ria. I saw her hand too. It happened in a flash, you see – just as I was turning to go – on my way out.'

'What do you think Ria was doing under the bed?' Payne asked in a matter-of-fact voice.

There was a pause. 'She wanted to see how I'd react. She intended to give me a nasty shock,' Camillo said slowly. 'She knew I'd go to the bungalow, even though she'd told me not to. I've had time to work things out. She knew I was terribly keen on her, so she expected me to turn up. I phoned her in the morning, you see, and told her I wanted to give her a Valentine present. I think the woman was some friend of hers. I believe Ria put her up to it – asked her to dress up as her, put on a wig.'

'You believe Ria decided to play a trick on you?'

Camillo swallowed again. 'Yes. She must have called her friend and asked her to dress up like her, so that she could have a good laugh at my expense. She wanted to see the expression on my face. I think she wanted to make me look a fool, to humiliate me, to put me off her for good.' Camillo hung his head miserably.

'Makes perfect sense. Miss Leighton does appear to be the kind of girl who leads people to commit extraordinary lunacies. Did you by any chance notice whether she moved at all?' Major Payne asked casually. 'Her head wasn't bobbing up and down with silent mirth or anything of that sort?'

'No. I didn't see her move. I didn't stop to look. I ran out of the room. It gave me such a shock – seeing her under the bed – a very nasty feeling. I was terribly upset – shaken up by the whole thing.'

'You didn't get angry with her? You didn't work yourself up into a state? It never occurred to you to go back later and have it out with her?'

Antonia bit her lower lip. *Could* Camillo have killed Ria? Hugh was watching the boy keenly. Camillo's hair was short and wavy and light brown. That long black hair on Ria's pillow wasn't his – whose *was* it? Had Ria had many lovers?

'No. I didn't get angry with her.' Camillo shook his head firmly. 'Or if I did, it didn't last long. I was more upset than angry. I then managed to think the matter over. Since Ria clearly didn't want to have anything to do with

154

me, there was no real point in me going back and making a scene.'

'I see. Most commendable. You accepted defeat in the manliest, not to say the most gentlemanly fashion. How interesting. Charlotte told us you were on the brink of self-destruction. She suggested you wanted to kill yourself.'

Camillo frowned. 'Kill myself? Is that what she said? I never said I wanted to kill myself. It was she who told me not to go and do anything stupid.' He sounded a little annoyed.

'Is that so? I bet she patted your hand?' Payne's left eyebrow went up.

'Well, she did. She seemed extremely concerned about my state of mind. She said I reminded her of her favourite grandson. I believe she was under the impression I was much more upset than I really was.'

'Her favourite grandson?' Payne grinned. 'She can't stand her grandson.'

'I feel such an ass –' Camillo broke off. 'What did you mean when you asked if I'd seen Ria move? You don't think she might have been dead, do you? Oh, my God. That she'd been killed and shoved under the bed? You don't think it was that woman who killed her?'

'Well –'

'That's what you meant when you asked whether I'd noticed her move, didn't you?'

'Tell me, was there a carpet on the bedroom floor?'

'A carpet?'

'Yes. White, with a deep pile?'

Camillo frowned. 'Yes, there was. I am sure there was a carpet. White, yes. That woman kept stumbling over it while she danced. I don't think she was terribly comfortable on her high heels. They must have been Ria's shoes.'

'Well, the carpet wasn't there when we went to the bungalow. That was about two hours ago. It is our belief that Ria's body was taken out of the bungalow in the carpet. What time was it when you went?'

'Midday. The church bell was chiming twelve,' Camillo said promptly. 'Do you think it was that woman – that big, bloated, truly awful-looking woman – who killed Ria?'

'It might have been her, though at the moment we suspect somebody else. *The bloated baggage.* Isn't that what one of the Macbeth witches says?' Payne turned towards Antonia.

'The way she laughed. She sounded gleeful – pleased with herself – *triumphant*. It all feels like a bad dream now – some terrible nightmare.'

'We know exactly how you feel. It's been like that for us for the past three hours. Gosh, is that *all*? Only three hours since Knight spoke to you?' Once more Payne addressed Antonia. 'It feels like *ages*.'

'I should have been braver. I should have confronted that woman,' Camillo said. 'Asked for an explanation. I should have asked who she was and what she was doing in Ria's bedroom. I should have gone back and looked under the bed – instead of running as if all the devils in hell were after me!'

'I'd have reacted in pretty much the same way if I'd been in your shoes,' Payne said reassuringly. He stroked his jaw with his forefinger. 'Who was the mad creature, I wonder? You have no idea?'

'No.' Camillo shook his head. 'I think she was Indian.'

'The first Mrs Songhera?' Antonia said. 'I mean Roman's wife. Her name is Sarla. Charlotte said Sarla was fat, ugly and completely bonkers. On the plane – don't you remember?'

'Of course!' Payne slapped his forehead. 'So it was her! Must have been.'

'Roman's wife? I've never seen her but I've heard about her,' Camillo said. 'She lives somewhere local. I don't know exactly where. I haven't been here long. Some of the other boys were saying she'd been banned from going anywhere near Ria. They too said she was quite mad. Yes. Why didn't I think of her?'

'You have had a bizarre experience of the ghastliest kind,' said Payne, 'but if you want my honest opinion, it's all for the best. It's put you off Ria for good and that's the healthy way to live. Am I right in thinking that you went to school in England? No, don't tell me which one. Say, "the most frightful collage of shadows" once more, slowly.'

Hugh's doing a Professor Higgins now, Antonia thought, trying not to roll her eyes.

'The most frightful collage of shadows.'

'Winchester? No – Marlborough.'

'Marlborough is right.' Camillo looked impressed. 'Though I did a year at Winchester first. That was before my father lost all his money.'

'So that rigmarole Charlotte told us about the con-quistador blood and you being of the *noblesse* was not a rigmarole after all?'

Camillo gave a faint smile. 'I suppose not.'

'I did think you were the real thing, but I convinced myself you looked too innocent to have been to an English public school.'

'So when you went to Ria's bungalow, she wasn't there . . . She wasn't – under the bed . . . Neither was the carpet,' Camillo whispered.

'We have an idea where the body might be. We may be completely wrong, but we intend to go and check. It might be a dangerous enterprise. Somebody's already been killed because of what they knew.' Payne waved his hand. 'It's an impossibly convoluted story. We'll tell you the details some other time.'

'Did Roman kill her – because of me?'

'We do suspect it was Roman Songhera who killed her, but not necessarily because of you. Ria was a very bad girl. She drove her father round the bend. She actually caused him to die of a massive heart attack, or so we believe. You are well out of it, old boy. Actually, I don't believe Songhera knows about your involvement with her. If he knew,' Major Payne reasoned, 'I don't suppose you'd be standing here, chatting to us. Still, if I were you, I'd make myself scarce at once – to be on the safe side. As I believe I made it clear, we don't think much of your boss. Things may become worse in the next couple of hours. Songhera may go berserk and have us all thrown to the crocs. I am serious. This is *not* a terribly nice place. It deserves the fire of heaven. No, that's not fair. Rather – Coconut Grove is one of those places where every prospect pleases –'

'– *and only man is vile.*' Camillo frowned. 'Is that Heber?'

'Heber it is. Now then, we don't want you to come to any harm. Have you got anywhere safe to go? I mean go at once, post-haste? How about England? If you haven't got the money, we could lend you some.'

'That's awfully kind of you, sir. I've got enough money – and a British passport too.'

'Couldn't be better. You won't have any problems then. What the hell have you been doing here? However did you decide to join Songhera's troupe of Turks?'

'It was an adventure – a caper.'

Payne peered at him. 'You look terribly white. I'm sure you were darker this afternoon. You had a tan at the party, didn't you? Same as your fellow waiters. Golden toast-like. Where's that gone?'

Camillo grinned. 'It came out of a bottle. I haven't been here long, so I needed to blend in. It washes off –'

'Out of a bottle? You mean a bronzer? Oh!' Antonia exclaimed.

'Do you disapprove?'

'Not at all – sorry – just an idea.'

'My wife writes detective stories,' Payne explained, looking at her curiously.

'Do you really? I love detective stories,' said Camillo.

'You could stay with us when you come to London.' As soon as the words were out of her mouth, Antonia was aware of her husband looking at her sharply. Jealous, poor thing, she thought, amused. Well, the boy was terribly good-looking. 'You could easily embark on a modelling or acting career.'

'Thank you so much. Mrs Depleche also invited me to stay at her house at Eaton Square if I ever found myself in London.'

'Did she now? You are all set then,' Major Payne said somewhat stiffly. There was a pause. 'If the Honourable Charlotte has an ounce of sense in her head, which I am not sure she has, she'd say no to this house deal and go back to Wiltshire. Post-haste.'

23

The Snow Queen

Some five minutes later they were walking across the hall towards the swing doors. There was no one about. The bearded concierge was not at his desk. Probably watching the firework display, Antonia thought.

Major Payne said that they were reaching the most dangerous part of their adventure. They were about to walk into the lions' den. Did they have any alternative? Could they afford *not* to walk into the lions' den? Could they toddle along to their room instead, have a shower, retire to bed, read a bit, then turn off the lights, wish each other a good night and go to sleep? The answer, they agreed, was no, a definite no – they couldn't. They needed to investigate and they had to do it *now*. By tomorrow morning the body might no longer be in the deep freeze. Then they would never know if they had been right or not.

'What shall we do if we do find the body?' Antonia said.

'No idea. No idea at all.' Payne looked grim.

They had tried to ring England on their mobiles but, again, there was no network. The doors swung behind them and they found themselves walking along a beautifully carpeted if inadequately lit corridor. 'Let's hope we won't run into one of Songhera's goons,' Payne murmured. Antonia noticed with some surprise that the walls were decorated with Rackham's illustrations of Hans Christian Andersen's fairy tales in silver frames. Ria had

had a book of Andersen's fairy tales in her room. Roman Songhera seemed to have bowed to Ria's taste, or did he perhaps share it?

There they all were. The steadfast one-legged tin soldier gazing besottedly at his beloved paper dancer. The sinister Shadow. Little Ida and her flowers, looking faded and exhausted after their midnight ball. There was the ugly duckling and the emperor whose new clothes no one could see. The Snow Queen and little Kay. Antonia was familiar with them all and she remembered the Snow Queen's chilling words, 'Now you are not getting any more kisses, or else I'd kiss you to death.'

Ria seemed to have been a fervent Andersen aficionado. Her name might have come from an Andersen tale, Antonia reflected. Ria had read Andersen's tales in bed. She couldn't have been entirely rotten then. No person who liked fairy tales was ever irredeemably bad. Was that a logical argument? There was also something touching in the fact that Roman had gone to the trouble of having Rackham's illustrations mounted so beautifully in their silver frames and hanging them on the wall in such a perfectly symmetrical way. It did look like a labour of love. Roman had gone out of his way to please Ria.

The first door they opened turned out to be a broom cupboard, but the second revealed a steep staircase leading down into what looked like a cellar. The storeroom that housed the deep freeze?

They started descending the stairs. Antonia leant on her husband's arm. How sore and tired her feet felt. We are descending into the very bowels of hell, she thought. She was a little hysterical – she was extremely tired – one always exaggerated and said silly things like that when one was nervous – it was a defensive reaction of sorts. The lights flickered and there was a faint crackling sound. She hoped there wouldn't be a sudden blackout. They had been warned about blackouts but of course one expected a place like Coconut Grove to be exempt from the kind of power cut that seemed to afflict Goa's lesser mortals.

Coconut Grove was after all the local Buckingham Palace. Roman Songhera *must* have his own generator.

The last step, thank goodness. No, the cellar at Coconut Grove did not bear a single similarity to hell. The temperature for one thing was lower than it had been upstairs; it felt pleasantly cool and airy. Antonia stood looking round. The walls were of a colour that brought to mind a winter sky in England and seemed to be covered in some insulating material since Hugh's jocular 'Point of no return' sounded particularly strained and hollow in the silence. She wished he didn't say things like that. If they started screaming for help, no one would hear them . . .

Everything was perfectly clean. Clinically so. There was the smell of some superior disinfectant in the air. A cool fresh fragrance. Alpine Breeze? They might have been inside a well-ordered private hospital. Antonia decided she didn't care for the hospital association either. Major Payne pointed silently to the row of tall shining metal doors. The deep freeze, must be. There were six doors, taking up the whole of the long wall, each one sporting the *New Millennium* logo, same as on Ria's fridge. Antonia's heart began to beat faster. She didn't like the idea of opening doors and finding out what was behind them – look what happened to Blue Beard's young bride!

Most fairy tales were rather sinister and they frequently had the surreal logic of dreams. Some of them were highly unsuitable for children. Antonia's thoughts turned to Andersen once more. To paraphrase what the roses said to little Gerda – *She's not dead. We've been in the ground, where all the dead are, but Ria wasn't there.* No. Antonia didn't actually believe they would find Ria's body in the deep freeze. This is all nonsense, she thought. A mare's nest. We are on a wild-goose chase. It was ridiculous to expect the deep freeze to yield a *corpus delicti*. Out of the question. Ria was alive. She was hiding somewhere.

She saw her husband open the first door. 'Ice cream. Vanilla. Belgian chocolate. Midnight cookies and cream.'

'You don't have to read aloud,' she said.

'Are you scared?'

'Yes.'

He reached out for the second door. She stood beside him as he pulled it, but the door seemed to have got stuck, so he pulled again –

The caviar probably, Antonia thought. The next moment the door opened with a sharp crack. Antonia felt an icy blast.

Some long object, taller than either of them, fell out amidst swirls of steam.

It was the rolled-up white carpet.

Antonia cried out and stepped back. This is not happening, she thought as she watched her husband catch the carpet before it hit the floor and lay it down gently. This is only part of the nightmare.

Neither of them said anything. Major Payne started unrolling. The carpet had frozen and it felt stiff and unyielding to his touch.

The girl's face was encircled by a sparkling aureole of ice and Antonia was put in mind of some strange flower that had grown in a glacier. The hair was no longer golden-brown but bluish-white with intricately patterned ice crystals. The cheeks were smooth and white. The lips were pale pink, slightly parted. She seemed simply asleep, an impression belied by her wide-open beautiful blue eyes.

The eyes stared back at them . . .

The fragrance of the flowers says the girls are corpses. Ding-dong. The evening bell is tolling for the dead. Andersen had such a morbid imagination! A very strange man by all accounts, from what she had read about him. Antonia thought she smelled hyacinths. A sweet, sickly smell. The smell of death? That now was *her* morbid imagination. Or was it the disinfectant? Perhaps she had been wrong. Not Alpine Breeze but hyacinths –

Ria was wearing silk red-and-black Brooks Brothers pyjamas with white pearl buttons. The top button was missing. Antonia suddenly felt like bursting into tears. Ria wasn't wearing a brassiere under the top. Silently they knelt on either side of the body. The throat was white, vulnerable, exposed. No, not entirely white. There were dark blue marks on either side of it, where somebody's hands (Roman's?) had squeezed the life out of her. So Julian Knight had told the truth. Ria was dead. She had been killed. She had been strangled. Oddly enough the face didn't bear any of the usual signs associated with strangling – it had not turned purple, nor was it distorted or bloated –

Antonia spoke and her voice sounded harsh. 'Julian Knight told me he saw Roman bang her head against the bedpost. He said he heard a crack. He didn't say anything about strangling.'

'Perhaps he got confused ... Let's check.' Raising Ria's head gently, Major Payne slipped his hand behind it. 'There's a swelling – at some point her head does appear to have met with some hard surface all right – though I doubt whether that was enough to kill her. Doesn't feel that lethal. It might have made her pass out ... I am no expert of course ... A doctor would be able to establish the exact cause of death, but I see no chance of a PM, do you? Hello, what's this?'

Payne reached out for Ria's half-closed hand.

Antonia thought she heard a noise. Looking up, she was startled to see their distorted reflections in the freezer's convex silver doors. Their faces looked ghostly, bug-eyed, ghoulish. But theirs weren't the only reflections. There was somebody standing behind them, at the bottom of the staircase. A man –

'Oh, my God.' Antonia's hand went up to her throat.

Major Payne turned round sharply. The next moment he was on his feet, his hands clenched into fists.

Roman Songhera was wearing a white dinner jacket and black tie. The theatrical turban had disappeared. He looked very sleek and suave. His hair was revealed as black and shiny. Oiled back. Too short – the long black hair on Ria's pillow isn't his, or he might have had a haircut, Antonia thought irrelevantly. Or had Ria slept with the James Bond taxi driver? That young man's hair had been long and black all right – he'd had it in a pony tail! Antonia's next thought was: *Roman is bound to have a gun in his pocket. He's going to shoot us.*

Only he didn't. What happened next was, in a way, rather unsettling. Roman Songhera hadn't uttered a word. He wasn't looking at either of them – they might not have existed. His eyes were fixed on the body in the red Brooks Brothers pyjamas lying across the white carpet. Roman's face was extremely pale. He took a step towards the body, then another. He held out his hand in a pleading gesture. Tears had started pouring down his cheeks. His shoulders shook. He took another step. He moved like a robot or a sleepwalker. He stopped beside the body.

Antonia and Major Payne moved away, to the left and to the right, respectively. They watched Roman Songhera bow his head and fall on his knees. The whole thing looked like some elaborate formal dance. *Dance Macabre* . . . The dance of death . . . Roman reached out for Ria's left hand and held it in his with great tenderness. He stroked each finger with his forefinger. He then cradled Ria's head on his lap. He was crying soundlessly; his tears were falling on Ria's face, on her bosom. It was all unbearably sad. Would the tears soak into her heart and thaw out the deadly lump of ice, the way it happened to little Kay in the Andersen tale?

Despite herself, Antonia felt a lump in her throat. She reminded herself that Roman was a bully and a hoodlum, the worst of thugs and very possibly a murderer, that he kept crocodiles in a lake and didn't deserve a scrap of sympathy, yet she couldn't help being filled with terrible pity. Roman's sense of loss was heartbreaking . . .

'Ria,' he said, then again, 'Ria. *Can the flames of the heart die in the flames of the pyre*?' He looked at Antonia, then at

Payne, his eyes dimmed by tears. A more unlikely poetry quoter Antonia could not have imagined. 'That's what she read to me once – it was from one of those tales she loved so much.'

His voice sounded choked, flat and hollow within the insulated walls. Now he was stroking the dead girl's cheeks, first one, then the other, very gently, with the tips of his fingers, as though she were a sleeping child. His hand then went up to her forehead and her hair. After that he touched her throat ... They heard him gasp. He had seen the blue marks. He turned his head towards Antonia.

'Who did this?' he asked. When she didn't answer, he repeated his question, on a threatening note. '*Who did this?*'

'Look here, Songhera, don't you think –' Major Payne began, but Antonia pulled at his sleeve.

'We don't know,' she said. 'We are trying to find out.'

'You are trying to find out?' Roman Songhera frowned – as though trying to collect his thoughts. His eyes held a dazed, hopeless, puzzled expression.

'D'you mean you don't know who killed her?' Payne said.

There was a pause.

'I kept ringing her, but there was no answer. She didn't answer her mobile, nor her landline. I wanted to go and see what was going on, but I was very busy. The party – Charlotte – the fireworks. Ria didn't want to come to the party, but she promised she would.' Roman's right hand now lay across the dead girl's forehead. He spoke in a halting voice, simply, without any affectations, no longer with the *faux* English public school accent. Antonia thought he sounded American.

'The party was about to start. I was expecting her. At first I was annoyed with her. I thought she wasn't answering on purpose. I thought she had decided not to come. Sometimes she did things to annoy me. I was getting angry. At about ten past six I sent two of my men to her house, to see what was going on. The fools didn't get back to me ... I waited ... They were making me wait! Why didn't the fools ring and tell me at once she was dead?'

'Perhaps they were afraid?' Payne suggested. 'Scared of what you might do? Shoot the messenger – that sort of thing?'

Roman Songhera stared back at him in astonished admiration. 'Shoot the messenger? Yes. I might have shot the messenger all right. How did you know?'

'Elementary psychology.' In your highly idiosyncratic world, Payne thought, but didn't say it.

'You are jolly clever.' Roman nodded slowly. 'That was what Charlotte said. That you were jolly clever. I knew it the moment I saw you. I noticed the way you looked at my tie. No doubt you thought it was – what's that phrase you use?'

'*De trop*?'

Roman's expression remained grave. 'Not a caddish thing to do?'

'That too. Wearing the tie of a school one didn't go to was certainly considered not on in my day.' Payne shrugged. 'I don't suppose that kind of thing matters any longer.'

'Oh, but it does matter. It matters an awful lot to me. I do wish you worked for me, Major Payne, then you'd have been able to advise me. You are clever too.' Roman turned towards Antonia. 'You write detective stories. You can get into the killer's head. You know how a killer's mind works. You have a better chance of finding the killer than anyone else. Will you find Ria's murderer for me?'

'This is a matter for the police,' Major Payne said. 'Where we come from, the police would have been called by now.'

'You mean Scotland Yard. The best police force in the world.'

'That's what foreigners think, but they aren't that good, actually. They sometimes shoot innocent people dead.'

'Our police do that all the time.' Roman waved his hand dismissively. 'Our police wouldn't be able to find their own noses. Their post-mortem would be of a highly dubious order – even if they flew someone over from Delhi. No, I don't want a formal investigation.'

Payne cocked an eyebrow. 'You are loath to draw attention to yourself?'

'I can't bear the idea of a forensic pathologist putting on latex gloves and groping Ria – gawping at her – cutting her body and extracting blood and skin samples – photographers flashing their cameras at her. No. She will *not* be defiled . . . *You* will investigate.' Roman pointed his forefinger at Payne, then at Antonia. With his florid dark good looks and portentous manner he brought to mind a Mafia boss. 'I want you to investigate. I will pay you. I will give you as much money as you want. Find the murderer. Tell me who it is. Give me a name, that's all I want.'

'Did you order your men to bring the body here?' Major Payne asked after a pause.

'I did. They didn't tell me at once that she was dead. I got a message saying there was a problem, a serious problem. Then another message – *Ria badly hurt*. They knew how I'd feel. They knew I was mad about her. They knew I adored her –' Roman broke off. His hand had gone up to his eyes.

'I am sorry,' Antonia said.

'In the end they came out with it, they had to. I thought it was some mistake. How could she be dead? It was only last night we'd made love! But I knew they wouldn't have dared say she was dead if she hadn't been. I knew they were telling the truth. They had no idea how she had died, they said, though they thought there was something funny. They said nothing about –' Roman pointed to the marks on Ria's throat. 'I told them to bring her here.'

'In the carpet?'

'The carpet was their idea. My men – I suppose you'd call them my goons? – are not entirely without enterprise, you know.' Roman gave a faint smile. 'All I told them was to do their best not to attract too much attention. I meant to come and look at her sooner, but I was so busy with the party upstairs. It's been hell, having to smile and chat to people, pretending I was fine, knowing all along she was down here, packed in ice, dead. She will be given a proper send-off,' he said very quietly. He touched Ria's forehead once more. 'What I want from you is to find me the murderer.'

24

The Wrong Man

'You won't make her disappear, will you?' Payne might have been talking about some conjuring trick.

'Disappear?' Roman scowled. 'I don't know what you mean.'

'Drop her into the lake or something.'

'I will do no such thing. I said a *proper* send-off, Major Payne. Ria was my queen, so her departure from this world will be commensurate with her status.'

A pyre? Antonia wondered.

'I don't suppose you will let her relatives in England know that she has died?' Payne went on.

'Her father is dead. She hated her father. There is a step-mother and an aunt, I think, but I don't believe Ria cared much about them. She had no one close. In that respect she was like me. Solitary, rootless, rebellious. No, Major Payne, I won't be letting anyone in England know. There'd be no point.'

'If we are to undertake this investigation,' Payne said slowly, 'we'll need to eliminate you as a suspect first. Can you prove it wasn't you who killed Ria?'

Hugh was pushing his luck. Once again Antonia cast an anxious glance at Roman, but he showed no signs of anger or agitation. All he did was place his left hand at his chest. 'You think it was me? You think I killed Ria?'

'How do you explain this then?' Payne was holding

something between his thumb and forefinger. 'A broken cufflink made of platinum, same as your tie-pin earlier on, and it's got the initials RS engraved on it. It's yours, isn't it?'

'Sounds like mine.' Roman didn't leave Ria's body. 'Where did you find it?'

'It was clutched in her hand. How did it get there?'

Roman went on stroking Ria's forehead. 'I have no idea. If you think I was there and we had a fight and then I killed her, you are wrong. The killer must have planted it, to throw suspicion on me. I was wearing the platinum cufflinks the last time I was with her. Last night. I didn't stay the whole night. I left my cufflinks in Ria's bedroom – forgot all about them – on her bedside table, I think.'

Major Payne cleared his throat. 'What if I told you somebody claimed they actually saw you strangle her?'

'I would say he was a damned liar,' Roman answered promptly, without any particular rancour.

'How do you know it is a he?'

'When could I have strangled Ria?'

'Sometime in the morning?'

'I spent most of the morning in Charlotte's company. I drove Charlotte round in my car. I showed her the sights. We started at nine. I'd have suggested you came with us, but you were still sleeping ... We kept stopping. We watched the solar eclipse ... You can ask her. You can check and double-check. I didn't leave Charlotte's side for a moment.'

Charlotte, Antonia reflected, was not exactly a paragon of moral probity. Roman could have easily persuaded her to give him an alibi. In her own admission, she had a soft spot for men that went too far. All Roman needed to do was don his turban and play the smouldering sheikh. But he sounded as though he was telling the truth. Antonia saw a puzzled expression on Hugh's face – the idea must have occurred to him too. The time factor. Once again she had the strong feeling there was something very wrong with the important times in this affair.

171

'Find me the murderer,' Roman said again.

'Do you have any idea who that might be?'

'It – it couldn't have been a robber, could it? I wanted to provide her with a permanent guard, insisted on it, but she said no. We had a big argument about it. She is – was – very independent.' Roman's voice shook.

'We found no signs of breaking and entering. What about Sarla – your former wife?'

'Sarla? She is still my wife, damn her. So you have heard about Sarla? Yes. She hates Ria. She is jealous of her. My spies tell me she's been doing some really crazy things. Visiting witch doctors and so on.' Roman paused. 'If you did find out it was Sarla, I would slit her throat with my own hand.'

Then he broke down once more and now his grief and despair were much worse than the first time. He called out Ria's name. He sobbed and howled and a flood of tears ran down his face. He was completely unselfconscious about it. He didn't seem to care that he was making a spectacle of himself, that they were watching him. His shirt front was wet with his tears. He picked up the dead girl's body, put his arms around it and buried his head in Ria's neck. He rocked backwards and forwards.

Antonia glanced across at her husband. Payne looked exasperated, though something like sympathy had crept into his expression. She signalled with her eyes: *Shall we?* He nodded and the two of them tiptoed out of the cellar.

It isn't Roman, Antonia thought. Roman didn't kill her. He is the wrong man. He wouldn't have kept asking them to find the murderer if he had. He had nothing to gain from their involvement. If he had been in denial, he'd have acted differently. She didn't think he was pretending either. But then who was it? Who killed Ria?

The long-haired taxi driver. Could it have been him? The young man with a dangerous penchant for speed had suddenly become subdued at the mention of Roman Songhera's girlfriend. A one-night stand on her part, something a girl like her did out of boredom, much deeper for him? Ria, Antonia imagined, had enjoyed her power over men. The driver was excitable and volatile. One supposed Ria to have been habitually transgressive. Didn't transgressive behaviour induce transgression in others? Strangling suggested a *crime passionnel* – something done on the spur of the moment – shades of Othello . . .

Or was it the discontented wife, mad Sarla, after all? She might have killed Ria and pushed the body under the bed, before 'becoming' Ria.

No. Neither of these solutions explained Julian Knight's claim. Julian Knight had insisted it was Roman who killed Ria.

The partial solar eclipse . . . Evil under the sun . . . Tan out of a tube . . . The fake tan was important somehow . . . Then there was the question of which shoulder Julian Knight had held higher, the left or the right . . . According to his Chinese landlord, it was the right, but she and Hugh thought it was the left . . . I need to arrange my ideas properly, Antonia thought; this whirlwind won't do . . . *This Masquerade* . . . A masquerade came into it, she felt sure, but it was also something to do with the sun, or rather with its disappearance . . . Why *did* she keep thinking about the solar eclipse?

'*Solitary, rootless, rebellious,*' Payne murmured. 'Interesting. That's the definition of a psychopath, d'you realize?'

'Is it?'

'Yes. According to Stafford-Clark. It's textbook material. Maybe a bit dated now. How did it go on? Um. *Plausible but insincere, demanding but indifferent to appeals, dependable only in their constant unreliability.*'

It was as they walked back into their room and turned on the light that the answer came to Antonia – as though illumination had come not only literally but metaphorically as well. She had remembered what the policeman had said and why she had thought it so important.

Julian Knight had died at the time of the partial solar eclipse, which had taken place at eleven in the morning and had lasted for five minutes. There was no doubt about

173

the time of the solar eclipse. Which meant that Antonia's encounter with Julian Knight couldn't possibly have happened when it had – after six in the evening, when the garden party at Coconut Grove had been in full swing.

But it *had* happened. She hadn't dreamt it. Julian Knight had told her he had witnessed a murder!

Well, that could mean only one thing – there had been two of them.

25

The Case of the Discontented Wife

Her exaltation hadn't abated – quite the reverse. The young man's sudden appearance might have had something to do with it, she wasn't sure. Such a handsome young man! Golden skin and lips like rose petals. Better-looking than Roman. Younger. She had expected Roman to turn up and make love to her, but he hadn't. She had no doubt that Roman would find her irresistible. Well, he might still come. She would wait –

No. Change of plan. There was something she needed to do rather urgently. I *must* say thank you, she thought.

Sarla's heart was beating rather fast. She wished she didn't feel so happy! When people were happy, they didn't want to do anything but sing and dance and laugh! She was happier than she had been ever before in her entire life. Happier than on the day she had married Roman. Happier even than when she had won the lottery.

The curse had worked. And how! The curse had brought along a murderer. It had made Roman and Ria's love-nest the focus of dark forces, of violence, of death and destruction and – as though that were not enough – Sarla had been there to see it happen!

She kicked off the high-heeled shoes and danced about the bedroom on the balls of her feet one last time, laughing and giving thanks to her masters, then she took off the whore's rags, ripping one apart in the process, what she believed was called a 'bustier', and pushed them into the wardrobe; that was where she had found them in the first place.

She changed back into her sari. She covered her face with her scarf to avoid recognition – in case someone saw her leaving the bungalow. One or two of Roman's men might be lurking around. Actually she didn't care a fig about Roman's men. She wasn't really afraid of anyone any longer – she felt confident – strong and powerful – invincible! Her masters were watching over her. She would never come to any harm. What can man do to me? Sarla sang out as she opened the front door and walked out.

It had been some minutes after nine o'clock in the morning when she came up to the bedroom window. She had been carrying a bag filled with powdered bones. Her *third* bag. She had kept repeating the curse under her breath. She had emptied the bag on the ground outside the bedroom. Apparently the curse was at its most potent if one brought the bones in the morning. 'I have become death, the destroyer of worlds,' she whispered.

She had assumed Ria was still sleeping, the lazy spoilt English girl, but she had heard a noise inside the bedroom. A very strange kind of noise. It sounded like someone gurgling, choking, gasping for breath. The window had been ajar – the curtains hadn't been fully drawn –

Well, she had witnessed the slut's neck being wrung in the same way as she (Sarla) had wrung the necks of all those chickens. Was that a coincidence, the manner in which the slut had died? She didn't think so! It was a sign from her masters. Her masters wanted to make it absolutely clear to her that it was all their doing, in case she started doubting. Sarla had also seen the killer. *Very clearly*. The killer's face was twisted with rage and suffused with red, like a cockerel's crest. Mouth open – teeth bared – like a snarling hyena's. It was a face she would never forget – *not as long as she lived*.

176

The slut hadn't reacted – she hadn't struggled – hadn't tried to push the killer back – no, none of that. She had merely lain on the bed, limp, lifeless, inert, like some life-size doll! Had she been stunned first? Oh, how Sarla had relished the sight of those strong hands around Ria's throat!

Sarla frowned. There had been someone else there. She had thought it odd. No, not in the bedroom. *Outside* the bungalow. Yes. She was sure she hadn't imagined it. The killer seemed to have brought a friend. An accomplice. A man had sat there on the porch, his face in his hands, shaking his head, weeping. The man had been very upset about something, in a real state, muttering to himself. Sarla had seen him as she had approached the bungalow with her bag only a minute earlier. The man had been completely unaware of her. The killer hadn't noticed her presence either. She might have been invisible. Perhaps she *had* been invisible? Yes – Sarla nodded to herself – her masters had seen to it – of course!

Sarla wanted to speak to the killer. She wanted to express her gratitude. She wanted to put her indebtedness into appropriate words. Perhaps when she kissed the killer's hand, some of the killer's super-human strength and tenacity would seep into her? She felt the overwhelming desire to *touch* the killer. She needed strength. She needed extra power. To defend herself, but also – to attack! She pursed her lips. Roman was next on her list. Roman was her enemy. Roman would be distraught when he found his beloved dead. He would suspect her, Sarla. He would have her killed. He had told her he would do it if she went anywhere near Ria. Well, what Roman didn't know was that there was someone more powerful than him – someone who was Sarla's ally and protector!

As a matter of fact she didn't desire Roman any longer. Roman hated her, despised her – as though it were her fault she'd given birth to a stillborn child! He said he found her revolting. Don't come near me or I'll hit you,

177

he said. She shrugged. What did it matter? She could have any man she wanted now. That beautiful young boy! All she needed to do was to . . . to . . .

She couldn't think what at the moment. She had lost the thread of her thoughts. She had actually heard the snapping of the thread in her head. She shook her head impatiently.

She tried to keep up a brisk pace, but the day was hot and muggy, suffused with sloth and sullen expectation, so her progress was not as fast as she wanted it to be. She was covered in sweat. She mopped her face with her scarf. Her body felt hot, wet and slippery. She felt itchy – far from comfortable.

Roman was to blame for *everything*. She had started putting on weight after he had left her – he had said such terrible, such hurtful things to her! He had said she was of 'impure stock'. Roman's men had been spreading the story that one of Sarla's aunts had given birth to a giant rat. He was still using her money but he showed no gratitude. He said her head would roll if she made any fuss about the money. She wanted Roman . . . dead! Yes. Dead, like the slut. No mercy. Perhaps a little word in the killer's ear? Killers developed a taste for death after they had killed once, they felt the urge to do it again, she had read somewhere.

A bond had been forged between her and the killer. An *unbreakable bond*. The killer had felt compelled to come to Kilhar and strangle Ria *because* Sarla had chanted the curse and smashed the bones with her feet and danced the dance of death. The killer had come from afar to oblige her. The killer had flown thousands and thousands of miles to bow to her will.

Sarla thought back. It was only when the deed had been done and the slut lay dead on the bed that the killer left the bedroom. There had been some muffled talk outside the bungalow – in English of course – between the killer and the man on the porch. She had then seen them walk down the road, the two of them, the weak and the strong.

178

The slut was still there, on the bed, in her red pyjamas, lying on her back. Sarla had been afraid Ria might come to and get up, so she had climbed into the bedroom and checked Ria's pulse. No, the woman who had ruined her life was dead all right. Sarla had slapped Ria's face, quite hard, to make absolutely sure. No, nothing. Just a little foam at the corner of the mouth. Dead as a doornail, as the English said. Sarla giggled. The English had so many silly sayings! Dead as a dodo and silent as the grave and a cup of proper coffee in a copper coffee pot.

Ria's golden-brown hair had been all over the pillow. Sarla couldn't see Roman wanting to stroke the hair of a dead girl. No, of course not. Which meant that her, Sarla's, hour had come. She reached out for her bag – her other bag – the bag she *always* carried with her. She had pulled out the golden-brown wig from it.

What happened next Sarla couldn't quite remember, not with any great clarity.

She had suddenly found herself standing in the middle of Ria's bedroom, reflected not only by the dressing-table mirror but by *all* the mirrors on the ceiling as well. She felt like an actress on a stage. She saw she was wearing the slut's fishnet stockings and the snakeskin high-heeled shoes. She looked really sluttish. Really beautiful. Her face looked different – no longer her own but a lovely peachy colour – the most seductive eyes and luscious lips ready for kisses. The blusher had made her cheekbones stand out and her face no longer seemed fat. All the make-up had come from the slut's make-up kit on the dressing table, though Sarla had no recollection of applying it to her face. No recollection at all. Wasn't that funny?

Sarla had screamed in surprised delight and slapped her hand across her mouth. Then she had started laughing. She hadn't been able to stop herself. How she had laughed! Tears had come out of her eyes. Once, not so long ago, she had felt unhappy, lonely, insecure, unfulfilled – no longer! She had stood examining herself in the mirror, then her mouth opened and she began to say things to her

179

reflection, words which she never thought she knew. Some really dirty words. Her father, the retired schoolmaster, would smash her teeth and rip out her tongue if he ever heard her use such language. *Bad language*. The funny thing was that it had felt so *good*.

She had then got busy. She had pushed Ria's body *off* the bed and she had kicked the body *under* the bed. She had then lain *in* the bed, among the cinnamon-scented silk sheets, admiring her legs made longer and slimmer by the high heels, waiting for Roman. She had heard the church bell chime midday. On a sudden impulse, she had got off the bed once more and started dancing around the room. It was at that point the beautiful boy had arrived. His face! He hadn't seen any woman as beautiful as her before, that much was clear from his expression.

Sarla halted. She saw two crows gorging on bright mangoes in a still, dust-green tree by the side of the road. Where had her feet brought her? She took stock of her surroundings. She knew this place. A white façade, which Roman had said was 'Georgian'. A Union Jack. Not authentic Georgian since the building had been completed in the early 1970s by an enterprising Indian businessman, without any real permission from the company running the original Brown's, which was in London. Dover Street, Roman had said. Roman had always pretended to have expert knowledge of everything that happened in England. She was standing outside the English hotel. *Brown's*. Of course.

This was where the killer was.

How did she know the killer was there? Well, this was the *only* place the killer could possibly be. Sarla too, in her own way, had become an expert on things English. On English faces. Such a *respectable*-looking killer. Upper class, without the slightest doubt. Someone her father would approve of.

'All I want is to say thank you and kiss your hand,' Sarla rehearsed her words. She was certain the killer's hands still held the Power. What she also wanted to know was *how it had felt*.

The next moment she saw the killer through the window. Sitting in the foyer, drinking tea and scanning an English newspaper. Not looking like a killer at all.

Sarla went in.

26

The Science of Deduction

It was the following morning.

The sun shone brightly and the sea sparkled, vast and green, and again, incredibly calm. Creamy waves curled up at the brink of the golden shore. The yacht *Caspar*, whose striped funnels brought to mind a children's book illustration, was still moored not far from the Coconut Grove private beach. The landscape was lush with flamboyant trees, highly decorative palms and bulbous banana plants poking up in dense undergrowth. The scent of hot lime flowers, or something very similar, filled the air. Major Payne decided it smelled like honey. Apart from the agreeable cooing of cape turtle doves and pigeons overhead, the silence and sense of peace were absolute.

'It's not right at all for the view to look so lovely, if you know what I mean. I'd have preferred a black canopy of low and swollen clouds,' he murmured. He sat slouched low in his wicker chair, legs straight out in front of him. 'Should I ask for a double brandy perhaps?'

'That would be most unwise.'

'Too soon after breakfast? Can you think of something else then that might cheer me up?'

'My book is going to be translated into Mandarin Chinese,' Antonia said.

'Really? How jolly. Are you serious? How do you know?'

'Got a text from my agent.'

'When?'

'Just now.' She waved her mobile. 'Perhaps Tang will read my book. Make sure he gets the tobacco you promised him.'

'I've seen to that. Manolo must be delivering the package at this very moment.' Payne glanced at his watch. 'So one can get texts. Are we allowed to send texts? I suppose we could text an SOS to Scotland Yard, if the worst should ever come to the worst?'

'Not Scotland Yard, SAS.'

'Then they could mount a rescue operation and get us out of here. They could bring choppers and things. Or is it the Task Force who do that sort of thing?'

'What should we consider the "worst"?' Antonia frowned. 'Being dragged screaming to the lake with the crocs?'

'He won't do that. He needs us to find out who killed Ria.'

Payne was feeling tired and dejected, in a strange sort of stupor. The night before he had had a nightmare in which funeral pyres, crocodiles, the Honourable Mrs Depleche and a sinister elderly man with sepulchral blackened eyes and whited face, like some figure from German Expressionist theatre or the horror films of Murnau and Pabst, had all played a part. Perusing the letters of the late Lord Justice Leighton to his daughter at bedtime had something to do with it, he had no doubt. He had the bundle with him now.

They heard a distant church bell chime nine. They had been having breakfast on the smaller of the two terraces at the back of the house: sliced melon, bacon-and-eggs done to perfection, golden toast, Oxford marmalade, a pot of gentleman's relish for him, fruit salad, freshly squeezed mango juice. They were sitting at a round marble-topped table under a large striped umbrella.

Major Payne laid down the last letter, poured himself some coffee and lit his pipe. '*De mortuis* and all that, but the late judge does emerge as an impossible fellow.

Obsessive, possessive, bigoted and didactic. He describes his sister Iris as "unreliable as the Poles and the Irish". Apparently he caught her telling a lie once, and never forgave her. He says she is "adept at deceit" and that lying is "second nature to her". Can't see how anyone could have been fond of him.'

'No saving graces?'

'Can't really see any. Oh, he is jolly fond of the theatre.'

'What about his great all-consuming love for Ria?'

'What about it?'

'Wasn't he ennobled by it? Didn't it make him appear human and vulnerable? More – likeable?' Antonia looked up from her diary. She believed she had managed to crack the Knight conundrum – but if she was right, the mystery only deepened and became more fantastical. Who *could* that man have been – and why had he done it?

'I wouldn't say it made him more likeable, no. It was the wrong kind of love from start to finish. Possessive and controlling. Damned unhealthy. One can't really empathize with Lord Justice Leighton, or feel sorry for him on account of his daughter earning silly money as a call girl and then graduating to gangster's moll.'

'How much did she earn, does she say?'

'Three thousand pounds a night. Sometimes four.'

'That's more than the advance I get for a book.'

'She might have exaggerated. She does appear to have led the judge on an awful lot. That's what his letters suggest. I bet she made things up whenever her news was not sufficiently shocking. She seemed to have tantalized and tormented him – thrown provocative perversities at him – related her unspeakable exploits in some detail. It is perfectly clear that her heart did *not* belong to Daddy. I wish I were able to take a look at *her* letters.'

'Perhaps one day they'll be published?'

'Perhaps they will be. The stepmother might decide to make a fast buck. Incidentally, the stepmother's name is Lucasta ... The judge complains about her ... Lucasta drives him round the bend with her fussing and she tries to run his life ... Or does he mean "ruin"?' Payne peered down at one of the letters. 'They should publish all the letters in one volume, both hers and his together. It would be the kind of correspondence that provides the gentle reader with a good cautionary tale. Ria's was a female rake's progress all right ... I think she as good as killed her father.'

Antonia nodded thoughtfully. 'Perhaps that was her intention all along?'

'The judge's deteriorating health is a recurrent theme in all his letters. He has heart trouble. He suffers from breathing difficulties and dizzy spells. He feels depressed for most of the day and when night comes, falls prey to insomnia. When he manages to go to sleep he has nightmares. He keeps thinking about his daughter. He writes that he would rather die than accept as truth the things she says she does.'

'That might have been emotional blackmail, but the fact remains he did suffer a massive heart attack and died.'

'*Pulmonary embolism.* That's what the unreliable aunt writes. I think the judge and his daughter deserved one another, don't you? One destroyed the other and vice versa ... Is that a terrible thing to say about people one has never met?' Payne poured himself more coffee. 'I cannot help thinking that Lord Justice Leighton was to blame for the way Ria turned out in the first place, that he was the architect of his own misfortune ... Each man kills the thing he loves ... The Frankenstein syndrome ... I may be completely wrong. I shouldn't judge anyone, really. Still, look at him!'

Payne had placed the photo, which he'd taken from Julian Knight's desk, on the table. 'He does look the part,' Antonia agreed. 'There's something very creepy about him. It's those boiled-gooseberry eyes, I suppose, but also the way he smiles ... So his letters give no evidence of any flashes of humanity? No little heart-warming details?'

'He refers to the fairy tales he used to read to her when she was little, which I suppose is warming in its own way.

He mentions plays he and Lucasta went to. They were quite taken with an adaptation of Mrs Henry Wood's *East Lynne*, he says, which they saw in Chichester. He raves about the cleverness of Anthony Shaffer's *Sleuth*, which they saw in Morecombe-on-Sea or some such place. Rep companies seem to like that sort of thing, don't they? He refers to a DIY job he did in his study. He says his hands are still strong. He never fails to complete the *Times* crossword.'

'How curious. You never fail to complete the *Times* crossword either.'

'True. All right, he was not utterly nightmarish then.'

'Was *East Lynne* the one where the disgraced Lady Isobel returns to her family home, disguised as a nurse, and is not recognized? Does anyone read Mrs Henry Wood nowadays?'

'I don't suppose they do. Unless for some Eng. Lit. university thesis on obscure Victorian writers. *East Lynne* is melodrama of the most turgid kind. It was on the best-seller list, apparently, when it first came out.' Payne puffed at his pipe. 'Am I right in thinking Agatha Christie used an equally improbable impersonation ploy in *Murder in Mesopotamia*? A woman marries the same man *twice* without realizing it? Husband number one becomes husband number two and, thanks to his intricate disguise, remains undetected?'

'Yes. Though I wouldn't have called Dr Leidner's disguise "intricate". He simply grew a beard and changed his name. *Mesopotamia* was one of Christie's two duds in the 1930s. The other one is *Dumb Witness* – unless one is fond of dogs.'

'I've always been fascinated by impersonation in detective stories. I have very mixed feelings about it. I don't think impersonation would ever work in real life. I suppose it is easier for a young person to pass themselves off as an older one, or for a man to impersonate a woman convincingly – though not the other way round.'

'Now then, do you want to hear my deductions in *re* Julian Knight or not?' Antonia asked.

'I most certainly do. I've been longing to hear your deductions. Last night you were damned mysterious about it all.' Payne frowned. 'He couldn't have been dead and at the garden party at one and the same time. If that is what I think it is, it puts an entirely different complexion on this case.'

'It most certainly does.'

'You have reason to believe that the body we saw in the morgue was not that of Julian Knight, correct?' Payne picked up the coffee pot once more.

'That was Julian Knight all right. It was the man who spoke to me in the folly who wasn't.' Antonia glanced down at her diary. 'Don't interrupt now.'

'According to the policeman, Julian Knight died yesterday morning between eleven and five past eleven. It was the partial solar eclipse that fixes the time of death so firmly in the mind. But Julian Knight was also alive and well at about six o'clock when he told me his extraordinary story about seeing Roman Songhera strangle his English girl-friend. Clearly,' Antonia went on, 'we are talking about two different men – one of whom, the *real* Knight – died earlier than we imagined.'

'How do you know that was the real Knight?'

'It wouldn't make sense if it were the other way round. The man in the folly managed to persuade me that his life was in serious danger. He said that he had witnessed a murder committed by Roman Songhera, the uncrowned king of Goa. He was scared. He feared for his life. He was convinced he'd end up dead. And what happens? No sooner has he finished his tale than he is called away on the pretext of a telephone call. He never comes back. He vanishes into thin air. We set out to look for him and we discover Julian Knight's dead body in the local morgue. He has been run over.'

187

'Cause and effect, eh?'

'That was the impression he intended to create, yes. You remember I couldn't swear that the dead man was the same one who'd handed me the diary? Well, I still can't. I did imagine he looked different, but then convinced myself that that's what happened when people died.'

'If the man in the folly wasn't JK, who the hell was he?'

'I believe that was the killer,' Antonia said. 'The *real* killer. After he strangled Ria, he came over here and told me it was Roman who had done it. His intention was to set up Roman. The killer had already managed to dispose of Julian Knight.'

'By running him over? Did he have a car?'

'No. By pushing him in front of a speeding car. He was walking with him. It happened in the morning at about eleven – at the time of the partial solar eclipse, when most people were looking up at the sky through smoked glass. Couldn't have been difficult, given that Knight was an alcoholic, most certainly in an enfeebled state of mind and body.'

'*The veiled one*. Good lord, yes. The killer disguised himself as a local woman! So the whole thing was carefully premeditated? The policeman mentioned a veiled one, didn't he? After seeing Knight disappear under the wheels of the speeding car, the killer managed to escape into the crowd – but not before removing the Boy Scout diary from Julian Knight's pocket?'

'He might already have done so.'

'Indeed he might. All that happened in the morning. The killer now has six hours to get ready for the next deception. He dresses up as Julian Knight, or rather puts on a shabby jacket, a soiled panama and enormous dark glasses. He gatecrashes the garden party, gets into the folly with you and makes an entry into the diary – describes how he has seen Roman Songhera strangle Ria and so on. Julian Knight wrote in block letters, clearly on account of his shaking hand, so imitating his handwriting must have been child's play.' Payne stroked his jaw with his forefinger. 'So, my love, we are looking for a man in his early sixties. An Englishman of theatrical bent who loves dressing up and hates Songhera. Um. What else do we know about him?'

Antonia glanced down at the open diary on her lap. 'He is not in terribly good health. He kept sweating and I don't think that was only because of the heat. And of course he is freshly arrived from England.'

'How do you know that he's freshly arrived from England?'

'You referred to him as Old Zebra Face because of the white stripe across his forehead. At close quarters his face did appear mottled. He kept dabbing at it with a tissue. The tissue was extremely grubby. He left it behind, you see, dropped it inside the folly. I do think his tan was fake, like Camillo's, it came out of a bottle or a tube –'

'What a terrifying bloodhound you are! Thank you, Augusto,' Payne said as the waiter placed a fresh coffee pot on their table. 'Coffee, old thing? I must say the CG coffee is awfully good. As good as the coffee they make at your old haunt, the Military Club.'

'No, no coffee for me, thank you. You're drinking too much coffee. It's bad for the heart. Coffee also makes one paranoid.'

'I haven't noticed. Does coffee make you paranoid? I suppose that's conducive to the writing of detective stories of your kind.' Payne poured himself a cup. 'I wonder if Lord Justice Leighton drank too much coffee. Did the redoubtable Lucasta keep nagging at him to give up? Was coffee to blame for his deteriorating health and ultimate demise? Why oh why do I keep thinking about the old horror? For some reason I can't get him out of my mind. Where were we? Oh yes. The bogus Knight applies a bronzer to his face. Without it, his skin would have been too pale or too pink. His intention was to blend in – to create the illusion that he'd been living in Goa for a long time? '

'Well, either it wasn't a very good bronzer, or his skin wasn't responding very well to it, because his face was streaked. I also thought his hands looked rather pale pink, the colour of monkey's paws . . . All the locals, including the real Julian Knight, who had lived in Goa for some years, are deeply tanned. The man's face in the morgue struck me as deeply tanned, under his deadly pallor.'

'Zebra stripes and grubby tissues . . . I don't suppose those were the only tell-tale signs? You wouldn't have built up a whole case on the evidence of zebra stripes alone, would you?'

'I wouldn't. There is more. Julian Knight was colour-blind – Tang mentioned the fact – but the man who spoke to me in the folly wasn't colour-blind. The man in the folly saw a balloon and he knew it was red.'

'You've got the eyes of an eagle and the memory of a jackdaw,' said Payne admiringly.

'Red on any surface except green or yellow is absolutely invisible to colour-blind people.'

'You should be on *Mastermind*.'

'Then there was the man's watch,' Antonia went on. 'It showed the wrong time. I noticed his watch and at first I thought it had stopped at one o'clock, then I saw it said five past one when mine said five past six. *Five hours*. Do you see?'

'That's the time difference between England and Goa. . . . We are five hours ahead here. . . . You mean the killer forgot to adjust his watch? Charlotte too had forgotten to adjust her watch – she did it at the party. It happens a lot if people haven't been in a country long . . . *Yes* . . . To sum up, we are looking for an Englishman of late middle age, not in the best of health, a lot on his mind, complexion pink or pale, hates Songhera, newly arrived from England – am I missing something?'

'He had a good reason to hold his hand in a fist,' Antonia said thoughtfully. 'He is also a man who knew the private detective well enough and was familiar with Julian Knight's diary and the capital letters he used. Julian

Knight clearly trusted the man and did not become suspicious when he appeared dressed up as a local woman
wearing a veil. I do believe the killer was one of Julian's
clients.'

Payne leant forward. 'You said Knight seemed
extremely upset when he talked about Ria's death, didn't
you? He gave the impression of being in some way personally involved with her?'

'Yes. And I don't think he was putting it on. He was
overcome with grief. That struck me as a bit odd. That's
what gave me the idea that Julian Knight might have been
in love with Ria. Only that was *not* Julian Knight. So why
did he look such a picture of misery and despair? Why did
his voice shake? He clearly had feelings for her. So why
did he kill her? Who was he?'

There was a pause.

'If I didn't know it to be a virtual impossibility,' Major
Payne said slowly, 'if I didn't know he was dead, I'd have
said that the man was Ria's papa. Lord Justice Leighton. It
all fits in perfectly. Think about it.'

27

A Talent to Deceive

He tapped the bundle of letters that lay on the table with the stem of his pipe. 'In one of his letters he tells Ria he would like to come to Goa and collect her. Let's imagine that he did precisely that.'

'He is dead, Hugh. You don't mean – he left his grave – his ghost? A revenant?'

'Let's assume he isn't dead. Let's imagine he gets a plane and flies over to Goa instead. He knows Ria's address because they have been corresponding. As soon as he arrives, he gets in touch with Julian Knight. Asks him to brief him about the latest developments regarding Ria's liaison with Songhera. Perhaps he asks Knight to direct him to Ria's bungalow. He then appears on his daughter's doorstep unannounced. She gets the shock of her life but lets him in nevertheless. He pleads with her. Begs her to go back. She says no, perhaps laughs at him or says something provocative, which makes him angry. They are in the bedroom. He slaps her face. She hits back. He puts his hands around her throat – pushes her back –'

'Her head hits the bedpost?'

'Yes. That's how she gets her swelling. Old Leighton has seen red. He is quite unable to stop himself. He continues pressing his thumbs into Ria's throat. *He has strong hands.* When he suddenly comes to his senses and lets go, it is too late. Ria falls back on the bed. She is dead. He is overcome with grief and despair. He breaks down – cries. He has killed his beloved daughter! Some preservation instinct then asserts itself. He remembers whose fiancée Ria was. He stumbles out of the bungalow. At the thought of Songhera, Leighton's anger returns. Songhera now becomes the focus of all his resentment and hatred. He convinces himself it was all Songhera's fault. It was because of Songhera, the filthy wop, that his daughter died. Songhera will have to pay for it. His anger gives him strength to go on. It also gives him a sense of purpose. He returns to the hotel –'

'Brown's Hotel?'

'The *soi-disant* Brown's, yes. Haunt of well-heeled expats and British tourists of the better class. He sits in his room and considers the situation. Knight has seen him. Knight is the only person who knows Lord Justice Leighton is in Goa. Knight also knows that Leighton has come with the sole aim of taking his daughter back to England. Knight knows too much. Consequently, Knight will have to die –'

'But Knight's death will serve another purpose as well,' Antonia interjected. 'Knight will play the witness who cooks Roman Songhera's goose.'

'Absolutely. Leighton comes up with a scheme. He phones Knight and asks him to get him a pass for the garden party at CG. Knight obliges. He obtains the pass from one of the waiters or the maître d', whom he bribes. Leighton asks Knight to bring not only the pass but his diary as well. He says he wants to look at Knight's notes on Ria. Leighton goes to their meeting garbed in drag. Knight doesn't suspect anything – he is probably drunk.' Payne took another sip of coffee.

'They meet and Lord Leighton manages to pinch Knight's diary,' Antonia said. 'As they are about to cross a busy road, Lord Leighton gives Julian Knight a sharp shove between the shoulder-blades and sends him under the wheels of a speeding car. Exit Julian Knight, formerly of Scotland Yard. Lord Leighton disappears in the crowd. All people have seen is a "native" woman wearing a veil. The stage now is all set for the next act. Lord Leighton dons his second disguise. He assumes Knight's gliding walk, but he makes the mistake of hitching up his *left* shoulder whereas it was the right one with Knight.'

'Leighton adored *East Lynne* and *Sleuth*, both of which involve impersonation.'

'That's certainly suggestive. Did he make me his confidante by chance?'

'Not at all. The Brahmin told you that when he arrived at CG, Knight inquired about you *specifically* – asked where to find you, remember?'

'I thought that was a lie!'

'Hope that teaches you not to be presumptuous. How could Leighton have known you were at Coconut Grove?' Payne held up his pipe. 'Well, he was on the same plane from London as us and his seat was not far from ours. He managed to get a good look at you. Charlotte was talking at the top of her voice, about your detective stories, about your imagination running riot and so on.'

'She said she would like to take advantage of my imagination . . . You think that's what gave him the idea?'

Payne gave a portentous nod. *'The proud have laid a snare for me, yea, and set traps in my way*. The Bible always gets it right, doesn't it? Charlotte also talked about CG and the garden party, so Leighton knew where to find you. He decided you would be perfect for his purpose. He hoped that you would bring Songhera to justice. That was going to be his revenge.'

'Who was the person who called him on the phone?'

'Leighton paid someone to call him from a telephone box. He answered the phone and then walked out of CG and disappeared. The Brahmin didn't lie about that either. Well, old Leighton was clever but not that clever. What he didn't count on was Miss Antonia Darcy and her consort outwitting him.'

Antonia looked at him. 'Hugh, Lord Justice Leighton is dead.'

'Is he though?' Payne drawled.

'Well, that's what his sister wrote.'

'Ah, Dear Aunt Iris. What if Aunt Iris told a whopper to her niece? The very use of the technical term – *pulmonary embolism* – is suspicious, don't you think? It suggests a degree of self-consciousness, of trying too hard, of over-doing it somewhat. As though she was afraid her niece might not be convinced. Why do we think that Lord Justice Leighton is dead? *Only* because his sister Iris wrote a letter to that effect to her niece Ria. We have no evidence.'

'All right. If she did lie, why did she lie?'

'The obvious explanation, my love, is that she was extremely concerned about her brother's health and she wanted to terminate the flow of letters which clearly caused him such great distress of mind. If she wrote to her niece and said her father was dead, Ria would stop writing. As simple as that.' Payne relit his pipe. 'Perhaps there was a particular scare at some point. Old Leighton might have had a heart attack – say, he *nearly* died of it, but eventually recovered. That is why the man in the folly looked ill! Leighton's brush with death might have given sister Iris the idea.'

'Or Lucasta Leighton might have asked her to do it? Less suspicious, coming from a sister who was not exactly her brother's favourite.'

'Yes . . . Ah, Charlotte!' Payne waved his hand. 'Good morning. How is your head?'

'*Terrible.*' Mrs Depleche sat down. She wore a tropical suit that was the perfect match for her sola topi. She kept her hand at her forehead. 'It feels as though somebody undid it last night while I slept and left it out overnight on a deckchair in a hailstorm.'

'Then you should be happy to have it back,' Payne said airily.

'Roman's vanished again. One of his myrmidons told me that somebody in his family's died. I caught sight of him down on the beach, looking dashing in combat fatigues. My head doesn't feel like my own. I am worried about it.'

195

'It's your liver you should worry about.'

'Roman won't be able to take us to his croc farm.' She sighed. 'Relatives do tend to pop off at the most awkward times. I have had most of mine buried, thank God. Pour me a cup of coffee, Hugh, there's a good boy.'

Payne picked up the coffee pot. 'Shall we order some breakfast for you?'

'No, no breakfast. Couldn't eat a thing. I'm sure a poached egg would kill me. I saw some of Roman's men carrying cans of paraffin, screwed-up paper and wood chips. I thought they looked ludicrously solemn. . . .This coffee tastes absolutely foul. Or is it me? Are they going to have a bonfire, d'you think?'

Ria's funeral, Antonia thought. A pyre. She'd been right.

'I dreamt of a clergyman in full canonicals last night,' Mrs Depleche went on. 'He asked if I would like to take communion. He had terribly sad eyes. Perhaps it's a sign I am going to die here.'

'Did he give you extreme unction?'

'I don't think so.'

'Then you'll be all right.' Payne took a sip of coffee.

'Today I don't intend to touch a drop. Last night the *Caspar* crowd were telling me about a funeral procession they saw. Elephants – the kind of flowers that look as though they are about to eat you – juggling marmosets in brightly coloured frocks. It was all very beautiful and a little unusual.'

'The juggling marmosets couldn't have been part of the funeral. They must have gatecrashed the funeral and should have been shooed off. You don't happen to know any Leightons, Charlotte, do you?' Payne said on an impulse. 'A Lord Justice Leighton?'

'There are the Wiltshire Leightons. Robbie and Maurice. There are others too, mostly men. Made extraordinary marriages, all of them. Then there's the Hertfordshire line. Toby and Iris.'

'I think these are the ones.'

'I knew a Lucasta Furness who married a Leighton, can't

196

remember which one – Toby, I believe. For him it was a second marriage. Odd creature, stayed on the shelf for ages. Rumoured to have poisoned her best friend. Clever and manipulative, or so they said. All clever women are manipulative.' Mrs Depleche looked pointedly at Antonia.

Annoying old witch, Antonia thought.

'Married to a woman like that would be either a blessing or a curse.' This time Mrs Depleche cast a speculative glance in Payne's direction, as though to ascertain whether he considered himself blessed or cursed. She seemed disappointed when his expression remained blank.

'Did Toby Leighton die?' Payne asked.

'He might have. I never read obituaries, such a lot of nonsense. Perhaps we could have a little walk on the waterfront and stop for coffee at this place everybody calls Brown's? Can't be the same one as in – as in . . .' Mrs Depleche yawned. Her eyes fluttered and closed. She fell back in her wicker chair and a moment later she was snoring.

Major Payne looked at Antonia. 'Brown's. That's where we might find Leighton. Unless he's gone back to England. I don't suppose he knows the body has been taken away from the bungalow. He probably assumes there will be a proper investigation – and he hopes that Songhera will swing for it. That's what they do here, isn't it?'

'I think so, yes. They do hang murderers in India.'

'He'd be anxious to be back in England when the British High Commission ring to notify him of his daughter's death. As her next of kin, he would be expected to fly over to Goa to collect the body.'

'But he is already in Goa.'

'Yes. It's a tricky situation. He wouldn't want it to be known he was in Goa at the time of his daughter's murder,' Payne said thoughtfully. 'He might wait till later today before he comes forward and declares that he's just arrived from England. I think we should go and put our theory to the test. It would be best to catch him unawares –'

'Go where?' Mrs Depleche asked, suddenly waking up.

197

'Brown's Hotel.'

'It cannot be the same Brown's as the one in Dover Street, can it?'

'An ersatz version, I imagine, and illegal to boot.' Payne picked up his pipe and rose from his seat. 'Wonder if Rocco Forte knows about it.'

'Good to see you wearing a hat, Antonia.' Mrs Depleche nodded amiably. 'This is a most extraordinary place. Yesterday morning Roman and I stopped and watched a bunch of fakirs put on a show. They seemed to get a tremendous kick out of walking across unsheathed knives and they chanted the while. I've never heard anything like it. It sounded like a tape being played backward at speed, but I rather liked their beards.'

'Did you and Songhera stay together all the time?' Payne asked casually.

'I think so. Yes. Roman kept stopping the car. I wanted to take photographs of things, you see. The solar eclipse and so on. *Such* an obliging boy. He thinks the world of you, Hugh. I so wish you and he could be friends. He told me he wanted you to work for him.'

'He asked me to tell him each time he did something caddish.'

'I adore cads. I don't think I have ever stayed at Brown's. I mean the one in Dover Street. I understand it is always full of foreigners. Americans and so on.'

'Here it's the haunt of English people of the better class, apparently.'

'How ghastly,' Mrs Depleche said. 'The oak panelling is bound to be riddled with dry rot. Termites everywhere. As a matter of fact, I have changed my mind. I won't come with you after all. I feel a little tired. I'll sit here in the sun and have another forty winks.'

'Something's burning,' Major Payne murmured as they set out some five minutes later. 'Can you smell it? A sulphurous smell. Bitterish. A hint of oleander and roses too.'

'I think it's Ria's funeral pyre,' said Antonia.

28

A Taste for Death

'Would you like more tea?'

'Yes. Thank you, *thank* you. This is such good tea!'

Lord give me patience. This is worse than yesterday. The way the creature gushes. At least she's wiped that rainbow make-up off her face. She wanted to kiss my hand again. So embarrassing. People stared. She keeps her eyes on me. Keeps staring. Her hand brushing against mine. Mustn't show distaste. She's doing it on purpose, I am sure. Seems to be fascinated by ... by my hands.

'Sugar? Milk?'

'Yes, thank you. Cream, please. I love cream,' Sarla said.

It was Sarla's second visit to the killer.

If only I'd looked at the window, I'd have seen her. Could I have done anything about it? Could I have run out and strangled her as well? I couldn't. A sympathetic witness. How droll. *Somebody who approves.* How perfectly ghastly. Don't feel terribly well. She seems to believe it was she who'd summoned me. Something to do with – bones in a bag? She is more than a trifle mad. What do I talk to her about? Ask her where she learnt her English? Yes. Small talk.

'Where did you learn your English?'

'My father was a teacher,' Sarla explained. 'He is an old man now. I don't like him.'

Treat her with caution. Humour her. Get her out of the way at the earliest opportunity. How?

'Your English is very good.'

'My father beat me. I hope he dies soon.'

'I am so sorry.'

'Will you kill my father?'

'More tea?'

Sarla leant across the table and spoke urgently. 'Ria was going to die. I had a feeling that morning. I knew it, but I didn't know *how* she was going to die. I knew it was coming to her. I didn't expect somebody like you.'

'This is all quite remarkable.'

A nod and a smile . . . Non-committal . . . Perfect poise . . . Preposterous . . . Say as little as possible . . . No other option, really . . . What is the time? What's poor darling doing? Won't speak. Won't even look at me . . . Must be strong . . . Such dreadful tension . . . Despised and detested . . . Mustn't burst into tears . . . Did it for the best . . . Impossible situation. . . . No winners.

'The woman who sold me the hex said, great power. She said, the masters know how to do it, you just wait. *Great power.*' Sarla was nodding over her chocolate éclair. 'You don't look like a killer at all. The masters choose the most – the most – what is the word?'

'The most unlikely means?'

Ridiculous, providing her with the *mot juste*. Get out of here, you crazy lump. You ugly fat monster. Your fingers are covered in chocolate. Your mouth too. You are starting on the sachertorte now . . . Dear God . . . Do you intend to eat everything within sight? Can't stand watching you stuff yourself . . . Makes me sick . . . Such puffy eyes . . . Smile . . . Wouldn't do to antagonize her . . . *Smile* . . . The maître d'hôtel is watching us, wondering whether to intervene. Waiting for a sign from me. All I need do is give a nod. *No.* The creature might turn nasty . . . A scene . . . The last thing I want . . . Must concentrate, reflect, make sense of things. What am I to do?

'You don't know Ria?' Sarla said.

'No. Shall I ask for more cakes?'

'You got the call. You *knew* you must come. A feeling – and a thought, yes? I was told how it works. You knew it here . . .' Sarla touched her voluminous bosom. 'And here . . .?' She touched her head now.

Humour her. 'Yes. You are absolutely right.'

The way she's pushing her breasts into the lemon tarts! She's wearing 'European dress' this morning . . . Lime-green frilly blouse, skirt like a tent . . . So greedy – dipping her fingers into the custard tarts – so *fat* – if she had been a man, the buttons would have flown off her waistcoat like bullets . . . Henry said that once, about someone at his club . . . How much longer? I'm getting desperate . . .

'You felt you had to come, yes?' Sarla went on. 'You gave up everything and got the plane. You knew you must come to Kilhar?'

'I knew I had to come to Kilhar.'

'I think you were in one of my dreams once.'

'Really? How interesting.'

'Sometimes I see things that are not there.'

It is clear that she is mad. The way she rolls her eyes. Such a monstrous lump. Some glandular disorder? How strong is she? Would she put up a fight if –? My wrist hurts. The way she goes on stuffing herself . . . Crushing meringues between her fingers!

'More tea?'

Can't go on like this . . . Hands brushing again . . . She's doing it on purpose . . . The glint in her eyes . . . Possessed by the spirit of hero-worship . . . If I had poison, I'd put it in her tea . . . Am I destined to be having tea with her till kingdom come? Doomed for eternity! That's what hell must be like . . . Mustn't become hysterical . . . *What am I to do?*

'That man,' Sarla said. 'Who is he?'

'What man?'

'You came together.'

Looks sly . . . Knowing . . . Seen us . . . Mad people can be very cunning . . . She knows too much . . . What's that, gleaming in the sun? Fruit knives? Yes. Sharp, very sharp . . . Yes, why not? As sharp as scalpels . . . Checked one with my forefinger last night at dinner . . .

'You told a lie, but it doesn't matter. I checked at Reception. I asked them your name. I won't tell anyone. You knew Ria. You have the same name as her.' Sarla put her forefinger across her lips and looked round. '*Leighton.*'

There was a pause then the killer said, 'What would you say to a walk along the beach?'

No one would suspect *me* . . . Plenty of suspects . . . Roman Songhera – though of course they wouldn't touch Roman Songhera . . . Everyone in this damned place seems involved in some kind of illegal racket . . . The police are notorious slackers . . . It will be all right . . . Murder *is* easy . . .

'A walk?' Sarla breathed. 'Only the two of us? I want you to kill my husband.'

'I will have to change first. Won't be a moment. Would you like to wait for me outside?'

A fruit knife, yes . . . In the back of the head, just above the neck . . . Quick as a flash . . . Somewhere on the rocks? Then shove her into the sea . . . What are those screams? Curlews and seagulls . . . Hungry, always hungry . . . Would they peck at her eyes?

29

At Brown's Hotel

The hotel with its white Georgian façade and Union Jack dangling limply loomed before them. It looked incongruous in the haze, like a film set – somewhat distorted – shimmering. It was as though a sheet of hot glass were stretched between it and them.

The air felt close and oppressive. Something angry in it, or so Antonia imagined. Some active malignancy was slowly gathering round her, throbbing to a white-hot head. She could feel it like a weak current from a battery.

They entered the foyer. Payne crossed to the reception desk at once. There was a queue.

Antonia stood, looking round. Potted palms, Persian rugs and big buttoned leather armchairs that brought to mind the Military Club. A man and a woman sitting on the over-stuffed sofa, not talking, each one with a newspaper. English of course. *The Times*, five days old. The *Telegraph*, ten days old. Like a couple out of Somerset Maugham. Not exactly a picture of marital bliss. Might have been strangers. Perhaps they *were* strangers?

She didn't think the air-conditioning was working properly. She really mustn't stay in the sun too long, not even in her new straw hat. She had spent ages putting on sun cream. She wasn't particularly keen on acquiring a tan. She remembered Miss Bingley sneering at Elizabeth Bennet for having grown 'so brown and coarse' as a result of travelling in summertime. People became delusional if they spent too much time in the sun. Mad dogs and Englishmen. A lot of mad-looking dogs had barked at them as they'd walked along the beach. Hugh had thrown a stick at one of them and that had sent the whole lot into paroxysms of rage. No RSPCA. Of course not. Dangerous place. Marvellous-looking beach, though.

'They are burning patchouli sticks again,' grumbled the Englishman on the sofa.

'It's *not* patchouli. It's something else,' the woman said.

'It's patchouli,' he said.

Their faces were hidden by the newspapers. He: mottled frog hand, signet ring and horizontal-striped socks. She: patterned silk dress, flat sensible tan-and-white shoes, varicose veins . . . Marital ennui . . . Conversation of numbing banality . . . Would she and Hugh sit in companionable silence on over-stuffed sofas in former outposts of the Empire one day? Would they ever run out of things to say to each other? I hope I haven't got sunstroke, Antonia thought. She dabbed at her forehead with her handkerchief. Why was it that one could always tell the English abroad?

What was Hugh doing? Still in the queue beside the reception desk.

Journey's end. They had reached the *metamenusis* stage, where the detectives were required to explain their reasoning. Time for the final surprise. It would turn out Julian Knight hadn't been killed by Lord Justice Leighton after all, but by somebody completely different. By, say, the adulterous Mrs Gilmour? Her husband had asked Julian Knight to follow her – she'd been having an affair with an Indian. Or why not a vindictive she-male from the notorious brothel where Mr Agrawal had been a habitué? Lady-boys, as they were also known, could be loyal to the death, Antonia had read somewhere.

No – the *faux* Julian Knight didn't fit in with any of these solutions. It *had* to be Lord Justice Leighton. *A somewhat outlandish denouement*. Would he have registered under a different name? He hadn't intended to kill his daughter. He had loved Ria more than anything in the world. He had wanted her back. It had been a spur-of-the-moment murder. Not even that. An accident – a tragic accident – he'd lost his temper –

'*Garçon, la même chose.*' The Englishman on the sofa had lowered his newspaper and was swirling his forefinger over his empty glass.

'Why are you speaking French?' His wife frowned. 'We are no longer in Monte. You're drinking too much.'

'You are talking too much.'

Antonia was replaying the conversation in the folly in her head. Lord Justice Leighton – in the guise of Julian Knight – said he had seen Roman bang Ria's head against the bedpost. That, he seemed to believe, was what killed her. But Ria had been strangled. He hadn't said a word about strangling. Well, they were not really sure how she had died, actually. Curious. Things like that bothered Antonia. She didn't like loose ends.

Hugh was talking to the receptionist. At long last! Antonia moved closer. He was asking if they had a Lord Justice Leighton staying at the hotel. The answer, after a brief check in the hotel register, was yes. Lord Justice Leighton was in his room. Would the gentleman like to leave a message? The gentleman wanted to see Lord Justice Leighton? Was the gentleman expected? No? Well, in that case they were not sure. (The Hispanic-looking receptionist kept employing the royal 'we'.) Lord Justice Leighton hadn't been feeling very well. Some twenty minutes earlier he had been outside, but had come back. The night before he'd had a bad turn. The resident doctor had been called. They had specifically been asked not to disturb him.

The couple on the sofa were talking again.

'That woman we saw earlier on. The tall one with the immaculate hairdo.'

'What about it?' The husband appeared uninterested. 'You know her?'

'No. She did something quite extraordinary. She glanced round, then quick as a flash she took one of the –'

'I am absolutely certain he will see me, my good man,' Payne said in impossibly clipped tones, what Antonia called his Plummy-Blah voice. Hugh was doing his military trick of standing as though on parade, bent a little forward from the waist, his arms slightly curved at the sides. She could see the receptionist was impressed.

'Would you please call him at once and tell him that it is about his daughter? Tell him it is an extremely serious matter. The name is Payne. Major Payne. He wouldn't know me, no. *And* Mrs Payne. From the British High Commission in Delhi,' he added.

So that was going to be their game. Antonia shook her head. Were they being irresponsible? It would be a cruel deception. On the other hand, why not? Hadn't Lord Justice Leighton played a cruel deception on her? Hadn't he made a fool of her in the folly?

The receptionist had picked up the phone. He turned his back on them as he dialled a number. He spoke in a low voice. A moment later he said, 'Lord Justice Leighton will see you. Room number 45. Fourth floor. Would the gentleman and the lady like to be escorted by the bell-boy?

'No, thank you. We'll find our way up,' Major Payne said.

As they headed for the lift Antonia heard one of the waiters say in perplexed agitation, 'There were six fruit knives, I swear. There are only five now!'

30

Thou Art the Man

The moment they entered the lift, a thought struck Antonia like a thunderbolt. 'He will recognize me! We spent at least fifteen minutes together in the folly.'

'Well, if he does realize the game is up the moment he claps eyes on us, he's bound to give himself away at once. That's what we want, isn't it?'

They were walking down the corridor now. Framed photographs on the walls. Cricket teams. 1903 . . . 1928 . . . 1935 . . . The Cricket Club of India . . . Lord Willingdon, the cricket-loving Viceroy, resplendent in dress uniform, his epaulettes, medals and crosses lending him a faint air of light opera . . . The Maharaja of Patiala (1891–1938). A chunky man in thigh-high boots and a bulbous turban adorned with a peacock feather. Face the shape of a heraldic shield, an aquiline nose, the thickest horn-shaped moustaches she'd ever seen and the boldest and lustiest of stares. A lady-killer, if ever there was one. The type, Antonia reflected, Edwina Mountbatten, Charlotte's maenad-mentrix, must have found irresistible.

Major Payne pointed to another photograph. 'Yadavindra Singh. The best cricketer the Patiala dynasty ever produced. He was a crowd-pleasing batsman in the aristocratic style, given to short but spectacular innings with lots of fours and sixes and as little running between wickets as possible. He had a passion for botany.'

'Can anyone be killed with a fruit knife?' Antonia asked suddenly.

'Of course they can. You must aim at the jugular or the nape.'

Number 45. A solid mahogany door the colour of dried liver. Antonia felt distaste bordering on revulsion.

'Pull your pretty bonnet over your eyes and keep a step behind me,' Payne whispered.

He knocked on the door twice.

As no one answered, he tried the door handle. The door opened and they entered the room.

There'd be a kind of poetic justice, Antonia thought, if they found him sprawled on the floor dead, either as a result of a massive heart attack or by his own hand.

It was an opulently decorated cherry-red room, which at the moment was sunk in gloom, an effect created by the coral-coloured curtains having been drawn across the windows and the balcony door. A fine black chinoiserie chest, late eighteenth-century, Payne imagined. Decorative gold-leaf garlands along the walls . . .

Lord Justice Leighton sat very still in a recently up-holstered gilt and ormolu armchair with his back to the window. The phone, a 1940s model, was on a little table beside him, on his right. On his left stood a larger circular gilt-surround occasional table with a coffee cup on it and several medicine bottles. Against the table leant a silver-topped cane.

He didn't say a word, just stared back at them. He might have been a wax effigy. The pale face brought to mind a death mask. He looked nothing like the Julian Knight who had talked to her in the folly, Antonia thought. A high domed forehead of the kind that might have been described as 'noble' – tufts of white hair – thin lips pulled down at the edges. The protuberant, bloodshot eyes were empty, devoid of expression. No – the eyes had a haunted look. (Gnawed away by guilty conscience? Tormented by his sense of loss?)

He wore a light blue shirt, a cravat the colour of chartreuse, white trousers and white slip-on shoes. She'd never have recognized him, Antonia reflected, never.

'Lord Justice Leighton?' Major Payne had removed his panama.

The figure in the armchair stirred. 'What is this about my daughter? What's happened?'

Antonia was mesmerized by the look and sound of him. Breathing not good. Wheezes. Hands pink and mottled, like a monkey's paws. Right hand across chest. Left hand on knee –

'My name is Payne. Major Payne. I am from the British High Commission. This is my wife.'

The tortured eyes gazed at Antonia indifferently, without a flicker of recognition. (Was he pretending?)

'Has anything happened to my daughter?'

What was that? Her heart started beating fast. *His little finger was missing.* So that's why he had held his hand in a fist throughout their conversation in the folly. She had assumed he was holding something, but he wasn't – his hand had been empty. He knew a missing little finger would attract attention, that it would be noticed and remembered. So it was him!

'I am afraid I am the bearer of bad news,' Payne said.

'What bad news?'

Antonia was put in mind of an Edwardian problem painting in the grand manner of, say, the Hon. John Collier – the kind of painting that spelled everything out with great clarity and attention to detail, leaving very little to the spectator's imagination. It would be called ... well, *Bad News* of course. It was the air of dated formality that she imagined hung about the three of them that had given Antonia the idea.

There was the upright grave-faced Major with his stiff upper lip, his greying blond hair sleeked back, clutching his white panama before him ... The Major's mem, immaculate in her pale yellow silk-and-linen dress and straw hat, whose black ribbon hinted subtly at the horror of the situation, her right hand cupped in a nervous gesture at her discreet cleavage ... The distinguished-looking elderly gentleman leaning back in the red velvet-and-gilt armchair, his white hair ruffled, his mouth agape, his right hand pressed against his heart, his left pulling at his elegant cravat, as though he were choking –

'Marigold Leighton is your daughter, isn't she? I am afraid she is dead.'

'No.' Lord Justice Leighton made a stifled sound and covered his mouth. 'Not dead. Can't be.'

'I am sorry, sir. She died yesterday. She was murdered.' Payne was watching the former judge closely. 'She was strangled.'

'Strangled? Oh – oh, my God.'

'We thought you should be informed about it as soon as possible. I am sorry.'

'When – when did it happen?' Leighton's speech was a little slurred. Had he been sedated?

He was going through the motions but his heart was not in it. He spoke his lines in a tired, distracted manner. He tried to appear shocked, grief-stricken, stirred to his depths, but it was a somewhat vague and perfunctory performance. Well, he had passed through it once already. He had been through hell, Antonia had no doubt, but that was yesterday; it was hard mustering up the right feelings at will, doing a repeat performance. He appeared exhausted – deflated – drained of energy – all passion spent. His eyes didn't focus properly.

'Your daughter's body was discovered this morning.'

'This morning? How – how did you know where to find me? How did you know I was here?' Leighton looked confused. 'Did the police get in touch with you?'

'The police contacted your sister in England. Your sister told us that you were here, the name of your hotel and so on. She rang the British High Commission in Delhi.'

'Iris contacted the British High Commission? But Iris has no idea – she doesn't even know –' Lord Justice Leighton broke off.

Payne pounced at once. 'Your sister has no idea you are here, has she? Of course she hasn't. You managed to keep your trip a secret from everyone! Well, we also contacted your wife at Noon's Folly in Hertfordshire. It was she who told us the whole story,' he went on improvising. 'About all the letters you wrote to your daughter and how you came to Goa to try to persuade Ria to go back to England.'

'You contacted . . . Lucasta? But you couldn't have!' Suddenly Lord Justice Leighton gave a thin reedy laugh. 'What nonsense is this? You aren't really from the High Commission, are you? Who *are* you?'

Antonia wondered whether Hugh would come up with some portentous phrase like 'pawns of destiny', but he didn't.

'We know exactly what you did yesterday morning,' Payne said.

'I've done nothing.'

'You killed your daughter.'

Lord Justice Leighton's hand went up to his forehead. 'I didn't kill my daughter. You are mad.'

'This we believe to be the sequence of events. Do correct me if I get something wrong.' Payne cleared his throat. 'You went to Ria's bungalow in Fernandez Avenue yesterday morning. She let you in. You told her you'd come to take her back to England. You had an argument. Things got out of hand. You lost your temper – you shook her – pushed her back on the four-poster bed. You were in her bedroom. Her head hit one of the bedposts and she passed out. Then – then you strangled her.'

Leighton rasped out, 'I want you out of here now, or else I will call Reception and ask them to – to . . .'

'You want to summon the law? Please go ahead.' Payne waved at the telephone. 'I am sure the local police would be very interested in talking to you. I hope you have a good alibi for yesterday morning?'

'I don't need an alibi. I don't know what you are talking about. Please leave me alone. I am awfully tired. I am not well. I have a terrible headache. I get *three* kinds of headache.' Leighton shut his eyes. 'This one is the fabled winged headache with red and green feathers and gold-black claws that clutch and squeeze while its heavy wings beat faster and faster *and* faster. It's causing me *agonies*. I sit in a dull haze and suddenly it comes. I have become an expert on headaches. I could write a monograph on headaches.'

'You are acting crazy now.' Payne clicked his tongue and shook his head. 'I don't think it will help you much.'

'You won't get a penny out of me. You are trying to blackmail me, aren't you?'

'Not at all. We are trying to establish the truth.'

'There is nothing to establish.'

'We are private detectives and we have been investigating your daughter's murder.'

'You aren't private detectives.'

'As a matter of fact you have already met my wife. You couldn't have forgotten my wife, surely? You met her only yesterday evening, at our employer's Valentine party. You had a long conversation with her. In the folly. Before you disappeared . . . Something of an actor *manqué*, aren't you?'

'I've never seen this woman before,' Lord Justice Leighton said firmly.

'You entrusted me with the diary of the man you killed and then impersonated,' Antonia said, taking the reddish-brown notebook out of her handbag and holding it aloft in her hand in a gesture that seemed vaguely threatening. How absurdly melodramatic. She might have been confronting Lady Isobel Vane of *East Lynne* notoriety.

The former judge fixed his boiled-gooseberry eyes on Payne. 'Did you say your "employer"?'

'That's correct. We work for Roman Songhera. He commissioned us to find his fiancée's killer. Which we now have.'

'Nonsense. I don't believe you.'

'Come along, darling.' Payne touched Antonia's arm. 'We mustn't make Mr Songhera wait.'

'*Wait*.' Lord Leighton seemed to have come to a decision. 'You are very much mistaken. I didn't kill Ria, but . . .'

'Yes?'

'I will tell you who did. I'm damned if I let her get away with it.'

There was a smell in the room and now Antonia became aware of it for the first time. Not medicinal. Was that what eternal damnation smelled like? It was some stately scent and, funnily enough, it seemed familiar. Now, where . . .? Antonia frowned. Not such a long time ago – at Ria's bungalow? *Yes*. In the hall, then in Ria's bedroom. Antonia had thought it an unlikely choice for a young girl of Ria's persuasion.

Did *he* use the scent? Antonia experienced a slightly creepy sensation. Lord Justice Leighton couldn't be a transvestite, could he? She had also noticed a kimono and lady's slippers beside the double bed, as well as a brooch in the shape of what looked like a triton, two diamanté hairpins and a jar of cold cream on the bedside table. A beaded scarf of the kind Moslem women wore lay on another chair. *The* veil? That was what he had worn when he killed Knight. Antonia cast round, trying to spot a woman's wig somewhere. An immaculate hairdo. Where had she heard something about an immaculate hairdo? Split personality? A Norman Bates kind of solution?

She was aware of a draught. The door behind her seemed to have opened –

Turning round sharply, Antonia gave a little cry. What she saw gave her such a shock that icy coldness passed right through her and broke out on her skin in gooseflesh. For a moment she couldn't feel her heart beating at all and then it seemed to pound with enormous rhythm.

A woman had entered the room. A woman whose stiff ghost-white hair looked like a helmet, which was a remarkable feat to have achieved in this hot weather. Her Roman nose was very red as a result of over-exposure to

213

the sun – it brought to mind a ferocious Red Indian. She wore a snuff-coloured khaki suit and, in addition to her handbag, she held a grey finely woven straw hat with an ivory satin ribbon. She was pressing a handkerchief to her left cheek.

The stately scent became more pronounced. It was her scent of course.

The woman seemed to have met with an accident. Her right hand looked badly scratched. Could she have been attacked by some animal? There was also an ugly gash across her left cheek and her handkerchief was saturated in blood.

31

The Veiled One

'Lord, it's you,' the former judge groaned. 'I thought I caught the Chimera whiff. I told you not to come back. Why is it you never listen to me? Why did you come back? Go away. I don't want to see you ever again. For as long as I live. Which won't be long now.'

The woman said, 'How are you feeling, Toby?'

'I feel rotten. I won't last the day. I see my future like an inch-long white ribbon before my nose.'

'I don't think you've taken your medicine. You promised you would without fail.' The woman spoke in a precise, measured, level way.

Too measured, Antonia thought – like one of those electronic voices issuing from machines. It must be his wife. Lucasta Leighton. Antonia watched her go up to the former judge and reach out for his forehead. Her manner had something of the sleepwalker in it.

'You are dripping blood all over me! What have you been up to? She drinks blood,' Leighton told Payne. 'She is a vampire. Dotty and doting. She takes advantage of my helplessness. I detest her. She is a monster.'

'Why haven't you taken your medicine?'

'She insists on sleeping in my bed. She's ruined my life. I keep telling her to go away but she doesn't listen.'

'Who are these people?' Lucasta Leighton was examining her bloodied hand with a puzzled frown, as though she had noticed there was something amiss for the first time.

'They have been sent by Roman Songhera. Well, Ria told me what he does to his enemies. Roman Songhera should be told about you, don't you think?'

'I think you need another injection.'

'No, not another injection! Don't let her go to the bathroom!' Leighton cried. 'Would you do me a great favour, Major? The bathroom floor's made of what I believe is called tessellated marble. I want you to go and smash each one of this human manticore's syringes and bottles against it, reduce them to powder with your heels, then flush all her witchy tinctures down the loo.'

Oh dear. Antonia felt the sudden urge to laugh. How perfectly awful. *Comedia horribilis*. A black farce!

When Major Payne made no move, Leighton said, 'These people work for Roman Songhera. They know everything about it, Lucasta.'

'There's nothing to know. Pay no attention,' she mouthed at Antonia and tapped her forefinger lightly at her forehead. She seemed to suggest the former judge was deranged.

'They know everything,' he reiterated. 'They know everything.'

'They are lying. Look at them! Just take a good look at them!' Lucasta's voice was higher now. A hysterical note had crept into it. 'How can you think they work for Roman Songhera?'

'We most certainly do not look the part,' Major Payne said. 'That's precisely the reason why he employed us. The money's awfully good. And we'll get more as soon as we give Songhera a name.'

'He's bluffing,' Lucasta said.

'They think it was me. I can see why. *I* thought it was me! They've been very logical about it.' Once more Lord Justice Leighton shut his eyes. 'Nothing matters any more, but I don't see why they should go on believing it was me.

216

It isn't right. You led me on. You deceived me. *It was you, not me.*'

'I am awfully sorry but I must ask you to leave, if you don't mind.' Lucasta Leighton turned towards the unwelcome visitors in a parody of graciousness. 'My husband is in precipitately declining health.'

'I refuse to take part in any sort of consolidated alliance,' Leighton declared, sticking out his lower lip. 'Especially one of a criminal nature.'

'My husband has a serious condition. Physical as well as psychiatric. He is on medication. Please –'

'I have, after all, devoted my entire adult life to law and justice. I will *not* betray my principles.'

It was you. You lied to me. Those were the words Mrs Gilmour had overheard. It had been Lord Justice Leighton and his wife. A middle-aged couple. Home Counties written all over them. The husband had looked distraught. *Of course.* Antonia held her breath. Lucasta Leighton had been at Ria's bungalow. She had entered the bedroom *after* Lord Justice Leighton had left it. Leighton had believed he had killed his daughter, but he hadn't.

'*Please*,' Lucasta Leighton said again, with greater emphasis, and this time she gestured towards the door. She took her hand off her cheek and Antonia gasped – it was an incredibly deep wound. Lucasta Leighton's cheek appeared to have been ripped apart.

'What – what happened to you?' Antonia couldn't help asking. 'Who did this to you?'

'Let me tell you first what Lucasta did.' Leighton had loosened his chartreuse-coloured cravat from around his throat. 'I will tell you *everything*. She destroyed my daughter and now she wants to destroy me. You should know about it, then you can report back to that filthy wop. Tell him it's the wicked stepmother who did it. Let him deal with her as he sees fit. Tell him I insist on something protractedly painful.'

'Oh, it's nothing, my dear.' Lucasta gave a dismissive smile. 'A little accident.'

217

'I understand Roman Songhera keeps crocodiles.' Leighton smacked his lips. 'He breeds them. Ria wrote about Roman's crocs in the most lyrical terms. You will be fed to the crocodiles, Lucasta, and they will tear you apart and they'll devour every bit of you until you disappear completely.' He spoke with weary relish. 'You are bound to taste foul but I don't think they are particular.'

'Now, Toby –' The next moment Lucasta Leighton winced. She must be in dreadful pain, Antonia thought.

Leighton laughed horribly. 'Oh dear. I keep forgetting you have been wounded. That woman struggled, I expect? You said she was big? Did she bite you?'

Had Lucasta Leighton committed *three* murders? It was she who had taken one of the fruit knives, of course, of course. *A woman with an immaculate hairdo.* Antonia felt a sick feeling in her stomach. She tried to catch her husband's eye but he appeared ghoulishly mesmerized by the spectacle of the warring Leightons.

'You wouldn't have thought it of her, would you? It wasn't all plain sailing, though. At one point she was seen.' Lord Justice Leighton gave the impression of having summoned up all his strength. 'There was a witness to Ria's murder. She told me about it. That wop's wife happened to be peeping in through the window. She called on Lucasta yesterday. They had tea together.'

'Sarla Songhera witnessed the murder?'

'She did. Mrs Songhera was quite amiable, apparently. Grossly fat but amiable and well disposed. She seemed to approve of what Lucasta did. She seemed to admire her for killing my daughter. She came again today and again they had tea together, then Lucasta came up to change – into her hunting outfit. Just look at her!' Leighton shook his forefinger. 'Aquascutum. Lucasta believes in being dressed for the occasion. Well, the hunting season opened this morning. *Vive le sport!* She was clutching something in her pocket. A knife, I think. I knew at once she intended to kill that woman. She had that look about her. Did you manage to do it, my precious?'

'I have absolutely no idea what you are talking about, Toby. I am afraid you are delirious.'

'How I got to marry her, I don't know. I admired her air of efficiency and sense of the theatre. We used to do impressions together,' Leighton confided in Major Payne. 'I couldn't believe my eyes when I saw her sitting downstairs, waiting for me. I'd just arrived from the airport, but there were great delays, so she beat me to it. She'd bought all the right things. Sola topis, mosquito repellent and antihistamine tablets.'

'You didn't tell her you were coming to Goa?'

'Of course not. I said I was going to Baden-Baden, for my health, but she'd found my ticket in my desk, damn her. She'd been rifling my desk, reading my letters, spying on me! She then followed me all the way to the subcontinent. One might have been excused for taking her for my bloody shadow. She hopped on the next plane apparently and that's how we ended up at this ghastly place.'

Lucasta Leighton went to the door and opened it. She looked at Antonia, then at Payne. 'If you don't leave at once I will call the management.' She was pressing the handkerchief against her cheek once more.

'I am nothing but a feeble-minded fool. No one would have thought I was once described as "possessing the finest legal brain in Britain". I thought the world of Lucasta's managerial qualities,' Leighton went on. 'She's not quite human. She's a demon. Never gets tired. Can exist on four hours' sleep a night – like that Thatcher woman! Disgrace to womanhood. I didn't feel too well that day, so it was she who phoned Knight. We weren't sure about the address. Knight showed us where Fernandez Avenue was, though he didn't come with us. We went together, she and I. I should have gone alone, then none of this would have happened.'

'I wanted to help you,' Lucasta said. 'I love you.'

'My brother-in-law is a fool but sometimes fools see the truth more clearly than the wise. I happened to overhear something he said. It was to the effect that Lucasta poisoned Imogen while nursing her – that's my first wife – in order to get me! I didn't believe it then, but now I wonder. I very much wonder.'

Antonia blinked. Had Lucasta committed *four* murders?

'Don't you believe a word of what he says. He is seriously ill.'

'My darling Ria – I miss her so much!' Leighton sobbed.

'Toby – darling – *please* – do not distress yourself.' Lucasta Leighton made an imploring gesture but the next moment she reeled back and leant against the wall. Her hand clutched at one of the chairs. Had she been overcome by nausea? Delayed shock? She needed to go to the hospital – have the gash cleaned and sterilized – stitched up – properly dressed – she must be given a tetanus jab – she might get blood poisoning.

Antonia was suddenly filled with dreadful pity for both of them. Love, she thought. The misery, the confusion and the horror of it. Oh God. The heart weeps.

'I told Lucasta to wait outside. I rang the bell. Ria hadn't changed one little bit,' Lord Justice Leighton whispered. 'Lovelier than ever. She got the shock of her life when she saw me. She didn't recognize me – thought I was a stranger at first – stared as though I were Banquo's ghost. Gasped. I wanted to kiss her but she wouldn't let me. She thought I had died, you see. Turns out that Lucasta and my sister concocted a scheme between them – a ruse – while I was in hospital – last November.'

'You nearly died!' Lucasta cried. 'It was her fault!'

'I collapsed in the woods, but it wasn't a heart attack – exhaustion, mainly – worry. I recovered fast enough. It was all Lucasta's idea of course, that letter. Iris hasn't got the brains. Cardinal Richelieu in a frock, that's Lucasta. She put Iris up to it – made her write a letter to Ria saying I'd died.'

'I did it for your sake. Your daughter's letters were killing you. Your daughter had no right to treat you the way she did. She had it coming to her. She didn't seem to realize that actions have consequences and extravagances

220

have to be paid for in the end. She was degenerate. I couldn't bear to watch you suffer!'

'You were right, Major. I asked Ria to come back with me. She refused. We did have an argument. She said some awful things to me and I got angry. I took her by the shoulders – shook her – she slapped me – I pushed her back – against one of the bedposts, as it happened. I didn't mean to. I thought I heard a crack – it was probably something else, but I – I thought she was dead. My sweet little Ria. My lovely girl. I got into a panic. I couldn't feel her pulse.'

'She had only passed out?'

Leighton bowed his head. 'The same thing happened with me last November, oddly enough. I collapsed in the woods and my sister couldn't find my pulse. She thought I was dead . . . I thought I'd killed Ria. I rushed out and told Lucasta. I wasn't myself. I'd become bloody dependent on her, that's the trouble. I asked her to go and check. I shall never forgive myself for that, never. To think that I *was* wrong! Ria *was* alive! It was Lucasta who killed her! She strangled her.' He covered his face with his hands.

'I did it for you. Your lovely girl was a blot on the escutcheon. Rotten through and through. She did shameful things, outrageous things, disgraceful things. And as though that were not enough, she set out to destroy you.' Once more Lucasta was speaking in measured tones. 'Can't you *see*? I couldn't let her go on. She'd have started writing to you again. She'd have resumed her torture tactics. I did what I did in good faith – finished her off – got rid of the rot. Please, darling – do try to understand!'

'I shouldn't have asked her to go and check, but I couldn't stand on my feet. I was shaking. Had to sit down on the porch. I felt a constriction in my chest, as if my vital organs were being squeezed by some malignant hand. Lucasta then came back. It was a minute or two later. She looked extremely grave. She said – she said that Ria was dead all right.' Leighton's voice quavered. 'I remember very little of what followed. We returned to the hotel. She gave me an injection ... She does it quite adroitly ... I never feel the needle ... She'd done a nursing course, damn her ... Suddenly I felt better – stronger – happier! She'd given me some bloody anti-depressant. Do you know what happened next?'

'She told you it was all Roman Songhera's fault and that he should be held responsible for your daughter's death?'

'Yes. She was right about that one. It *was* his fault. Roman Songhera – the high khan of Kilhar. He lured my little girl away to this dreadful God-forsaken place. Well, I agreed to everything Lucasta said. She talked about revenge and retribution. She said they would strap his legs, stick a bag over his head and crack his neck on a rope. But first we had to make sure people knew that he had killed Ria. It sounded good. It made sense of things. Lucasta seemed to have hit on the right course of action. I was broken with grief but I pulled myself together. I threw myself into it. Lucasta took care of every single detail. She masterminded the operation. She kept going out, buying things, making phone calls –'

'Did you know she intended to kill Knight?'

'No, not till she'd already done so. She brought his diary to the hotel. She told me what to do with it. I was going to become Knight.' Leighton turned towards Antonia. 'I told Lucasta about you, you know, that you'd be staying at Coconut Grove. She is a great fan of yours. She said at once – *Why not make Antonia Darcy your agent of justice? She would be perfect for the job.* We were on the same plane, you see. Your friend was holding forth about your all too vivid imagination.'

'We guessed,' Antonia said drily.

'Lucasta's got a genius for jiggery-pokery. As devious as the devil. She even thought of putting one of Roman's cufflinks into Ria's hand, didn't you, my dear Lady Macbeth? To suggest struggle.'

'*Are* you Antonia Darcy?' Lucasta Leighton was looking across at Antonia. The front of her khaki suit was stiff with blood.

For a wild moment Antonia feared Lucasta might come up to her and shake her by the hand and tell her how much she admired her books, but she remained standing beside the wall, one hand pressed against her cheek, the other clutching the gilded back of the chair.

She didn't take any of her ideas from one of my books, did she? Antonia felt at once chilled and fascinated by the thought.

'I went through with all her plans. It seemed the right thing to do. I wasn't myself. I was moving in a fog.' Leighton was becoming rather breathless. 'She put the bronzer on my face. Told me to keep my hand in a fist because of my missing finger. It was the kind of thing people *would* remember, she said.'

'You didn't adjust your watch,' Antonia pointed out. 'It was five hours behind. It was still British time.'

Lucasta made an exasperated sound. 'You fool! I did tell you to set your watch!'

Could he have *wanted* to be caught? Antonia wondered. One of those inexplicable subconscious urges?

'It was your wife who rang Coconut Grove, wasn't it?' Payne said. 'When they called you to the phone?'

'Of course it was her. Who else is there? Julian Knight needed to disappear. It was only later, when we came back to the hotel, that I realized what she had done – that she'd deceived me – that it was she and not I who killed Ria. She kept talking about Ria being *strangled*. There was a smile on her face when she thought I wasn't looking – smug, gloating. It suddenly dawned on me then. She admitted it. She had to, to prevent me from giving away the whole show. I had started shouting, you see. I was beside myself.'

'She killed your daughter and left you thinking you'd done it.'

'Yes, Major Payne. That's exactly what she did. I could have torn her limb from limb there and then, but I suddenly felt ill. Had to sit down, nearly collapsed. She likes it when that happens – then I am in her power. We were downstairs, in the hotel lounge. There was some dreadful woman there, listening – a platinum blonde of a certain age – brown as a nut – lots of gold chains round the neck. Lucasta was worried we'd be rumbled.'

Antonia found herself thinking of the ending of 'The Cardboard Box'. Sherlock Holmes solemnly wondering about the meaning of it all. *What object is served by this circle of violence and misery and fear?*

'I've never heard so much nonsense in my life. I'll get the injection now,' Lucasta Leighton said briskly. She seemed to have recovered. 'Then I'll make you a drink. Then – perhaps a nap?'

'I will kill you if you come anywhere near me!' Leighton reached out for his silver-topped cane and waved it in the air. 'Where are you going?' he cried as Major Payne took Antonia by the hand and led her out of the room. 'Don't leave me with her! Please – don't go . . .'

They left them together in their gilded room, the woman with the ripped-out cheek and the man with a face like a death mask. The last thing they heard was Lucasta Leighton saying it would be perfectly all right, the tiniest prick, he wouldn't feel a thing – then the sound of smashed glass, followed by a cry.

The door the colour of dried liver slammed behind them.

As they walked quickly past the cricketing groups and the Maharaja of Patiala smiled down at them from the wall, Payne said by way of a Parthian shot, 'As punishments go, that's much worse than the crocs, don't you think?